Death by Chapters

Will Thurston

Fidus Publishing, 2019

Death by Chapters by Will Thurston

First published in Great Britain in 2019 as eBook and paperback by Fidus Publishing

ISBN 978-1-082416-43-9

The stunning knife shown in the cover image was handmade by Alexander Noot. To learn more about his handmade knives and belts, visit his website at http://www.lxblades.com or follow @lx_emergency on Instagram.

Acknowledgements

Writing a novel of any length is an arduous task. It's an uphill struggle to get from your initial idea to a carefully crafted climax. Breathing life into characters and following them, seeing what they do is the fun part. It's not always what I expect them to do when I start out!

I could not create these novels, and enjoy the ride, without the help and support of several people. These are as follows:

- My wife, Lisa, who seems to love me through everything I do, good or bad, and seems to love everything I write as well (which I'm not sure I agree with, as I'm pretty sure some of it's awful).

- My children, especially the boy who is anxious to be old enough to read my stories, and who comes to me with small story books he produces himself, just as I tried many times when I was his age. A mention should also go to my daughter who combines with my son to produce noise sufficient to aid me in developing patience and an ability to concentrate and write in almost any circumstance.

- My parents and in-laws who read and critique my works and help me make them better, making me a better writer along the way.

- Lesley Grainge has provided some of the best feedback I have ever received, which has helped to improve this book in several ways. Thank you Lesley!

- Tristram Johnson also deserves honourable mention here for reading a book outside of his interests just because I asked.

- Alexander Noot, the next fan of my books (hopefully) who graciously allowed me to use one of his knives in the cover image, despite shrinking it and covering it in blood! He was even prepared to send one to me to use for the photography, such is the level of service you get from this man when you show an interest in his beautiful hand-crafted knives.

- My day-to-day employer that I can't mention by name, who provide me with a job and an income that means I don't have to live in complete poverty whilst living my dream of authoring books.

- Fidus Publishing for believing in me enough to put my material out there for the world to see. I know thus far it's not been seen by millions. The hundreds or thousands so far is enough.

The fact that anyone who isn't related to me can read what I write and enjoy it seems unreal and at the same time validating, so finally, thank you to you, the reader. Without readers, there would be no point in writing anything and I would have to find something else to do with my warped imagination!

Death by Chapters

Will Thurston

Prologue

He was almost there. The place. Serene, but once the site of chaos, and of a most significant kill. Nostalgia seemed to be in the crisp, cool morning air before the general populous would rouse themselves, defiling it again with their exhalations and with their pointless lives.

There had not been another living soul around in a few short minutes of driving. Maybe they had all gone. Wiped out by some overnight plague. A wicked half-smile formed. *If only!*

A peaceful euphoria flooded through him, adrenaline ready to gallop through his veins like a pack of spooked wild horses.

The sky was dressed in a light yellow and pale blue ensemble, promising to usher in a clear, warm day. The morning mist hugged every low-lying field with the occasional tall tree or building popping up through the haze like the hand of a newly minted zombie, stretching through the soil of his grave, reaching for the freedom of the roaming undead. In the distance the not-so-flat fields gave way to angular, dramatic hills, like some giant beast had torn and chewed up the edges of the landscape in a fit of rage.

Anyone of a duller but purer mind might stop the car and photograph the scene, suitable for the cover of a travel brochure and framed perfectly by the windscreen of the speeding vehicle. How many times would others have captured the valley on film, archiving the result in some cheap imitation leather photo album, destined to be forgotten?

Beauty in any of its forms was there to be appreciated, celebrated even, but life was filled with poor imitations. They failed to draw the attention of the eyes and thus left countless hearts and minds untouched. A photograph could only capture so much of the panoramic views. The scent of lavender would be lost. The views of Wild Angelica and Roseroot at ground level would be omitted.

Eighteen months into a new century, digital photography was starting to push its way to prominence, but the wave that threatened to sweep aside traditional photography was nowhere near ready to lap at the shores of reality. Its inevitable innovations would soon trade dusty albums for clogged up memory cards and computer hard drives.

He slowed the car and lowered the window, taking in a lungful of the sweet aroma emanating from the local flora and fauna.

Take in the beauty now. Live in the moment. The past and the future are irrelevant.

The road he traversed would soon snake around, descending from the hill's midpoint. The sound surface stayed fairly level and smooth, nature's efforts to reclaim it falling to do any more than crumble its edges. Purple, white and yellow flowers found impossible homes amid the near-sheer rock face to the right. Gravity defying trees blossomed in pale pinks and blues to his left, dotted along the very steep drop.

Drinking in the view, the smells, the peace and quiet would be enough for most. There was yet another reason to revel in it.

I could visit here more often, but what is the old adage? Never return to the scene of the crime?

Was it an unnecessary risk? He shook his head. Utterly absurd, especially after the passage of so much time. What could the police do? Install a roadblock and accuse every random traveller of involvement in a death, deemed an accident, from years prior? A preposterous postulation.

His foot pressed a little harder on the accelerator pedal as he approached a sweeping bend to the right. His second-hand Audi sports car represented the last of his meagre funds, his inheritance a depleted part of his past.

Realising that either the memories or the scenery had caused him to hold his breath, he exhaled and then filled his lungs with air again in a slow and deliberate manner. A smile spread across his face. The view, dead ahead, outshone everything else on the approach.

"This is the place where the direction of my life changed," he said aloud to no one.

The road in front seemed to disappear behind his imagination for a moment. The resting state of his mind often flashed this scene again, sometimes at inopportune moments, teasing him to re-watch. He relented, indulging in scenes inherited from the years-old drama.

The scents of the hot rubber on the road, the spilled petrol and of burning oil reached his nostrils anew as if causation had only just occurred. The sounds of the crunching metal and the shattering of glass echoed in his ears once again.

The car in front swerved, veered and over-corrected. It flipped onto its side and then its roof, and then it summersaulted again. It was as if the vehicle was thrashing around, trying to free itself of an inner demon that possessed it.

An odour of rich copper-scented blood was carried by the breeze, almost overwhelmed by the stronger smells of fuel. Even so, the scent was detectable to those with a satisfactory olfactory sense.

The rough tarmac underfoot was scarred but intact as he crouched by the wreck. Life was draining from the eyes of two people in that overturned car. A husband and wife, together in death.

There was something fascinating in watching someone surrender their mortality. It was a moment comparable in beauty to the vista to his left. An omnipotence had threatened to overwhelm the occasion on that day, his own injuries incidental.

One fateful moment. Two new deaths. A lifetime ahead to indulge in his new passion. Everyone needed a hobby.

A void in his life that had grown until it had felt all-encompassing, had been filled by a new mission, a purpose. Before that moment in that place, his own life lacked direction and meaning. His mere continued existence had seemed untenable. In one moment, he was transformed from suicidal to homicidal.

As he finished rounding that gentle bend in the road, the only survivor of that mid-afternoon crash was casually jogging in his direction. He sneered as his foot followed instinct and pressed the pedal to the floor. The young man from the back seat, the one that was missed first time around, all grown up. Right there in the crosshairs. What were the chances?

He and the lone survivor more or less shared a birthday, and only two years separated them. In another life, they could have been brothers. In his early twenties, he had a bright, diametrically opposed and promising future ahead of him. *Let's see what I can do about that.*

With an alteration to his steering, the runner was in the centre of the windscreen. His right foot squeezed down harder, the toes of his right foot curling inward with tension. Maybe the car had more to give. *Time to complete the task. Finish collecting the set.*

The confused look on the young man's face gave way to shock and then to full-blown fear. The whites of his eyes stood out in the last of the dim morning light like cat's eyes at midnight. Eyes only widened that much, that quickly, when death was grinning at them, scythe in-hand. He stopped, head spinning around like a confused bird, looking for any means of escape. But desperation would breed disappointment.

To his left was nothing but a jagged, sheer wall of grey, miserable stone. There was no way he could climb that. There was not sufficient time for him to get high enough if he could. He would be crushed between a rock and the hard surface of twisted metal.

To his right on the other side of the road was a low steel barrier and a one-way trip to the valley below. Maybe he could survive a fall, maybe not. Terror was etched on his face as it dawned on him that there would be no refuge, no deliverance from his fate.

He turned back on himself and charged down the road, almost tripping himself up as his jog transformed in an instant into a breathless run for his life. The sprint in a pathetic zigzag would do nothing to improve his chances. He was driving a car, not aiming a weapon at the man.

Hands gripped the wheel like they were wringing a neck. *Attempts at escape are futile. I will get you.*

The gap between the two grew shorter and shorter. The runner was about to be mown down, like roadkill. It had to be. How could anyone hope to outrun a sports car?

With no gap between his foot and the floor, he pressed his teeth together, eyes bulging out of his head. He was inches from the young man's heels. Closer, closer until the moment of impact.

He had expected to hear a satisfying thud. Instead a clip of his heels sent the target tumbling off to the side, over the steel barrier and out of sight.

Deflated, he slammed on the brakes, tyres squealing and sliding across the road in complaint at the abuse. He sighed and then stuck out his bottom lip, letting his shoulders hunch. The tension immediately drained from his entire body. *What an anti-climax. You get so close to taking a life, only for gravity to rob you at the last second.*

Disappointment in the quest for a kill was not a new sensation. On this occasion, acting fast could still dispel his dismay.

Opening the door, he breathed in the rubber-scented air like it was a beef roast on a Sunday afternoon. *Ah, the memories!*

He stood at the edge, peering down at the figure. A gnarled tree, part of the way down had broken his fall. He lay in some kind of heap against it. He was probably thirty yards away.

He clapped his hands together and rubbed one palm against the other. Wasting no time, he stepped over the low barrier, holding on until steady. He then started to make a more careful descent than that of his adversary. *This might not be over yet. Time to recover the body and check for signs of life.*

Chapter 1

Her eyes shot open like a trapdoor, sending her thoughts hurtling in a downward spiral. Something was wrong. Her heart was pounding, her breathing was heavy, and her forehead and cheeks were cold and damp with perspiration. *Where am I?*

The smooth white ceiling, the matching walls and a section of blue and grey sky seen through a large picture window, was all clean, new and unfamiliar. *This isn't my home, my bedroom.*

The heart pounding increased as everything blurred. *What was I doing yesterday? Why can't I remember? Did I choose to be here?*

Broken pieces of memory floated around, waiting to be plucked out of the air and reassembled.

Sounds of distant traffic and trains just about made it through the thick glass of a nearby window.

The man. The man on the train. I knew him from somewhere.

Pain shot through her head but receded quickly into a dull ache. It would return, like a tactical opponent, playing the long game.

Blinking did nothing to abate the blur. Obstinate optics threatened to never focus on anything again. Heat built up behind stinging eyes, trying to escape.

Her heart was still beating like a kid thought it was a new drum set. No idea of location. No clue on conveyance to this place. *Am I alone? Can I get out and run for home?*

It was time to move. Time to get up and get out of this strange place, whatever the cost in personal pain.

She lifted her head. A spasm of pain followed her forward momentum, darting to her forehead, screaming through her cranium as it went, forcing all movement to cease. The pause provided instant relief. Every movement was maligned by an invisible, ethereal attacker. The same tactics: Strike and retreat.

A silent sigh escaped. There were no signs of immediate danger. Maybe she had more time. *I can't get up and run for the door. Maybe I can figure out why I'm here.*

A hypothetical newscast rang in her ears.

A local girl, Samantha Barkes, was beaten up, dragged off and dumped in some high-class private dentist's waiting area last night. She was last seen on a train in the company of a man, six feet tall, with greying short black hair. The man had greying designer stubble, a la George Michael or Steve Jobs.

Ridiculous. The truth was a mile away from that, but the details were close. The sensation was old but new: A hole in the memory and a heart full of shame. Both had been constant companions once. They had returned like old friends just breezing in through the door.

The horrendous feeling bore symptoms incident with intoxication. The consequence of her choices, not those of a madman. She frowned. *If only I remembered what those choices were.*

The usual methodical planning out of the window. The structure of routine had been shattered. Indecision, as constant as a shadow, had vanished with last night's setting sun.

"We're not far from my stop."

"Mine too."

"Manchester?"

"Maybe this conversation can carry on for a while yet."

"I'd like that."

…But I don't do this! I don't sleep in the homes of men I've just

met.

Laying on a sofa, still fully dressed in yesterday's light blue jeans and pale yellow jumper, all she could do was turn her head to the side and look. Blurred objects became clearer and took on something closer to a familiar form.

Beetham Tower stood proud, its cantilevered construction suggesting the apparent top-heavy structure was prone to toppling. Deansgate Square was vying for attention. The gothic clock tower of the Town Hall seemed to be poking its head above the parapet of newer surroundings, trying to sneak a peek at its new neighbours.

The familiar Manchester skyline, but from an unfamiliar vantage point. The bright late spring morning threw sunlight over several angular skyscrapers as well as a distant field of homes, broken and unbroken.

Distant tower cranes and a smattering of scaffolding were complicit in destroying the Manchester of her memories. Steel and glass replaced brick and slate, a newer and more fashionable city emerging from the ashes of an upscaled mill town. The city, growing up with its residents, boasted a sophisticated skyline, the product of disingenuous design. Shining and incredible edifices, exemplary architecture, if not profligate.

Normality nagged at her senses. *This is different. Different is bad.*

"You're Larry Llewellyn!" I just blurted it out, sitting opposite the most famous person I've ever met.

He was sitting there, looking as charming as the photo in the back of my book.

"I'm Sam. I must be one of your biggest fans." Did I really say that? How clichéd. How obvious.

There was a smile. He offered to sign my book. We had a conversation of sorts. Did that somehow get me here?

She gritted her teeth. *Time to try moving again. I can beat the pain.* Stunt drivers and death-defying acrobats could expect an adrenaline rush at a key moment. Could adrenaline be afforded for the lifting of a heavy head from its pillow?

Pushing past the nausea, she continued lifting until she was sitting up. Her clammy skin peeled away from the white leather sofa beneath as she moved at her glacial pace.

She blinked away the last of the blurriness in her vision. Time to identify an exit route. There it was, the other end of a narrow, high-ceilinged room with white walls.

The carpet, the furniture, everything was white to match the walls with only a partial splash of colour, the harsh morning light making everything gleam with the intensity of a thousand pins to the eyes.

The route to the entrance required navigating around a kitchen area, a long table with eight chairs and the coffee table. But the first task was to get up from one of the sofas. All of it had a surreal organic quality, the kitchen, the table, chairs and sofas a perfect bright white, seeming to grow out of the walls or the floor. It looked like someone had forgotten to colour it in.

The stark, clinical look was broken by two paintings on the wall, original and seemingly of nothing other than random shapes in strong, vibrant primary colours. One large crimson rug on the floor stood out like a stain at a crime scene, its thick pile, the texture of woollen pom-poms she had made as a child. *I don't like this place. How do I get myself from here and out of that door? What do I do then?*

Her mind wandered, staggering around the task at hand like a drunk man on an indirect journey home. Anything and everything provided distraction to her dehydrated brain.

"Just don't tell me how it ends," I had said. We were talking about the book. The new book I had in my hand.

I remember: "Yeah, the hero's going to SURVIVE this time, isn't he?"

A stiff neck became evident as she looked down, staring into the High gloss coffee table beneath her eyes. Imperfect features were reflected imperfectly, with a shimmer and a wobble, bringing back thoughts of staring into frozen puddles on the bitterest of winter days.

The tips of her dark brown hair were just long enough to sway forwards and reach the edge of her view. Her green eyes stared back at her, clear and full of self-loathing. Nobody looked good at that angle, but any reflection was a reminder of being stranded somewhere on that landscape between thin and obese, between the celebration of beauty and body-shaming.

One of your biggest fans, indeed. What did he think when I said that?

She scrunched up half of her face, feeling it become a slight smirk. *What did Harry from uni say? Cute and curvy? I'm happy with that.*

She sighed and the smirk faded. *But what did Harry's sister say? Your BMI Doesn't lie!* A balanced diet was annoyingly enough for the fault-finding Britney. In stark contrast, it was tiring, running up the downward escalator of weight management, expending so much effort on merely staying still. No fad diet, no healthy eating regime ever did quite enough.

"Good morning!" said the cheerful, handsome man to her left, the other side of the large room. Where did he appear from? How long had he been there, watching? She faked a smile, pushing away the scowl that had been lurking. *Kidnappers probably don't greet their captives so cheerfully. But then again, how would I know?*

Standing there, facing her from the other side of a breakfast bar, was the charming man from yesterday's train.

The same greying black hair and stubble. The same squared jaw, pronounced cheekbones and deep brown eyes which combined in the look of a man that was hiding something. There was an air of awkward confidence about him.

Hardly the typical criminal I study about at uni. Do those of a murderous persuasion use books, a conversation and a typewriter to lure people in? Do they make their victims breakfast?

The hidden clinks and clatters of plates, cutlery and pans, though tempered, still made her wince. Even the most mellow of everyday sounds was a hard blow to the head.

The morning light started to dim as a swarm of thick clouds rolled in. The oncoming gloom settled on every sense and put a damp coldness on everything.

"Full English okay with you?" he asked.

As the familiar fry-up smell reached the end of the open plan space, Sam nodded twice and then winced. There was no excuse for moving such a fragile head that fast. The dizziness and pain were still there, biding their time, preparing to strike again.

Fragments of fuzzy memories tumbled and bounced around her brain like coloured glass in a Kaleidoscope. Apparent random collisions and patterns seemed to organise themselves, lining up to enable a review of every recollection coherently. After several seconds, she could evoke yesterday's journey, the wilful abandon of her normal, over-thinking, timid self.

This man, shy but famous, confident but withdrawn, had let her in, but why?

The headache and the nausea still waning, the aching in every joint, all paled in comparison to something larger as she watched the man plate up breakfast. Something was lurking there, communicated by the senses but somehow undetectable. *Something is wrong here.*

There were clues in yesterday. Anything there might provide a point of origin for her odd, ominous rumination. The devil was without doubt within the detail, and quite possibly on the other side of that breakfast bar.

Chapter 2

Marvellous train journeys were the stuff of fiction. Reality was mundane. No exciting strangers. No thwarting of a terror plot. No destination of magical proportions. So many stories had been inspired by this mode of transport, but not by this model of train. Nothing to inspire the great Larry Llewellyn here. Nothing to validate or add value to the day.

Wasteful meetings with annoying agents had never pretended to be very useful either, except for possibly inventing new ways to kill an agent. He insisted on face-to-face meetings in far-flung London.

"You're trying to lecture me about modern technology?" Shaun King had said, laughing. The man's short bleached blond hair with its cowlick did not complement the bright blue frames of his glasses. The wide royal blue and white stripes on his crooked tie also looked at odds with his plain lilac shirt, like he only ever put the office worker's noose around his neck in preparation for a meeting. There was a permanent wide-eyed look etched on the man's face, like someone who was in over their head.

Larry could only shrug in response.

"You?" Evidently this man's mother had not told him it was rude to point. Maybe she had. Maybe he ignored her too. "The guy who still delivers novels a chapter at a time, typed sheets from that ancient contraption of yours?"

Larry shook his head. "Owning today's tech and choosing to use it constantly are two very different things. This meeting, though, could have taken place over the phone or even using video chat."

"Do you even know how to use Skype, FaceTime, Google, WhatsApp, OoVoo?"

"What the hell's an OoVoo?"

Shaun nodded with the smirk and the raised dark brown eyebrows of someone who had won an argument. It was the smug look of someone who should expect to be punched in the face within seconds. "Exactly my point."

He gritted his teeth instead of fighting back. According to his dentist, both teeth grinding and fist fights were bad for the teeth. He chose the former. Less damaging consequences. *I do my research. I know more about today's tech than this man would understand.*

Some facets of modern life, the sociological as opposed to the technical, were bemusing. Social media fulfilled an essential and otherwise difficult role in book promotion. Occasional dabbling in the occasional fictitious account in the name of book research could be useful. That was all. Peering into a handheld device with every spare second failed to fascinate. With time to kill, the best thing was to work it to death. Writing, creating, was far more useful as a pastime than perusing non-stop news feeds and wasting brain cells on celebrity gossip.

He looked back at the smug agent. *This is what I get for my fifteen percent. Surely the money could be put to better use.*

The high-class office with glass walls, sharp angled walnut desks and space-aged mesh and stainless-steel chairs, the UHD flat screens on each office wall and the cream leather sofas filled otherwise empty offices in the same manner as the disease of social media filled empty lives. The company claimed success over many years, but the floor had been close to empty of clients on every visit. *I've never seen anyone else here. Just how much of this am I funding?*

The smug face of the obstinate agent was a blight on the view of the large, impressive new buildings that formed the City of London's iconic landscape behind him. Working in the shadows of the Shard, the Gherkin and the Walkie-Talkie came at a price. The agency had relented. Not just to the lease, but to keeping this barely capable individual, styling himself on a bad police E-FIT, on payroll.

Larry shook his head. There was no sense reliving the rest of the egregious exchange. He tipped his head back and looked at the ceiling. *Put it behind you, like the farm buildings and the millionth tree whizzing past.* There was no benefit in looking at the watch again. It would say nearly the same thing, but how could there still be over half an hour remaining? What else was there to do inside that cage on rails?

He picked up his pocket notebook, thumbing through its scantily used pages, glancing at each half-baked idea with a sneer and a shake of the head. He flipped it closed and chucked it back on the table. *Why do I even carry this thing around?*

Another brief stop. Another dying station welcomed the train. Another Saturday evening horde finished boarding, on their way to the next chapter of their humdrum lives. The beeps and whistles sounded, the doors slammed shut, and the train rumbled and complained, continuing its reluctant struggle to move forward.

Thinking time could be a boon for an author, unless the mind of that author had already been ransacked, any good ideas having already been carried away in the swag of a previous muse. That next bestseller, like the answer to a quiz question, travelled from the tip of the tongue to the recess in the back of his mind, entrenching itself all the more with each retrieval attempt.

Thus far, critics had been fairly kind. On the grand landscape of literature, the books were trash, and everyone knew it. Even so, when the reading public demanded more, what was to be done? It was tiring, living in a game where every effort expended was solely to appease the masses. A life at the mercy of the mob, with the stakes forever raising, could not continue forever.

The old Royal typewriter, heavy, solid, dependable, would be a willing travel companion but he would be the strange one for carting such a contraption around. There was no battery to expire, no news or other alerts to distract. Just sheet after sheet of paper, begging to be used. The laptops and tablets used by almost everyone else offered only fake paper, fake news, distractions galore and the promise of a battery that expired when creativity was charged up and ready to go.

Failure was lurking, laughing at the man who could not adapt, who could not write. Many a victim had been created and captured. Maybe he would be the next washed-up writer to fall out of favour, from the pedestal of the public eye and into the pit of has-beens and obscurity. *I need a new character. My muse, my next victim, and I need it soon.*

The almost-white plastic moulding and the bright, possibly Caribbean-inspired patterned fabric conspiring to cover pretty much everything, the countryside, it had all remained unchanged since boarding. The notepad still sat on the table where it had landed. Urgency and apathy could only combine to any great effect when the pressure piled on. Reading even his own notes was enough to turn his own stomach these days. *Damn this pathetic motion sickness. I wish I could write on trains.*

The creaking but refit carriage, the window, the watch. The carriage, the window, the watch. There had to be something else to look at, something new to see. Maybe the watch would hold good news this time. It was like it was shaking its head, putting on a glum face. Still half an hour to go.

What if smoke billowed from the front of the train, every passenger scrambling to the back so they could breathe?

What if a passenger opened a window, hoping for fresh air, only to let in a toxin that wiped out everyone on board?

What if the train driver had passed out? What if no one else could do enough to take over or to stop the train?

What if one of the red-uniformed staff snapped, trying to decorate the inside of the carriages to match the colour of their coat with the innards of passengers?

What if a man chopped up his victims by leaving their bodies on the track, knowing the high-speed wheels on the London line would cut them in half?

He shook his head. Even thoughts of death couldn't lift the mood. But there was something over there. Something he had not noticed earlier.

A young woman on the opposite side of the aisle with shoulder-length dark scruffy hair and a slightly chubby face was wearing the palest of pale blue jeans with embroidered flowers on its extremities and a pale yellow long-sleeved top. All of it was too figure-hugging for a person of her build. A mid-brown leather jacket was lying crumpled atop the grey backpack on the seat next to her.

Uninteresting enough. Nothing special, except for the book. That book. The cover art had only been approved a matter of days ago alongside the almost-adequate agent. It had been on general sale for less than a week. She was into its final pages.

Those same words, the characters, the scenes, had become real to him over recent months. At times, her eyes widened. At others she would smirk. At others she would recoil or grimace. It was all becoming real to her. She was not just reading the words for entertainment. She was living them.

It was the first time in a while that a smile spread across his face when thinking about it. The final words being embedded into the final page by the thin arms of his typewriter often marked a dark period. There would be mourning for their death, there would be wallowing in the shame of taking the life of another for the purposes of entertainment. It mattered little whether that person was real or imaginary.

It was not polite to stare, and yet it could not be helped. Watching someone else's fascination was empowering. The polite thing would be to divert attention again. Look out of the window, pick up that notebook, do anything else.

But then, she looked up and she looked right at him.

He looked away but it was too late.

A moment later he let his eyes dart back in her direction. Her eyes were still locked on him, a curious look on the young woman's features. Her gaze shifted back to the book with a speed that reminded Larry of an excited bird. She shoved the final few unread pages to her left, using her index finger as a bookmark, until she was looking at the inside of the back cover. She looked up, and then down, and then up again. She was comparing the author's photograph to the person in her eyeline.

The woman stared open-mouthed at him far longer than most people would find comfortable. She closed her mouth, furrowed her eyebrow slightly and pointed at him and then at the picture. She then mouthed the words, "Is this you?"

A partial smirk and a single nod of the head later, she was scrambling across the train carriage, a mess of bags, coats and sundry items swaying on a brief trip across the train carriage, heading in his direction. She almost fell on her face as the carriage shifted under her feet.

"You're Larry Llewellyn!" She said, almost panting, falling into the seat on the opposite side of his table.

"I know!" He wore an awkward smile. "Have been for some time."

She shook her head, looking cross with herself for her lame introduction. She held out her right hand. "I'm Sam. I must be one of your biggest fans."

He shook her hand. It was soft and damp with perspiration. *One of my biggest fans? You're certainly not the smallest, but I've met heavier.*

"It's nice to meet you, Sam." She was still holding the book with her left forefinger wedged inside. He cleared his throat. "Would you like me to sign the book?"

The young woman stared at the hardback book, wearing a pensive look. *Maybe she's not that big a fan of mine after all.*

She bit her lower lip for a moment and looked towards her feet. She gave him a cute, quizzical look and said, "I would much rather have a conversation with you. Pick your brains for a few minutes. It would be more valuable to me than even *your* signature."

Larry half-smiled whilst holding out his right hand. "Young lady, you shall have both."

She handed over the book, resigning to the idea of needing to re-find her page. "Just don't tell me how it ends," she said with a smile.

He raised an eyebrow and smirked as he removed his good pen from his pocket and signed the title page. "Yeah, the hero's going to *survive* this time, isn't he?"

Sam let out a short laugh before her cheeks seemed to go a little red. The girl was cuter than she had originally seemed. Set in her symmetrical face was a pair of large, light green eyes with flecks of grey like polished Malachite. They were eyes that commanded attention when met by the gaze of another.

"So, Mr Llewellyn," Sam asked, looking more confident, "Do you have to kill off all of your main characters?"

"Do you think the stories would be any better if they survived?"

Half of Sam's mouth curled up before she said, "You might have a point."

Larry put his Mont Blanc Meisterstuck in his pocket, placed the newly signed book on the table and slid it towards Sam. He then leaned back in his chair, waiting for the inevitable rush of obvious questions from the girl.

"Do you think they're all a bit far-fetched?" Sam asked.

"The stories, the characters or their deaths?"

"Let's start with the stories."

"They're based on reality, so if they seem fake, what does that say about humanity and the world we occupy?"

She raised her eyebrows, paused for a second and then nodded.

"The characters are eccentric caricatures of real-life people. The circumstances of their deaths are also mirrored in the real world."

"You're better looking in real-life than your picture suggests," she said, changing topic so fast that Larry's head was almost spinning.

He smirked, feeling his cheeks getting warm. "That last comment is *not* based on reality. Maybe your eyes are still adjusting from reading."

She smiled. It was a pretty smile. There was something interesting, engaging about this girl. She softened his outlook. Like maybe there was more to life than just death. *Could she be my next character? Could she be my latest muse?*

"You know, I'm too young to be a best-selling author. That's what people tell me."

Sam looked puzzled.

"The general public expect me to be older, to have more life experience, like those stuffy old successful novelists. So, my agent had this brilliant idea of making my hair look grey, using makeup to make me look at least a decade older. Allegedly it's helped sell more books."

"Or maybe people are more bothered about a good book than a few strands of hair and some wrinkles?"

"Thank you!" Larry said with enthusiasm and a hint of sarcasm. "Where were *you* when I had that meeting with my agent?"

There was quiet for a minute. The countryside had morphed into red bricks and tarmac during their brief exchange. The encroaching city gloom could cause a passenger to wonder whether the serenity of those green fields had been some sort of apparition.

"We're not far from my stop," Sam said with sad eyes.

"Mine too," Larry said, reaching for the notebook on the table and putting it into his jacket pocket.

Sam looked at him. "Manchester?"

He nodded. "Maybe this conversation can carry on for a while yet."

Her smile returned as her head nodded in reply. "I'd like that."

Chapter 3

Her fingers skimmed the smooth top of the desk, reminiscent of an insect gliding on the undisturbed surface of a pond. The light cream glossy finish was not as reflective as a still pool of water, but there was little worthy of reflection in that room.

Aside from the rush-job flat-pack desk with its matching under-desk drawers and a tall set of bookshelves, the room was bare. The walls on all sides were smooth and clean. There was not a blemish in the darker cream painted walls, hinting at the possibility that no picture had ever hung from any part of them.

She cast a sharp shadow over an ancient typewriter in the centre of the desk, courtesy of the brilliant sunset streaming through the window behind her. The silhouette missed a pristine pile of paper to the right, still bathed in an orange glow.

The paper sitting in the warming light of a setting sun, yearned for a chance to be involved in the next story to fall from this man's fingers. Classic methods were still employed in that setting, the central contraption still dominant in this corner of an increasingly digital world. Twelve bestsellers had been created in such a setting. Everything there seemed to crave the opportunity to be involved in the next iconic, ironic death.

"So, this is where your ideas come to life?"

Larry gave her a stern shake of his head, maintaining eye contact. "My dear, this is where my ideas come to *die*."

Her lips curled slightly as she looked up to the ceiling. "Do you *always* have to be so dramatic?"

Larry only offered a resigned shrug as he stood near his guest in the almost-empty room.

Somehow the writing sanctuary should have been more than this. "It's all a bit... sparse, isn't it?"

"You were expecting the National Gallery?" Larry said, his voice thick with disdain at her apparent lack of understanding, turning to face several rows of reading material, classic and modern.

This man had achieved the remarkable in a decade and a half. Mere words from him toyed with every emotion, achieving anything from conjuring contentment to giving rise to rage. He had scaled greater heights than others. Somehow his words pulled the reader in and gave all an invitation to every adrenaline-fuelled moment. The author was, without doubt, one of the finest at introducing irony into the deaths of his protagonists. People knew what to expect and they kept asking for more.

He turned to look around the drab room again as if searching for some elusive apparition on one of the walls. "You need to focus your imagination, look beyond the bland and visualise the elements of your story. By doing this you cut out the distractions."

"But surely *I'm* now a distraction." A frown featured heavily for a moment.

Larry looked at her and paused before dismissing her suggestion with a shake of the head. "You're not a distraction. You're a part of life that needs to be lived to find new ideas."

"That all sounds like a distraction to me," the words softened with a shy smile and a shrug.

It would have been so easy to go all Llewellyn-geek on the guy, to play around on the typewriter responsible for so many stories, sold to millions all over the world. Any fan would jump at the chance to load a crisp sheet of paper and hammer away at those uneven circular keys, hoping to unearth their own bestselling character.

Twelve critically acclaimed novels, millions of now blood-thirsty readers, gradually desensitising, one story at a time. How many others would love to use that very typewriter?

But that would not be happening. Larry was effectively standing guard, unwilling to let her touch anything, like a grumpy museum guide. There might as well have been a velvet rope and a security camera. Then, seeming to remember his role as host, he exited the room saying, "Would you like a drink?"

He was out of sight, and the machine was on the desk, crying out for attention. Her left hand seemed to almost take on a life of its own, reaching for the top row of keys, like a hand hovering above oven-top hobs, checking whether they were still warm.

"Don't touch the typewriter," he said from the next room, as if he could see through the wall. The hand withdrew, defeated. How did he know? She almost waddled into the next room and flopped onto one of two white sofas.

The confidence exuding from his stories did not carry over into conversation. The real-life Larry was withdrawn, timid, a meagre portion of the personality prevalent on every page he produced.

In spite of his shyness, he was charming and witty when he put forth substantial effort in entertaining. Here was a man, attractive, intelligent, funny, rich and despite it all, he was single. Women must surely have been drawn to him, but where were they?

Larry, the enigma, was sitting in front of her pouring a glass of wine for each of them, almost begging to be studied like one of those profiles from her Criminology studies.

People were a complex breed. Every one of them, even the vilest of villains, was a melting pot of history, genetics, experiences, nurture and education. Good and bad, troubled and carefree, poor and privileged, all contributed, for better or for worse, for praise or for punishment. Understanding them was less important than finding the good in them, however deep it may be buried.

Hers was a life undone by upheavals. Rebellion had been easy. The turbulence of troubles and misunderstood moments had led to a label that had threatened to stick for good. The impossible task had been fighting free of the mire of negativity.

As the evening continued, alcohol had started to numb the uncomfortable feeling of having infiltrated the man's inner sanctum almost instantly. Was his circle of trust small and already overcrowded, with rarely anyone but himself inside? Was she just the latest person he allowed in, fooling herself that genuine friendship might be possible with the celebrated lone wolf?

I can't be the first fan of his fiction to be here. Others must have been invited to get a glimpse of the real Larry Llewellyn.

They talked about their own favourite authors and stories, they discussed grammatical errors from social media that drove them both nuts and they laughed about the most ridiculous moments they had ever encountered in books or in movies.

Wine was flowing freely as the sun was setting over the Manchester skyline, casting oranges and pinks into the air, colouring the clouds and making silhouettes of the tall buildings. With each glass the finer details of the location, the company, the distant disquieting feeling and the time she was spending were blurring into the background.

As the edges to everything became fuzzy, conversations continued. Maybe there was some sort of agreement or arrangement between the pair of them. Disagreeing had been as difficult as continuing to sit upright.

She laid down and closed her eyes. The sound of an

evening train leaving Manchester Victoria Station travelled through the open window. The peace that accompanied a drift to sleep was absent. Instead, regret spread through every thought like wildfire. Maybe that inward fire would burn out. Maybe hope would return to douse those flames. Or maybe there was no removing that regret that followed meeting this man on a train.

~ ~ ~ ~ ~

The clatter of the pans in the kitchen echoed the screech and clatter of steel wheels on a rail.

There she was, sitting at the glossy white dining table, thanking Larry as he walked over and put down a plate of fried food.

The aromas were appealing to the senses, prompting an impatient stomach growl. But the reticence in partaking, in even being there still, would not leave.

The large rectangular table was so clean that it could be used for surgical operations. Larry, the willing and perfect host, had taken up the seat at the opposite end. Three well-spaced seats remained empty on each side, occupying the length of the lacquered surface. Why did a loner need a table for entertaining so many?

Besides the food, the table was bare except for a glass bowl containing grey translucent pebbles for a house-styling reason few could claim to truly understand.

She smiled as she turned her attention to the plate in front of her. *At least he's creating the illusion that I have personal space. I can breathe, and I can doubt myself in silence all over again.*

That voice kept nagging. *Time to get out.* She took a sip of orange juice and picked up her knife and fork. *Anything could have happened here last night.* She shook her head. *I wonder if he can sense my embarrassment.*

"So, did you sleep alright?" He asked, far too loud and cheerful. He put pieces of sausage and fried egg on his fork and raised it to his mouth, chewing at an eager speed. He was staring at Sam in anticipation of her answer.

Sam cut some bacon and pushed it onto her fork with a few beans. Her head swayed from side to side for a second. "About as well as anyone could probably sleep when they're drunk on a sofa."

He smiled and raised an eyebrow. Taking a break from chewing, speaking out of half his mouth, he said, "I suggested the spare room, but you refused to move."

She next attacked a hash brown and a fried egg, watching as the yolk burst and seemed to run away in three different directions. Even the clattering of her own cutlery against the porcelain made her wince.

She looked up again and frowned. "Why don't you look as rough as I feel?"

He paused from cutting his half of the grilled tomato, looked at her and raised an eyebrow again. "I didn't drink half as much as you did. You were really knocking them back."

"Surely an honourable man would have stopped plying me with alcohol and would have arranged a taxi to take me home."

"Two things," he said. "Firstly, I attempted limiting your alcohol intake. You went hunting for more. Secondly, what makes you think I'm an honourable man?"

She continued to pick at the food that was becoming less palatable with every bite.

At that moment Larry could have been anywhere on the scale between the fabled knight in shining armour and the typical leering lager lout from the local pub. *Nice guy or jerk? You decide!* Maybe further verbal exchange over the remnants of breakfast would yield sufficient evidence to come to a conclusion.

She glanced up at him in between chasing food around her plate. "I suppose you could have been *less* honourable."

He smirked, still looking down at the sausage he was partway through cutting. "How so?"

She shrugged. "You know. A single girl, drunk, in your home, no one else around…"

He stared at her looking genuinely puzzled, whilst continuing to eat.

"You could have taken advantage of my drunken state." Her eyes met his before a rush of awkwardness pushed her gaze back to the plate.

He placed his cutlery on the side of his plate, finished chewing his food and rested his elbows on the table either side. He steepled his fingers and bounced his chin off them. Straight-faced he replied with, "I did."

Sam's hands seemed to spasm open. She dropped the knife and fork. The noise of the cutlery colliding with the edges of the plate made her flinch.

Her heart was beating harder and faster. The air might have just been sucked from the room. Breathing had become impossible. Her head ached with a pulse that matched her increased heartrate, like some tiny person with perfect rhythm was inside, going berserk with a hammer. *What has he done? How could I not feel…? How could I not remember?*

He laughed and threw his head back in a move performed only by villains in cheesy movies before looking her in the eyes again. "Not in a physical way," he said. He resumed eating as if the conversation had been commonplace.

Constant confusion was taking a toll. The muscles that

moved her eyebrows were starting to ache. "What other ways are there?"

"Oh, there are *plenty* of other ways. I might have taken advantage of your good nature and drunken state when I asked you something."

The air had returned enough to fill a couple of lungs. Now the heating seemed to have been cracked all the way up. Uncomfortable was not the word. This was worse. Like accidentally ending up watching a porn movie with your mum.

Now words were barely audible over the hammering of her heart. "What did you ask me? What did I agree to?"

Larry held out his hands, palm down and pushed down on some imaginary cushion in front of him. "Calm down. This isn't some Hitchcock movie. I've not asked you to kill anyone."

Sam said nothing. Further explanation was necessary. Such inner storms were only hushed by hopeful words.

He resumed the breakfast he had nearly finished. "I asked if you would like to *be* killed."

Sam stared at him again, open-mouthed before staring at the half-finished food on her plate. *What the hell has he put in my food? What kind of psycho kills someone they just met?*

"I mean in my next *book*," he said behind a self-conscious half-smile. "I asked if you'd be my next main character."

Sam's shoulders drained of the tension they had accumulated. *That was an intense thirty seconds. Thank God he only kills people in literature!*

"Are you going to say anything?" Larry asked, both eyebrows raised slightly. He looked like a ten-year-old, wondering where his dad had hidden the new bike on Christmas morning. "Do you remember me asking?"

Sam, took in a couple of slow, deep breaths. The slow process of her lungs filling and then emptying, the sensation of her chest expanding and sinking all brought back a more human feeling. Then a smile broke out. "It would be an honour to have a character based on me."

Larry pointed the prongs of his fork at her. "And you're alright with what will happen to that character?"

Sam nodded. "I expect a good, gruesome, ironic death."

Larry nodded once, looking pleased. "Then Sam, you shall have your good, gruesome, ironic death."

They hypothesised about dire situations and circumstances in which the fictional Sam would find herself. She would throw out the occasional random idea, only for Larry to politely decline. He was the writer. He would decide.

The cooked breakfast had all but banished the effects of the hangover. With plates empty and returned to the kitchen, it was time for Sam to return to her own reality.

With their first but elongated encounter at an end, Sam exited in a taxi for which Larry had paid. He had waved her off like he was bidding farewell to a relative he didn't expect to see for a while.

This private hire vehicle was a class above the type she had used previously. The clean interior had been looked after. Light cream leather seats looked so new that they might have been fitted moments prior to picking up the passenger. Even the driver was dressed smart and was clean-shaven and polite.

She closed her eyes, took a deep breath and let it out slower than before. Tension sloped from her shoulders. A surreal twenty hours had drawn to a close. The famous author had proven to be anything other than the one portrayed by the media. Chance had thrown them together but had not offered answers to any of her questions. Why was he not more confident, living in luxury? Why was everything about him so understated?

A couple of beeps and a vibrating sequence signalled her phone vying for her attention. The text message sent to her dad the previous evening had preceded an extended ignorance of the phone until the silent ride home. *Five calls and a text message. I don't think he's very happy with me.*

A father's near rage could distract and distort, cause worry and trepidation. But the worry was already there, waving away every other emotion. She picked up the book which had come from the typewriter she had just seen. How would it end? Could the story be any more interesting than the past few hours?

The words bounced around as the taxi progressed. Even when still, they stayed rooted to the page. They could be read over and over, but they failed to drown out the one thought that filled every one of her senses.

One thought popped in and kept pushing its way to the front like a loud, impatient European, unaccustomed to waiting in line: *I should never go back.*

Chapter 4

Excerpt from MEAT IS MURDER by Larry Llewellyn

Light from the single, hanging bulb flooded into Andrew's eyes as the hood was removed. The bulb was a dull forty watts but compared to the blackness of several seconds ago, he might as well have been staring into the sun.

Even with the pain in his eyes as they started to adjust, he couldn't help but take in as much of his surroundings as possible.

The two minutes, sitting in the dim room but in near complete darkness, told him as much as his eyes could have communicated. The parts of rough concrete floor under foot were familiar. The sound of a constant drip-drip in the corner and the smell of damp, old stone had been encountered every day for decades.

There was no doubt, even before the big reveal, that the place of his captivity was commonplace rather than creative. *I was only down here earlier. Why am I back here?*

His mind was so caught up in confusion that he failed to consider the danger inherent in it all. He could not help but wonder why someone would stage such an elaborate kidnapping, only to return him to his own place of work, still dressed in the white trousers, shirt and apron, splattered with blood. For some reason unknown to him, his black socks and shoes had been removed, leaving his bare feet to feel the effects of a cold floor.

He shrugged his shoulders, his restraints preventing him from doing much at all. *I suppose anyone can be held prisoner anywhere.*

"Why am I here?" he asked.

No answer.

"I know someone's behind me," he said, before shouting, "Why am I *here?*"

His heart was beating harder and faster the longer his questions went unanswered. He couldn't shake one simple thought, forcing itself through his mind again and again, almost in time with the drip he had not fixed. *I'm here to die… to die… to die…*

The conversation earlier that day thundered through his mind like an out-of-control meat grinder.

It's kidnap insurance, he had said, slapping his belly in a comical manner.

You never know what those animal rights nuts will try next. At least most of those skinny weirdos couldn't shift someone like me.

How many times had he said something like that? If you say something enough, does it make it true in some crazy sort of a way?

Looking straight ahead, and then to the right and to the left, Andrew had still not had sight of the person responsible for the kidnapping. Was it some crazy hoax? Was it a publicity stunt? What other reason could there be for kidnapping a pillar of the local community, a giver to charities, a friend of the mayor, and the man who had owned the family butcher's shop for the past forty years?

He felt a chill in the air. He could see his own breath misting and fading in front of him. On several occasions his small-rimmed glasses started to fog from the effect before clearing again.

A perplexed mind was rushing through the possibilities. *Would a ransom demand be made? Could the whole thing have been a mistake?*

Neither would turn out to be true.

At the point at which Andrew's questions were driving down his odds of surviving at the same time as driving up his blood pressure, the kidnapper emerged from the shadows somewhere behind him.

The lowly butcher took in a sharp, cold breath. *It's her? Why her?*

The spindly, blond-haired nutcase had been a blight on his business for too long. She who had campaigned to provoke action and reaction was stood there looking as scruffy and feeble as usual. The same frayed blue jeans and ugly light brown, tatty woollen top had heralded a time when his life was about to get more difficult.

Why can't she find a new hobby? He looked on that ugly sweater yet again. *Anyone wearing that scratchy top might be inclined to feel grumpy.*

Her expression was as stern as it was skeletal. Casting his mind back over recent events, he had never seen her even smile. He had never seen her hair look anything other than the mess that it was in.

Surrounding the seat in which Andrew was bound, he could see familiar tools and implements. He had used them all, one floor up, on numerous occasions. The implements used day to day for cutting and shaping meat had been sharpened and cleaned. They had been laid out carefully on the surface of a stainless steel trolley.

Staring down at the tools of his trade, he could not help but see them in a new light. They would certainly be used for the carving of meat and flesh, and they would be devastatingly effective. They were weapons.

The nutcase woman, Crazy Kimmy, had that look in her eyes. He had upset her one too many times, possibly more. *She has never been dangerous. Never a genuine threat. Have I pushed her too far?*

The man could do nothing but listen to the rehearsed monologue of the ashen-faced activist as she explained in detail the way she had felt after every single embarrassing incident, all in her southern, upper-class accent and manner of speech.

Andrew found it difficult to concentrate on the words of this woman with her high-pitch whine, her increasingly manic tone.

"You know what you've done to me," Kimmy said. "You know the effect of the years of belittling, verbal abuse, the insults, the mockery…"

Andrew scowled at her. "No one takes my words seriously. No one."

"That's what you think!" she screamed back in his face. "You have damaged my efforts so much. You and your little carnivorous corner shop!"

Andrew's mind wandered from the restraints and he tried to shrug, before remembering the difficulty in doing so. "I'm just trying to run a business."

"Was the pig's blood stunt business?" She spat at him.

Andrew repressed a smile. That one was inspired by Stephen King's debut novel, Carrie. He chose not to share that with his captor.

"What about the animal intestines in my car last summer," Kimmy said, "or the defacing of my posters?"

There was silence for several seconds before Andrew said, "So what now? What are you going to do to exact your revenge for all these little things I've done?"

In a low, evil-sounding tone she said, "I think you know what's coming."

Andrew laughed in desperation. "I do a series of small practical jokes, and your response is… this?"

"Small jokes?" She walked over and picked up the meat clever as if she was picking up a pencil. "Here's a joke for you. Private pain for public humiliation!"

She loosened a strap and positioned his hand on a steel surface slightly elevated from its previous resting position on the chair arm. There was no question that Kimmy was stronger than she appeared. Maybe it was the adrenaline. Maybe it was her sheer rage.

With the restraints on the chair still tight enough, Andrew was powerless to move it more than an inch. She brought the razor-sharp implement down until metal crashed against metal.

Andrew was surprised that he did not yell out in pain. He did not faint. There was no significant drama in the seconds that followed. That was, at least, until the sight of his own blood registered in his mind. He had seen plenty of blood in his line of work, but it had rarely been his own, and not in such a large quantity, spreading so quickly over the steel, overflowing and yet trying to cling to every surface like a well-made gravy.

In a delayed reaction, furious pain shot through Andrew's hand and arm and every nerve in his body seemed to scream to be freed. He had just lost a finger. He would lose more.

"How do you feel now?" Kimmy asked in a sarcastic tone, her voice becoming more manic with each word. "Are you hurt? Upset? It's only a little finger! It's not that big a deal!"

Andrew wanted to say that the occasional embarrassing episode in the centre of the town did not equate to the punishment of losing body parts, but he felt too light-headed, too distant to respond reasonably. He had become subject to paralysing shock.

"How about I keep going, taking one bit off for every time you made me look a fool?"

Piece by piece, she cut off extremities and placed them in a large plastic barrel in the corner of the room. With every finger and toe removed, the pain intensified. With every amputation, his mind clouded and he became faint.

By the time she moved on to removing the hands and feet, he was shivering with an uncomfortable numbness. Severed nerves at every limb meant pain jumping around his body like random forks in a lightning storm.

She adjusted the straps, one at a time, positioning them where they could still be of most effect after each limb had been removed in its entirety. Blood covered every surface and was splattered all over the woman's clothes, arms and face. Combined with the angry look on her face, she looked like someone far removed from a good cause. She looked like the evilest person alive.

"The animals at the shelters, the ones you said should be turned to burgers, sausages and steaks…" She picked up the clever, wiped it on a nearby rag, and reached for his left forearm. She rested the meat clever on the elbow joint and drew it back. After a second, it came crashing down, only cutting halfway through the joint. She yanked at it, pulling free and then she swung again, then again until she had successfully found her way through. "Those animals will eat well tonight!"

Andrew had never taken delight in the slaughter of an animal. There had never been any sense of power in the cruelty he undertook in the name of feeding others. Yet, Kimmy was doing exactly that. She had spent substantial energy in complaining to the world that Andrew was some blood-thirsty monster. From where he was sitting, she was the only one taking delight in shedding the blood of another living being.

Kimmy was without doubt off her rocker. Andrew had learned, far too late, that it was not only a bad idea to get on the wrong side of an unstable person, but that it was a worse idea to stay there, waving a flag and dancing.

This woman would take him, in pieces, to the local underfunded animal shelter in which she volunteered. Ravenous, starving animals would be fed on his flesh.

Andrew, in life and in death, would provide meat for the masses. He would learn that even he could be reduced to the sum of his parts. He was made up of meat, and he could be part of the grand recycling regime of carnivorous creatures, referred to romantically as the Circle of Life.

Chapter 5

"You think it's okay to carry on like this?" he said with his voice raised.

He was almost shouting in her face. At around half an inch taller and having worked in the building trade his entire life, the man could be intimidating. His pale blue eyes and thinning fair hair did nothing to soften the hardened expression on his reddened, angry face.

"How old do you think I am?" Her own loud shrill tone made each syllable bounce back at force from the hard Magnolia woodchip walls and the high ceiling. After assaulting each other's ears, the sounds echoed and faded as they travelled along the tiled floor.

He stood blocking the entire length of the turn-of-the-last-century hallway in their terraced house, the inside rejuvenated, the outside the same dull brick.

To the left was the lounge in which her father would have spent several hours watching out of the window, wondering what his little girl was doing. Straight ahead, the stairs he would have climbed to go to bed, wondering when she would return home.

To the left of the stairs and further ahead, the kitchen where he had prepared his own breakfast alone, still thinking the same thoughts as the night before. *Where is she? What is she doing?*

He shrugged and turned to walk away, adding in a softer, quieter voice, "How old are *you*? Apparently *not* old enough! Still making the short-sighted choices of a teenager."

"It wasn't some random stranger, Dad." She was rooted to the spot. "It was Larry Llewellyn."

He nodded sarcastically as he dragged his feet down the

hallway. "Oh, I see. It makes *perfect* sense that you should spend the night in the home of a man who is single and spends all day writing stories about killing people?!"

The next noise was somewhere between a sigh and a frustrated groan. "If it's any of your business, nothing happened. Not that you've shown much of an interest in me until recently. I can take care of myself, you know. I'm not a six-year-old girl that falls down the stairs anymore."

Those final few words forced her father to stop in his tracks. He turned to stare daggers at his daughter. Those ethereal words turned into something tangible as they travelled the hallway, something solid yet invisible seemed to collide with him, knocking him back a step. He stood there, looking back, bewildered.

There was history in the words she had almost spat at him. Only three people in the world knew the hurt in those words, and two of them were right there, embroiled in an increasingly furious exchange of verbal blows.

With his brow furrowed and his teeth clenched, the old rage nearly resurfaced. Somewhere inside was something dormant, waiting for the chance to explode out of him again.

For the longest of awkward pauses, neither of them said a word. He just stood there, taking deep breath after deep breath until the redness in his face dissipated somewhat. The traffic outside continued. Birds still sang away, all as if this was not the most important conversation in the world ever.

"This is about more than your misguided belief that you can look after yourself," he said, turning around; struggling for a moment to catch his breath, wagging his right forefinger at her as he spoke. "Your mother and I are concerned for your safety. In addition, your conduct reflects on us. Did you pause to consider that at all before getting drunk in the home of a stranger?"

Sam started her reply with an exaggerated sarcastic nod.

"Oh, I have a lot to consider! You're not worried about me. You never have been. You're more concerned for your *reputation,* aren't you?"

The man was visibly shocked and offended, too much so to offer any words in response.

The sarcastic tone continued. "Ooh, look at Samantha, the daughter of the reputable builder. Look at her sleeping around. Is *that* what you think they'll all say?"

She stormed up to her room, slamming the door. The late response was bellowed from the base of the stairs. "You'll regret meeting up with strangers!"

She leaned against the back of the door. He was still shouting at her. "I can guarantee you'll wish someday that you'd made better choices! You'll feel as disappointed and angry with yourself. Just like I feel right now!"

She stepped away from the door and stood near the middle of the pastel pink bedroom. The light oak-styled double bed, large chest of drawers and bedside table were shiny and new, as disingenuous as her father's distress at her absence.

There were ancient and once-loved teddies on top of the drawers. An old Disney princess cushion was sitting on the bed, the one that she remembered hugging on those nights her parents didn't know she could hear their arguments. Posters of Belle and Ariel, her former Disney heroines were on the walls, giving her hope of a better existence. The old clutter had been put in place by him, hurrying to prepare a room fit for a student.

It was an odd combination of new and old. Her new bedroom was caught dithering between the lines of freedoms granted to University students and the stifling of an overbearing parent. The old childish trinkets and memorabilia were merely signs that the interior designer for this project had refused to let go of the little girl who had once shared his home.

She shook her head. *It wasn't supposed to be like this.*

Having been accepted at Manchester University, the time seemed right to reconnect with her father. Doing so would reduce her student debt and allow them to catch up on many years of missed daddy-daughter time.

Instead, we have nothing in common… and I'm not that little girl anymore!

A single tear ran down her cheek. *Maybe I was naïve to think he would hug me and tell me he loved me. He stopped doing that a long time ago.*

She took up a seating position on the end of her bed, the bookshelf straight in front. Once again it was cheap furniture failing in its attempt to look like expensive oak. The bookshelf was his. The contents of most of it, beyond the kids' books she hadn't read in over a decade, were hers. There was the name of the man who had been the cause of this contention. Right there on the spines of a dozen dark-coloured books.

Her phone vibrated. Her mother's oft-used phrase came to mind. *Speak of the devil and he shall appear.* She shook her head. *What a ridiculous notion. If Satan truly existed, could he really be summoned in a manner like that of the comical Beetlejuice?*

She picked up her phone and read the incoming message.

> Hello, my latest victim! :) I would benefit a great deal from a fact-finding day. I would like to know more about you and your background. There's method behind the ways I make my characters leap from the page. You would, of course, be able to ask me anything about the writing process for your own amusement and benefit. I'll pay for travel, food, everything. Are you free this coming Saturday?

Her hands typed out a reply, as if they had power of

attorney and no longer needed a firm decision from her brain. Typing the words, 'Yes I would love to', she hit the send icon with an amount of force that was unnecessary.

No chaperone. No father ruling on alleged indiscretions or the muddying of the family name. What right did he have to speak in such a way? He had barely even been a part of her life. This new, and mysterious man offered her a ticket out of her uncomfortable home life for a day and she was going to take it.

Chapter 6

The windows of the stationary car were fogging up with condensation which threatened to obscure their view of the narrow street. In truth, there was little within the scope of Larry's view that could be deemed sufficiently interesting to capture his imagination.

Humble red brick houses flanked them with twelve in an unbroken line on each side, house after house a near-identical clone of its neighbour, every owner seeming to choose their own colour for the large stone lintels above each window and door. Each owner seemed to have been engaged in the futile exercise of trying to personalise their property, attempting to make their own slice of the street look uniquely theirs.

Twenty four front doors and seventy two windows, in similar styles, faced and opened out onto the patchy tarmac, pot-holes exposing the old cobble stones beneath. The repeatedly resurfaced road was all but hidden by two near-unbroken strings of parked cars.

The street was wide enough to allow for three cars travelling side-by-side, but as was typical of modern-day Manchester, Liverpool and probably every other city, parked cars reduced the usable space to that of a tiny country lane. The designers of the neighbourhoods had not considered a car-filled future. There was no accommodating the automobile. Just row after row of mass-produced houses for the masses.

A colourful ceramic plate on the wall let them know they were parked one house away. It was as close as they could get to the end terrace house that Sam once called home. She had admitted to having no idea who occupied number 23 these days. An irrelevant detail.

The street mirrored so many in the modern age with

curtain-twitchers on the verge of calling the police at the slightest shadow of unexpected movement, such was their need to protect themselves and their property.

Looking beyond the grey slate roofs and red brick chimneys in almost every direction, an accumulation of cumulous clouds provided another layer of grey gloom. The place already had an air of neglect, as if even an apocalypse would leave it alone.

"It's been a long time since I was last here," Sam said, fidgeting with the belt that matched her white and blue floral cotton dress.

Larry nodded, the spring of fresh frustration barely showing in the way he held the steering wheel. There were so many ways to respond but he just tapped and squeezed and waited.

"I've seen it in home videos. We had fun here. We washed the car together right there; we ran around in the back yard and in the park down the road. It's just difficult to look at it all positively, given what happened."

Larry turned to her, asking the question he had been waiting to ask for the past fifteen minutes. "Exactly what happened here?"

She shrugged. It seemed as if she wanted to let it all out, but she was struggling to do so.

"That's all you're giving me: A shrug? What can I do with that?"

She slapped her palms against her lap and turned to face him. "What do you want me to say? I was probably five or six. I don't know what really happened."

A soft voice was needed. Like that therapist tone he had used before. "Just tell me what you *do* remember. Is being here bringing anything back?"

She looked down at her hands as she squeezed and pulled at her fingers. Her voice trailed off, her words like the soft mumble of a guilty child. "I remember I was messing around at the top of the stairs. There was a safety gate, but it was open. I turned too quickly and before I knew what was going on, I tumbled head-over-heels until my dad had hold of me to stop me from falling any further down the stairs."

She separated her hands, her left hand subconsciously finding the scar on her right arm, near her elbow, stroking it gently. A permanent reminder of an incident she could never forget.

"I remember there was a lot of arguing that night," she continued, "and every night afterwards whenever they thought I couldn't hear them. Not long after that they divorced, and I was forced to move away."

Tears were running down her cheeks falling on to her hands which were lying still, gripping each other so hard her knuckles were turning white.

He waited until she turned to face him again. Her eyes were wide and glistening with tears.

The eyes of a crying person were fascinating. A window of opportunity existed in gazing into the moist, tear-filled eyes of those with a self-inflicted vulnerability. That moment, easily missed, afforded the briefest of glimpses into their inner child. There was a tragic beauty in the mournful stare of a subject at any age.

"Shall we go somewhere else now?" he asked.

She nodded, looking away.

~ ~ ~ ~ ~

Pulling up by the side of a pleasant leafy street, a large new sign stood just inside a tall green railed metal fence. The sign displayed in large ornate gold-effect lettering the words "St Joseph's" and "All-girls school" smaller underneath. The mere suggestion of uppity little girls swarming this street in their perfect uniforms would make him groan with disgust. *How many could a driver run over in one go if they tried?*

Sam's old school was housed in a vintage building set back from the road from a time in the mid-to-late 1800s, an era when effort was expended to add ornate touches to even basic amenities. Equivalent water towers and toilet blocks built in recent times lacked the aesthetic qualities of their ancient counterparts. A tasteful dark green paint was used on the intricate carved wooden edgings as well as on many surfaces around the buildings and sheds.

The grounds were neat and well-kept. There was never much fun to be had in that playground. How could there be with everything staying so neat and clean? There was probably a janitor or groundskeeper lurking behind a shed or a bush, day and night, waiting to sweep up every leaf as soon as it hit the ground, ready to comb the blades of grass forming that perfect lawn so that everything was once again neat and straight.

The detailed leaf and branch pattern carved into the wood ornamenting each roof, door and window was so fascinating that it grabbed the attention more than the girl pouring out her heart in the next seat.

The memory that screamed to be free, trying to leak out through the liquid of her tears, was that of abrupt goodbyes, barely able to bid farewell to her friends. Her sense of loneliness was exacerbated by the move of school in addition to the forced move from the family home and the city she had lived in since birth.

She had soon ended up in a house she hated, in a town that was uninteresting, with potential friends who seemed to judge her before she had uttered more than a mouthful of syllables by way of greeting. In a matter of days her world had fallen apart and the only person who could understand was her mother. They mourned the passing of their previous lives together. Sam blaming herself for the fall that started it all, her mother passing a guilty verdict on herself for causing the rift.

As they travelled around the city, every street in that immediate area held a memory of Sam's that seemed to have been kept under lock and key until the Saturday he prodded and peered into her past. Close to half of the shops and restaurants that had been frequented by the happy family were still standing. Some had long-since been taken over, some nationwide brand obliterating a part of her heritage on their way to establishing a foothold in every retail park in the country.

Sam's facial expressions had said enough before she had uttered a word. Times that were once happy had been put through the wringer of wasted love to the point that there was nothing remaining but regret and misery.

The back-story of her parents, as far as she could remember, was shared as they nursed drinks in a new Starbucks on the outskirts of the town.

It made sense to suggest somewhere foreign, unfamiliar, somewhere that hadn't existed when her life fell apart. She could expound, fill in the blanks.

He flipped his pocket notebook closed for the final time that day. The parts of Sam's past, when the contents of those pages were assembled in the right order and assimilated, would result in a pitiable portrait with which his readers could sympathise.

Every choice she made, every action she undertook, every word she uttered seemed to have roots in that moment she tumbled down the stairs of her family home all those years ago. An entire life trapped behind a tumble.

The young woman's experiences had built a strong,

resilient character, ripe for committing to paper. A perfect protagonist.

~ ~ ~ ~ ~

Standing near the centre of the pink bedroom, Samuel let out a laboured sigh. Sometimes it helped to release the tension from his shoulders and neck. This time it made no difference. A slight grimace started to paint itself on his face, mirroring his mood. *Why did I have to be so harsh on her?*

Experience educated on occasion, proving that the little things made a difference. The affectionate touches, the hugs, the kind words, they all helped to show love and genuine affection. The opposite to this, the worst thing to do, was to mimic a bull in a china shop.

Either energy or enthusiasm drained away. It was difficult to tell which. He took a step back and was soon sitting on the edge of her bed. He put his heavy head in his hands. *What's wrong with me? I want to tell my daughter that I love her and that I'm worried about her, but instead it all comes out wrong!*

What was the saying? If you want to make God laugh, make plans? Today was a free Saturday. It was a gift. The perfect chance to spend time together, to put things right. They would revisit that old café that was still going, they would enjoy those classic milkshakes. But did she even like milkshakes anymore?

New eyes looked around the room with a fresh realisation. The Disney posters, the teddies, the children's books all spoke of the interests of a little girl who was no longer around. He shook his head. *What was I trying to do here? I kept this stuff because it meant something to me. It probably means nothing to her.*

He took his phone from his pocket and woke it up with a double tap. He brought up the contact with Samantha's details. She smiled at him, all the way from her social media profile. It was easy to just stare at the image for a long while without calling, without sending any kind of a message. The screen timed out and he looked away, shaking his head. There would be a chance for apologies, for making up, later that day. An evening apology that was offered when face-to-face would be better.

But what about the other woman, not far away, the other blood relative? There had surely been chances to put things right there as well. Chances that had not been taken. Distance had grown between brother and sister, but neither could really explain why. Over time, resentment had crept in where familial love should have been.

A line of books in front of him, if it had eyes, would be glaring. They were by *that* man, the one who was out with his little girl. What did anyone really know about Larry Llewellyn? The world wide web had a few answers, but the man lived a secluded life. The author only ventured out to talk about death and destruction. How could such a disturbed individual be a good influence?

Even so, he was a male who had shown an interest in Samantha. Maybe if more interest was shown to her by her father, that father would not be sitting on her bed, filled with regret. She had chosen to be with this unusual man instead of her own flesh and blood. What did that say about the nature and the future of their relationship?

Reaching for the unattainable. That's how it felt. Like being dumped in the middle of a bad dream. There had been enough of those to last a lifetime. Even with his little girl right there, the idea of connecting with her, loving her in the way a father should, all seemed elusive. The conscious decision not to crowd her with emotion, to give her space to settle, had not paid dividends over the previous three months.

An outsider looking in might see a parent and a child

sharing a home, talking, trying. But there was a nagging sense that their emotional distance was increasing, faster than it could be wished away. He wiped a tear from his eye with his hand. *I lost her years ago. I'm not going to let someone else steal in, so I lose her again.*

He stood up, smoothed out the duvet to remove signs of his visit, and walked out of the room.

At that moment, a mental To Do List was imagined with the ultimate goal of reconnecting with his daughter:

1. *Apologise to Samantha and arrange to spend some time with her, just like we talked about over the phone during the summer.*

2. *Help her see that people like the famous Larry Llewellyn simply cannot be trusted.*

3. *Win back the affection and attention of my daughter whilst doing points one and two.*

~ ~ ~ ~ ~

Larry was standing in his gleaming white and grey kitchen, holding up a bottle of red wine with an inquisitive look on his face.

Sam laughed as she continued her languid stroll across the lounge before dropping to the sofa. "Not after last time!"

"I can't imagine why," Larry said with a smirk.

Sam rolled her eyes.

How can a day like this be so exhausting? All I've done is sit around, talking about old memories.

Her life had been spent jumbling the pieces of her memory in the hope that it would all make sense. Today, the whole puzzle had been deconstructed, examined and reassembled. Even so, there were still ominous gaps.

Some pieces did not fit, even after their re-introduction that afternoon. What child could make sense of their parents separating? What would anyone think of their dad moving on, starting a new life without them, complete with a new house and a new girlfriend? What had happened to that woman anyway?

She forced out a deep breath. Letting go was a necessary step. So much tension drained from her shoulders that it was a fight to stay awake. *Maybe I'll never see the whole picture.* It was a wish to be relinquished, the whole truth of the past destined to always be elusive.

Despite the positives of new friends, attempts to reinvent herself, and setting a pathway to her future career, a coldness continued to return as memories of a former life and its incumbent friendships resurfaced.

Larry retrieved a small glass from a kitchen cupboard and poured himself something strong. Larry's consumption of a small amount of the dark amber, translucent liquid suggested that it was more expensive than Pinot Grigio or White Lightning that formed a liquid diet for many a student.

Larry took up a position on the sofa opposite Sam and held the drink in his right hand. "It's been a long day," he said with a sigh, looking out over the Manchester skyline. The sun was setting in a splash of colour, silhouetting the high-rise structures dotted along the landscape. For a few moments it resembled a primary school collage.

Sam nodded. "A very long day."

They had spent the day reliving several traumatic scenes in just a few hours, all for the benefit of literature. Pangs of sorrow and remorse came and went. *I've cheapened the experiences by sharing them with someone I barely know.*

Her life's history would be written, read and replayed in

the name of entertainment. How could someone agree to such a thing? How could they not hate themselves?

"Thank you for today," Larry said, turning to look into Sam's eyes. It was a genuine expression of appreciation. However much this man put on a mask, she had been privileged to see the real man behind the printed word today.

Sam shrugged, looking down at the thick white carpet. "It's good to talk about it I guess," she said.

"You don't sound convinced," Larry said.

Sam's shoulders dropped. She also sighed and looked somewhere between the window to her right and Larry's position on the sofa in front of her. "I just feel…"

"Like a sell-out?"

Sam's head spun in a quick, almost instinctive movement as she stared at him. "How did you know I'd be thinking that?"

Larry smiled. "I would be surprised if you *weren't* thinking something like that. It's normal for my future victims to feel that way, like they've been duped into providing their most intimate thoughts to appease the masses."

"And what do you usually say to them?"

Larry smirked. "I say thank you, obviously."

Larry held out his drink for a second as if making a toast to her company. "You need one of these," he said, standing up. "I'll get you one."

She waved her hands in protest. "No, no thank you. I need to get home."

Walking towards the kitchen with his back to her he said, "I insist. Just the one. It helps you relax and not to fret about your privacy being violated."

He walked into the kitchen and removed another glass

from the cupboard.

On the coffee table in front of her were two phones sitting next to each other. There were problems with so many people using near-identical phones. Why had that never been an issue until now?

She scowled for a moment before taking a guess, picking up the phone on the right.

As she turned it on and swiped at the screen, the home screen was not hers. Larry had also seemingly ignored the advice of security experts on TV.

On the small screen she could see part of a conversation between Larry and someone named Steve. She read the most recent message:

> Larry: Too right. She should just be happy to be getting any attention at all!

Who was the girl so desperate for attention? A scroll through the previous messages would shed some light.

The conversation centred around a girl with 'a big heart and a body shape to match' who had 'a nice personality' and 'nice eyes'.

She was described in unflattering terms and then Larry had added 'that's where the good stuff ends'.

Sam's eyes widened in horror. *This is me. I'm the girl.* She read on; Larry was still distracted in preparing a drink she didn't want.

> Steve: Why are you using her as your latest victim?

> Larry: She has no idea how many people I promise will be main characters.

> Larry: Most are ecstatic to be in there somewhere after the final edit, but I can't promise this one that she'll

make the cut!

The phone almost fell from her hand as she turned off the screen, hiding the brutal conversation.

With shaking hands, she replaced the phone. She picked up the one on the left. She put it into her bag as her hands clenched into fists so hard that she was digging her fingernails into her palms.

Her jaw clamped shut. Her heart was pounding. Her face was getting hot. She was so full of rage at that moment that she could have done anything.

With every available muscle clenched, every deep breath seemed to encourage instead of quelling the rage that built inside. She squeezed her eyes shut. *Verbally or physically assaulting him will achieve nothing. Violence is not the answer.*

Larry returned with the drink she had already refused. Without saying a word, Sam stood up, picked up her bag and her coat and stormed towards the front door.

"What are you doing?" Larry asked.

"Getting as far away as I can," said Sam in reply, her voice on the verge of breaking with emotion.

"Why?" Larry asked in the loud voice of an arguing parent.

Sam reached the door, opened it wide enough to fit a hand through and stopped. She turned around, looked at Larry and said. "I apparently have nice eyes, a nice personality and that's where the good stuff ends?"

Larry made some sort of noise between a laugh and an exclamation of disbelief, but he did not extend an apology.

"Are you really going to try to deny what you've been saying about me to your friends?" Sam asked.

"Those comments weren't about you," he offered in defence. He didn't even look like he had convinced himself by the words as they fell from his lips, let alone his guest.

Warm tears ran down her cheeks. "You don't get it, do you? I've had years of insults and abuse about my looks and my size. I've learned to live with it. I had just hoped you were different."

She opened the door wider and turned to walk out. "I was wrong. You're worse. You *pretended* to think differently and then you tricked me."

Larry's face was turning a darker shade of red. He was used to getting things his own way. "I was going to immortalise you. People everywhere could've fallen in love with you and cried at your death. Now, they'll just have no idea who you are when you meet your fate."

Sam stormed out of the door into a neat and newly refurbished hallway, making sure to slam the heavy door for added effect. Residents of the other three flats on that floor could probably hear the raised voices. They might even be looking out of their security peepholes in their doors, seeing a crying woman fleeing.

Tears blurred the approach to the elevator, but tissues were buried in the bag. They would have to be found and used later. The bigger issue was getting away from there, regardless of anyone seeing.

She pressed the button hard enough that her fingers hurt. The wait was only several seconds prior to the doors sliding open. She entered and pushed the button far harder than was necessary again, like it was the face of that man staring back at her, smirking.

The tears were stopping as a scowl etched itself on her features. To the left was a mirror that confirmed the hardening of her face. *I will not be a victim of this man!*

Crying was okay, especially now, but the woman reflected back, scowling, could choose another path, leading far away from self-pity. *So much for the great Larry Llewellyn. I'm much better without that monster in my life.*

Chapter 7

A life of disingenuousness might suit someone whose entire livelihood was derived from contrived characters and plot pulled from thin air. This was not how Larry viewed his life. The emotions, the people, the character traits, the settings, every particle populating the stories that began in his mind, all of it was as real to him as the phone in his hand.

The phone had been used on many occasions but to useless effect over the remainder of Saturday. Another attempt to get through. There wouldn't be many more. He puffed out his cheeks. *It's hard to sound sincere in a voicemail message, especially when you're not.*

It was her voice that answered, but it wasn't her. Voicemail again. There were two pre-scripted messages sitting in her inbox by now. He shook his head as he ended the call. His phone had done nothing wrong, but he glared at it like a dog that had chewed the furniture, like a best friend who had betrayed a confidence. *She should not have seen them in the first place.*

A writer's time was a precious commodity. There had to be space for reading, for writing and for procrastination in the name of writing. Minutes wasted on other people and projects soon became a knife attack on a creative mind. Too many hours and days wasted in the company of precious-minded potential protagonists would inflict severe wounds on the writing process. Maybe this time the ethereal part of him could stagger, bleeding and gasping, over the finish line of the next big story. Maybe, but only if the time-wasting stopped.

The seconds ticking by, those spent fact-finding and backstory building, those spent with a phone in-hand apologising again, were more important than the feelings of some easily offended female. Yet, if the apology worked, the hours spent in the woman's company would not have been wasted.

The notebook that had captured the character of Sam was staring up from the coffee table. He poked out his bottom lip. *Could I still use it? She hasn't specifically revoked permission.*

He shook his head. Too many legal complications. The book stayed still; his eyes fixed on it as he paced around the low table. *The occasional court case can provide ample free publicity, even with the eventual cost.*

Dizziness drowned determination as he paused his pacing and leaned against the window. The left sofa, not as worn-in as the right, had been used by her. It had been her bed on one occasion. It had been the place where she had been poking around in someone else's business.

He shook his head, waking up his phone again. *One more apology and then I'll move on to someone else.*

There was a rueful acceptance of hearing her recorded voice once again as the phone dialled. But no, not this time. His head snapped back slightly as she spoke.

"Sam, it's Larry," he said before rolling his eyes. *Of course she knows it's me!*

"What do you want, Larry?" The tone from Sam was harsh with a hint of despair.

"I wanted to apologise."

"I suggest you get on with it then."

"I'm sorry for the hurt I caused you. I was joking around, over-egging for friends. It was all nonsense you read in those texts. I hope you can believe that."

"But it was about me, wasn't it?"

He paused and took a deep breath. "Yes, it was. Even though the messages were sent privately, I should not have sent such horrible comments. Not about you, nor about anyone else."

"Thank you for your apology, and for your honesty," Sam said, sounding calm, almost defeated.

"Thank you for listening to me," Larry replied.

"There's one thing that still concerns me though," Sam said. "If this is how you wanted to write about me, how could I possibly say yes to potentially having such terrible things put in print for the world to see?"

"It's not really how I see you," Larry protested. "When I saw you on the train you had something pretty, something engaging about you. I wanted to find a way to capture that on paper."

"So, I was a challenge? A conquest of sorts?"

Larry shook his head. "That came out wrong. I just meant you had a presence that I warmed to instantly and I could tell you would be the perfect person-"

"The perfect person to use? To abuse? To insult?"

He waved his right hand dismissively. "No, not at all. Look, I know you probably don't want to see me or to speak to me again. I fully understand."

"I've just known a lot of guys who only ever seem to think about one thing. Girls are a means to an end for gratification, but it's only worth keeping them around if they're attractive enough."

"That's not true of everyone," Larry offered. "When you start saying all men are this, or all men are that, doesn't that make you as guilty as them?"

The conversation hit a lull. It was either heading towards a full-blown argument or it was heading to an awkward impasse.

Sam sighed. "Get on with it then," she said.

"Get on with what?" Larry asked, trying to sound puzzled.

"The real reason for your call. It wasn't to apologise, was it?"

"I called to apologise... But could I ask another question? Could I still base my main character for my next novel on you?"

Promises were about to be fired at her. The character would change. They would be more beautiful, charming and funny. Before any of it could be spoken, there was no one to hear the words. Sam had already hung up. *Bitch.*

He tossed the phone onto the sofa. Tension spread from his balled fists up his arms. His face felt warm. His heart was pounding. *So much for recovering wasted time.*

Chapter 8

She trudged into the centre of the pink room. The décor could prompt a smile or a grimace. *I know what he was trying to do here. This is borne out of love, not a need to cling to the past.*

The room was an apology without words, a recognition that the man had let too many years go by without being there for her. She stuck out her bottom lip as her eyes again threatened a tear or two. *How many moments have we missed?*

Her father stayed out of her way as she rushed to her room in her earlier tear-filled state. He had then offered something to cheer her up. The walk around the corner to the café and the ordering of large milkshakes seemed childish, but it had worked.

Full of chocolate, milk and cream, the bookshelves, a particular row of books, looked different. They seemed to loom large, casting a shadow, instead of looking on from their small spot in the corner, resting on fake oak.

She pursed her lips. *Maybe it's time to clear some space for academia and to get rid of the collection of books by a certain author.*

The rustle of a tree drew attention to the ajar dormer window. Nothing there but the top of a tree and the red bricks of a house across the street, illuminated by an orange streetlight. The outdoor lighting clashed to some degree with the pale pink of her own bedroom walls.

She continued to stare out of the window for a moment. What was there left to see? A thousand gazes out of that window had not added anything. She shook her head. Whatever she had expected to see in the dimly lit street was not there. It was always good to make sure no one was lurking in that tree. It was easy to spiral into paranoia. Trust was scarce at times. *It's bad when you can't trust your family. It's worse when you can't trust yourself.*

Cue the arrival of the real dad, the one from all those years ago, earlier that day. Missing for so long, even when present, the man had shown up in person, but not in mind nor in enthusiasm. Gone were the misunderstandings and crossed words. In their place, tenderness and compassion.

The framed picture by the side of the bed gloated of a once happier time. A young Samantha was sitting between her parents on a bench in a play park in Manchester, grins all around. She let out a heavy sigh. *Twelve years is a long time to miss out on treats, hugs and piggybacks on-request.*

Her face drained to a miserable expression as she again spun around. The other books on those shelves. *A few missed years of bedtime stories from those old books too.*

And yet, like the oak pretence in plastic covering the MDF that held those books, behind every happy memory was another two or three of angry outbursts.

When ensconced in another rewound reverie, determined effort could focus the mind on the milkshakes and hugs instead of the mistakes and the hurt. Life had torn her away from the first man she had ever loved, and had been cruel to only reunite them when all common ground seemed to have long-since eroded.

The books still looked on as she flopped down until she was sitting on the edge of her bed. Her eyes were burning into the spines of harmless, printed words. *Has this author hurt anyone else en route to creating these much-loved titles?*

What about those characters? How did those heroes and villains live? *Have past protagonists been real? Have they been cast aside?*

How would they have felt when they read their names or the caricature of their personalities in words seen by the entire world? Every detail, every mistake, every flaw belittled and broadcast to be consumed by an insatiable public appetite for Larry's brand of death and destruction.

The books had drawn her in like powerful magnets until she knelt by the shelves. She ran the fingertips of her right hand across the uneven line created by their spines. She sighed and then approached book number one. She plucked it from its place. It was Larry's first novel. *Bowled Over.*

Sam smiled. Craig Pinnock was the central character. After meeting his girlfriend in a local bowling alley during one of many ten pin bowling competitions, a relationship blossomed. The introverted Craig was a fantastic bowler. Strike after strike and a near-flawless technique had taken him to the verge of the national championships.

There came a point where 'Crusher Craig' as he was dubbed, needed to choose between his obsession with the sport and the pregnant woman in his life. He chose a wife and a family over the passion of his youth and young adulthood and he never looked back.

Over a decade later, the famed bowling ball, with a blue and black marbled finish and engraved with his nickname, still sat on a shelf in the closet. In the years to come he would show his three children the videos of him in action, then he would dust off and show off the heavy ball that had not seen the light of day in some time. His wife had suggested displaying the ball more prominently in the house, but in Craig's mind, doing so might reignite his first real passion to the detriment of those whom he loved.

Retrieving a pair of smart shoes from the back of their packed closet for a night out with his wife, Craig found himself caught on the strap of a bag. Yanking his arm backwards, he stumbled, fell over another bag and lay flat on his back with his head just clear of the door. Winded but otherwise fine, he lifted his head to see his prized bowling ball, which had rolled off the front of the upper shelf, falling towards him, no more than five inches from his face.

With no time to do anything other than widen his eyes, the heavy ball collided with his head with the same kind of force it had known when colliding with pin after pin all those years earlier. Strike! He laid on the floor, blood pouring from his head. The engraved lettering 'Crusher Craig' was visible in reverse on his forehead. It was as if the bowling ball was exclaiming "Vengeance is mine," as it rolled from the dusty shelf.

Sam replaced the debut novel and picked up his second, *The People Decide*. It told of the charismatic Don Wagstaff, an overweight, American Senator with a reputation for womanising, destroying lives and homesteads of many for his own benefit and getting his own way. The man was running in a US presidential election.

His campaign manager had more than once left Don alone to "do whatever he does" with another female voter. This time that veil of privacy would prove to be a problem. After being nominated by his party following months of campaigning, election day had arrived. Don mistakenly found himself in an unmonitored voting booth where he was strangled, dragged to a back room and left for dead by a desperate voter he had left divorced and penniless. He won the vote for the job of a lifetime, but his life ebbed away as he heard the victory cheer of his ignorant team.

Touching but not removing book number three, *Cuts and Losses*, she recalled the story of Gerald Hill, the sleek, young executive, and the most impressive in the history of Culbertson Motors. He had achieved, through cost cutting measures, the highest profit margins they had ever seen. The cars were rumoured to be unsafe, but he didn't care. Turnover was better than ever, and he was universally praised by those sitting in the comfortable chairs of the board room. His joining their ranks was a foregone conclusion.

He arrived one morning in a brand-new executive saloon from a rival company. That night he took the hill road home to his lavish mountain-side home, only to find that his brakes were not working on the steepest of drops. He hadn't trusted his own company's car and he had died as a result of his opposite number saving money on a crucial component: the brakes.

Sam ran her fingertips over books four and five, which told two similar stories. *They're After Me* told the story of Kevin Wise, a paranoid Schizophrenic who hired his own bodyguard, only for the same bodyguard to get so agitated that he killed him.

Ben Ferguson in *A Dangerous Place* became a hermit, afraid to venture outside because of the exotic diseases rife in the world in which he lived. After becoming such a recluse, he had no one to whom he could turn when he punctured the skin on a rusty nail and died a painful death from Tetanus.

Sam stopped and looked down at the books as if they were misbehaving children. *A part of me wants to get rid of you all, but I've loved reading you. Should I have to move on, just because I don't like your creator?*

Larry Llewellyn had been a successful published author for over a decade. Over that time, he had been prolific in bringing his ideas to life in the printed word. Sam was to be the main character in his next bestseller.

Sam smiled at the irony contained in those novels on her shelf. The smile faded with the name Larry Llewellyn in embossed gold lettering on each. Those words in the messages. What were they supposed to achieve? Who would do it? *Why am I surprised that a man who constantly tries to find ways to kill off the hero would turn out to be a horrible person?*

The tips of Sam's fingers continued to brush the books on her shelves. Past Llewellyn's novels she touched the spine of *Peter Pan; or, the Boy Who Wouldn't Grow Up* by J.M. Barrie. Much had been told about this man. Adopter of orphaned children, giving the copyright of his most famous work to

Great Ormond Street Children's Hospital, a pillar of the community and clearly a kind person.

She touched the spines of *Great Expectations*, *A Christmas Carol*, *Oliver Twist* and *A Tale of Two Cities* by Charles Dickens. By all accounts, the prolific author was another decent human being, campaigning for children's rights, education and social reform.

The famous plays of William Shakespeare were next. *Romeo and Juliet*, *Hamlet*, *A Midsummer Night's Dream* and *Julius Caesar* were there. Here was a man of which little was known of his private life. He may have been kind, helpful, giving, or he could have been selfish and mean. What had been said of the man was that he was dedicated to his work and that his legacy had come under somewhat unfair scrutiny since his death with claim after claim that his works were not his own.

How would it have been to meet one of these famous authors, asking them questions in some imaginary, leafy park on a perfect summer's day?

Sam: Charles Dickens, what an honour it is to meet you, sir.

Charles Dickens: It's a pleasure. What can I do for you?

Sam: Mr Dickens, you seem a kind person. What do you think of a man who shares your profession, who would insult a female in secret messages sent to a friend of theirs?

Sam shook her head. *Surely I would have better things to talk to him about than that. Let's try that again.*

J.M Barrie: It's nice to meet you lass, I hear you have some questions for me.

Sam: Did you really talk like that? I know you're Scottish but isn't the thick accent a clichéd stereotype?

J.M Barrie: I'm afraid I don't know what you're talking about. This is all in your mind. How could you know how I talk if we've never met?

Sam: I suppose you're right. Anyway, I wanted to tell you that the story of Peter Pan is amazing.

J.M Barrie: Thank you. I'm glad you enjoyed it.

Sam: My question is whether you think men like Larry Llewellyn will ever grow up or whether they will continue to act at a level of immaturity that would put a Neverland resident to shame.

J.M Barrie: That sounds like a conversation you'd need to have with him.

Sam smiled and grimaced in equal measure. *I can't seem to imagine meeting a famous figure from history without Larry somehow invading my mind and becoming the topic of conversation. Hopefully in time he'll leave me alone and I'll let him.*

She walked to her bedroom window again. The solitary tree was still moving in a light breeze. She let out a sigh. *It's been an emotional ride but at least it's over now.* Those books, even if ignored, would become the elephant in her room. *Maybe I'll donate them to a local charity shop.* She wore a wicked smile for a moment. *Maybe I should make up with the man for long enough to get them signed, and then I can sell them online.*

With renewed determination, she hurried back to the shelf. She snatched at the books, plucking them free one-by-one as if trying to rid the shelf of some sort of spreading infection. She half-slammed each one onto the floor, creating a rough pile.

They were good stories, written by a bad man. What was to be done with them? A final decision could wait. They just needed to be off that shelf where they could no longer mock her with their silent sit-in protest in honour of their creator. *Larry Llewellyn is out of my life and I'm out of his.*

She sat on the floor. There was space to fill with other

books. It was time to find a few worthwhile additions to fill that void.

Time to move on. Hopefully, Larry will be doing the same.

Chapter 9

The interview replayed again.

"What goes on in the mind of Larry Llewellyn?" the woman had asked, her wavy blonde hair bouncing on the shoulders of her business suit with every slight head movement, the bright lights of the studio catching the wisps of hair and turning them for a moment into molten gold.

"I think you can see from my stories. With the things I've lived through, I'm just grateful that I can draw on that pain and produce something real. It's a privilege to have so many enjoy the products of my messed-up mind."

The memory faded. If only they knew the truth. They had no idea what was locked inside.

In the minutes sandwiching the witching hour, most people would dream of nothing more than a good night's sleep. Larry was different. His muse, relentless, drove him through the barrier of tiredness and onto the extraordinary. This being, invisible to most, had an insatiable appetite for his ingenuity.

The muse, as real as the words in his mind and the paper on his desk, understood him. His best work seemed to seep from his fingers as he overworked them in the hours when his only companions were a loud typewriter and an enveloping darkness, chased away in one spot by a green glass-topped desk lamp.

The instigator of invention, the constant nagging nobody that fed on the thoughts dumped onto paper, was not easily articulated to the satisfaction of others. As the keys clacked and lettered arms collided with ribbon and paper, he let out a heavy breath. *What could possibly fill the void if my muse ever left me?*

Every new idea was expected to be given due

consideration and suitable development. An idea trapped inside the mind was nothing more than a waste.

The inked imprints inspired by his disturbed mind stared back at him. The public had been shielded from the worst of them. They had to be. *I can't let people see this side of me. What would my readers, my fans, and any potential reader think if my darkest creations were unleashed?*

Truth made people recoil in horror. Honest words brought media hounds to the door. When those in the spotlight spoke their mind, there was outcry. Some things were best hidden.

There was truth in that interview. It was his truth, anyway, regardless of the opinions of others. The genuine, heart-wrenching grief of a troubled soul was returned during his reflections. If there was a point that life changed, it was then. It was right there. Tragedy tormented until the pain needed an outlet. Inner pain destroyed from the inside. Other damaged individuals turned to substance abuse or self-harm, but his release had always been writing: Self-soothing that was creative and destructive in equal parts.

Tonight, the terrible taskmaster would not relent, restricting reminiscing. The idea had hatched, and the little monster would soon be running rampant through his mind. Pushing it out onto paper was the only way to set it free.

Replacing the paper with a fresh sheet, thoughts were settling and organising themselves. He was staring at the classic typewriter. He was the hero in a Western, looking towards the nemesis at high noon, fingers dancing an inch from a holstered weapon, eager to let fly. Fingers were close enough to touch the keys, ready to fire off another round. The result, another direct hit with his audience.

There was no such thing as an easy novel. The anguish, the contemplation, the thrill of discovery, all culminated in a crescendo of creativity that could push the story forward.

Characters, their motives, the settings were all invented, and then followed through their world. An author's job was to record that journey as those beings took on a life of their own.

With a working title of *The Girl Who Knew Too Much* typed on that first crisp, clean sheet of white paper, the trusty old Royal Model P typewriter with its almost gunmetal colour was almost pulsing with the excitement of being put to work. With every key in full working order and with a new ribbon in place, he started to type the name that would appear throughout the first draft.

Samantha Barkes would be woven through the fabric of this work of fiction like a golden thread. Her personality could draw in the typical reader. After all, she was one of them. The woman herself, flat and uninteresting when compared to the invented version, may have withdrawn her consent but it was a small detail. Names could be changed. The young woman projected onto the page was self-absorbed, self-righteous, with a warped sense of her own self-worth. She was a woman who would be considered plain, a little overweight and strange.

She would make mistake after mistake, trying to avoid the author, the idol who would turn her dream of being a protagonist into a nightmare.

Chapter 10

The hum of a distant lawnmower could draw attention from study books without even trying. The noise from the open window was an invitation to any event at all taking place beneath a perfect blue sky.

Birds were chirping, content with the warm weather and keen to tell anyone who would listen. Cars made their lazy way along the road on that bright, cheerful Sunday morning. Even the scent of freshly mown grass seemed to sit on the breeze, ready to follow anywhere the wind would take it.

The wind carried the scent to the study desk. A glance at the window and another at the books prompted some study-centric soul searching. *On such a gorgeous day, maybe the criminal offence should be staying inside and studying!*

The day, so full of possibilities, had given up only an hour to university texts. There was still time. It was barely ten o'clock. It wasn't even too late for breakfast yet. Stomach growls suggested priorities should be placed elsewhere. The kitchen beckoned.

A nonchalance accompanied her meander down the stairs. Trotting to a typical breakfast had rarely felt so calm. The hate and anger of the previous day had melted away with last night's milkshake. The first meal of the day, basic in ingredients, could be enjoyed without a comparison with the cooked breakfast by the man she was pushing out of her head. Cereal boxes would be standing to attention on the shelf, ready and willing if called upon to fulfil their role in filling a stomach.

As the final few carpeted wooden steps creaked and moved ever so slightly under foot, a merry rhythm was being tapped out by her right hand without any conscious effort to do so.

The smile that had spread from her face to her fingers remained, but a darker undertone crept in. Inquisitive elements started to write themselves on her features. Dead-ahead, just inside the front door was a rough-textured grey mat. Laying there, as if it demanded to be picked up, was a white A4 envelope, the brightest thing at the end of the corridor amid the dark browns of the floor.

She rolled her eyes and let out a laboured sigh. *Great. A letter for Dad. Now I'm going to have to find him, hand him whatever's in that envelope, and have him reprise last night's 'I might seem overbearing, but it's only because I love you' conversation.*

She plodded over and reached down, picking it up. The weight of the paper was more than it had seemed. This was more than an invoice or a simple letter. She pursed her lips as she stepped away from the mat. There was no need to fear the next conversation, but it was difficult to feel enthused about it at such a fragile stage in their father-daughter relationship. *Last night was like a clean slate. Maybe things can work with us if I try harder. Maybe we should arrange to do something together. Something a tad more suited to my age than those sugar coma-inducing drinks down the street.*

She turned it over. Her eyebrows raised. The handwritten address was as expected, but the name above it was anything but: Samantha Barkes

It was too early in the day for so much frowning. There was probably no return to the cheerful countenance of moments ago. Reason suggested that this would be nothing, but some lurking curiosity suggested that this ominous item was a Schrodinger's Cat situation in an envelope. Maybe the contents would provide a positive change. Maybe it would be an anchor, a millstone about the neck to slow down a pursuit of happiness. Unless it was opened, no one could know either way.

Consternation would not shift during the walk to the kitchen. The easy-peel flap was almost entirely open by the time she had missed the base of the stairs and had successfully descended the remaining single step.

Putting the puzzling item down, she poured herself a generous portion of some supermarket brand of honey nut cornflakes and she took a seat at the old metal table built for no more than two. The chair wobbled slightly atop the old tiled floor.

As she took spoonful after spoonful of the crunchy cereal, she paused occasionally to tug out a small stack of papers and to examine them. In the bold but uneven letters of an old typewriter, the top of the first page first revealed words familiar to every avid reader: CHAPTER ONE. Those words had only been seen in printed, bound novels prior to this point. *Who would be sending me a manuscript?*

Occasional glances at the pages accompanied breakfast, a casual interest maintained whilst eating. Towards the end of page one, her own name was typed out in that same uneven print. She paused mid-chew.

The wretched woman described was not her. This self-indulgent, pathetic female who wanted success at the detriment of anyone and everyone else, was far removed from the woman sitting at that little table. This was a tale of a woman who had too much faith in her own abilities, a horrible human being who was being set up for a fall.

Eyes, hungry to see anything else, darted around the room. Maybe on some level there was a need for a hiding place, or some need to make sure she was alone. *What should I do with this? Surely reading on will only bring me bitterness and annoyance, but I can't bring myself to leave it alone.*

Like driving past the aftermath of a collision on a motorway, looking away did not seem to be an option. What would befall the fictional female? The cereal became a casualty of curiosity as she became engrossed in what she could only believe was the latest work of Larry Llewellyn.

There were tuts. There were full-on shakes of the head. *So much of this isn't right. It's not even close to what happened.* The author had clearly been offended somehow. He was seeking his revenge. But surely the only offence caused was her own.

She shook her head again at the Sam on paper, weighing each incident against the truth.

Meeting an author on a train. True

Visiting his flat. Also true.

Spending hours laughing and drinking with him. True.

It was at this point that the truth and the story diverged. The Sam in real life had spent an innocent night on his stark white sofa. The Sam on paper had thrown herself at the author she idolised. A crass and shameful passage followed that described what she could only refer to as a steamy night of passion between fan and idol. The vulgar words stood out from others printed on the page like dandelions in a manicured lawn, causing her cheeks to turn red. *How could he have even thought about me like this?*

The fictional Sam had awoken the following morning, ashamed of her actions. She had flown off the handle, believing somehow that she could do better. She had stormed out, shouting accusing words at the author, claiming seduction at best and rape at worst before heading home.

The Sam who existed in word only was far looser with her morals, far more ridiculous. She was a preposterous caricature of the real woman. *I'm convinced no version of me, in any parallel universe, whatever my flaws, could ever act the way THIS Sam is acting.*

Sam bit down hard and clenched her jaw. Her cheeks felt hot. She started breathing harder and faster. Her left hand had been holding her cereal spoon, but it was now empty and balled into a fist. Her teeth were soon grinding, her eyes almost bulging out of her head. *Larry had no right to turn me into this.*

There were more words to read. Her warm cheeks returned to normal. Her forehead went from hot to cold. Two trickles of sweat travelled down the middle of her back at race car speeds. Her heart was still pounding in her chest. *This man, this author described on the page, is not the man I believed him to be. What happens if he publishes this? What will everyone think of me?*

There was a monologue of sorts, the thoughts of a mad author, let loose in the leaves of the elongated letter. The imagined man was not the stereotypical writer. He was not some soft-hearted, never-picked-a-fight-in-his-life wimp of a man who only battled with his typewriter. He was different, and he would show Sam.

There was a promise of revenge, of making her pay. This, again, reflected those final few words as she exited his room, attempting to navigate the hallway through her tears.

Some sort of strange boast claimed that the man behind the words had helped others meet a sticky end. There was a hint that quietly, away from prying eyes, he had caused some very real people to suffer some very real, gruesome deaths. The bitter man had hidden behind his typewriter, making audacious claimed confessions, believing them as his fingers fabricated. Maybe he let out some sort of crazed laugh as he imagined himself as being more than a man that made stuff up for a living.

The author's author, the crazed man on paper, had been incensed by the ethereal Sam. Fictitious as much as furious, he would help her to realise the error of her ways. He would teach her a lesson that she would not live long enough to forget.

Her already miserable existence would be manipulated until she was ensconced in her nothingness, until she surrendered her self-respect. Superiority would be supplanted by humility. He would find her limits as he forced her past them, until she begged him to take away the selfish little life that she had lived.

Sam dropped the pages onto the edge of her cereal bowl, sending the soggy flakes and milk across the table. The milk soaked into the corner of the final couple of pages and the ink started to run. *Let the liquid ruin the lot.*

Sam's fingertips turned cold and numb. A shiver stemmed from the base of her spine. Her heart was pounding in her chest harder than ever. *Just who is this Larry Llewellyn? What does he want from me?*

Footsteps grew louder along the hard floor. Her dad was approaching. With quick, fumbling fingers, she picked up the pages, brushed the worst of the milk and the cereal from them and shoved them back in the envelope. *I can't let my dad read these words. He'd think they were true. He would judge me even more.*

She hurried to clean up the mess she had created on the table and then she retreated quickly to her bedroom.

She paced around her room behind the closed door. *What do I do? Who can I talk to? Is this real? Is it all just a horrible joke?*

No answers yet existed to those questions. Pacing brought her to the pile of Larry Llewellyn books where she paused. A deep breath, and then another. Time to think. Time to reason. Allow thoughts to clear.

A smile sneaked into one side of her mouth. *I'm giving him exactly the reaction he wants.* She laughed and shook her head. *He's not going to kill me... Is he?*

She shook her head again. *It's a work of fiction. It's all pretend. He's trying to mess with my head and I'm letting him succeed.*

She walked over to the silver-coloured wastepaper bin next to her small desk and dropped in the envelope. *That's how I responded to the school bullies. It's how I'm responding to him. If*

I ignore him, he'll find someone else to pester and he'll leave me alone.

Chapter 11

Beyond the morbidly fascinated, few would allow their thoughts to centre around an untimely demise. Whilst it was true that death waited for every living soul, most of them had no desire to dwell on the possibility. Larry was cut from different cloth.

A unique outlook, possibly, but death filled the mind with fascination, solace, comfort, even happiness.

Of course, there was joy to be found in the act of taking a life when it belonged to someone deemed unworthy to continue in the world of the living. Characters were nothing more than apparitions in an antagonistic mind, at least that was what the public had chosen to believe.

He felt a smirk, pondering those whom he had manoeuvred beyond mortality. *They don't know the truth.*

The horrors of a person's past could drive them to do any number of things. Many of the world's leading entrepreneurs had a difficult start. Many of the world's prisons were filled with people who shared similar origins. What was the difference? Personality. Perseverance. Some gained inspiration from trials whereas others filled up a bucket of feeble excuses, ready to unload it on anyone as a means of justifying a pitiful existence.

The inner compelling to contemplate past choices did nothing to improve anything. There were times when he was a spectator in key moments in his own life. Who wouldn't wish for the chance to rewind and jump into the game anew? Alas, it was necessary to resign to the restrictions of reality, being unable to do so. Instead, the only option was to watch the re-run, to reflect, to reimagine and to regret.

The cathartic purpose behind writing had rarely been more than a footnote in interviews. Those short stories all those years ago had taken off in a manner unanticipated. Putting pain down on paper had kindled a fire that could not be doused, not even with a dose of deathly dramatics. Thusly thrust into the world of popular culture, duty was now equal to death.

Rooms accessed from the corridors of his mind contained unspoken, sickening horrors, only part of which he had dared to draft into a story. Yet, every room, despite its furnishings and content, was essential. Each door opened on an indispensable part of the process.

Every character, starting as a clumsy, moving jumble of thoughts, took on human form and became real over time. There was a thrill in imagining their final breath in the beginning. However, when the moment came, when pronouncing their death sentence, the keys became harder to press, the pen heavier. But the public were thirsty for blood. Having grown accustomed to shrugging off his misgivings, the moment of reluctance usually passed before shoulders slackened.

Whether death came by way of retribution or as a sweet release from conditions tantamount to torture, relief would come in the end, regardless of the victim.

The ugly typewriter, set in the bland room, stared at him in expectation. If the thing had human arms it would be sitting there tapping its watch. Time to get on with it. *I could romanticise over the feeling of reaching the end, but that won't get it done.*

All of the scratching on paper, hammering at keys, all of the wistful groans had failed to combine into anything useful. Time for his fingers to take five. Time for the imagination to go into overdrive. The smooth, uncluttered wall became his canvas. Blood and horror were the paints.

He frowned and pursed his lips. *Perhaps Sam could trip and fall in front of the train she was supposed to be catching.*

Perhaps she could encounter a real-life criminal who would mug her and push her from a railway bridge in front of her train. She would learn first-hand, seconds before she collided with the train, that she no longer needed her fancy degree to know something of the workings of an evil mind.

Mulling over the idea allowed it to develop further and further. Other possibilities, other dramatic deaths and murders involving infuriated ex-boyfriends came to mind. Some of the what-ifs developed, sufficiently worthy to be written down. Soon several pieces of paper would be scattered across the desk.

Then, like a knife in the gut in the darkness, the most brilliant of ideas seemed to penetrate his core. His eyes widened. His heart rate increased, as did his rate of breathing. He hurried to scribble down enough detail to recall it later.

After a couple of frantic minutes with a pen and paper, he slid the sheet an inch or so farther from him. He placed his weighty pen to the right, perfectly parallel against the paper's edge. He leaned back in his chair and put his hands behind his head and smiled at the ceiling.

The smile faded. Every success seemed to invite the demon doubt to creep around its edges. He looked down at the words committed to paper again, a knowing smile was re-writing itself onto his face. *No, this is good. I've just decided how I will kill Sam.*

The writing would recommence within minutes, but this moment of silent victory was one a writer should choose to cherish. Every achievement warranted celebration, even if their fullest extent had yet to be realised.

He wheeled his chair back and headed to make himself a drink. The smile seemed glued on. *Sam is living on borrowed time.*

Chapter 12

Her eyes opened. The expression no-doubt crossing her face could not have appeared more apathetic if the words 'WHY BOTHER?' were tattooed across her forehead. Incidentally, any attempt to answer such a question would be duly ignored. She pulled the duvet over her head and rolled over. *Why did I pretend to ignore that first chapter?*

There were better ways of dealing with a build-up of concerns, considerations and questions. An outlet of some kind, whether vocal or physical, would have released some of the steam building up in that pressure cooker of intense thought. Instead everything had swirled around in her head for the rest of Sunday and throughout that night.

Strange dreams had resulted. One singular somnambulistic situation included the first printed chapter in her waste bin morphing into a house-sized paper-based monster, akin to an abominable snowman, determined to strike her down. The creature had been about to chase her from her room until she realised that she could punch through its surface and tear it to pieces. She then screwed the whole thing up into a small ball of wastepaper and chucked it into the bin by her desk.

Another dream featured Larry's face on her father, her aunt, the postman, her few friends at university and on every stranger. They looked like him. They spoke like him. They all tried to hand her an envelope. The faces disappeared but her name was then included above shop windows, in newspaper headlines, and on every pair of lips on the bus. No amount of vandalism, erasure or demands for quiet could stop the name she had known since birth from being used in vain.

The final dream depicted Larry feeding her into his old typewriter like a sheet of paper before punching her to death by pressing keys. Sam had seen the arm of each letter approaching at high speed, feeling each one hammer into her skull until she awoke.

She sat up and shook her head while rubbing her eyes. *I need to talk to someone about this. I also need to avoid eating bananas before bed!*

With the Monday morning to attempt to clear her head before an afternoon of university classes, Sam sauntered through her morning routine before plodding down the stairs. *What about some Google-powered dream analysis?* She shook her head. *I don't think I even want to consider the results of that!*

As the worn texture of the carpet of the fourth step made contact with her right foot, it came into view. On the doormat was another one. Her eyes widened and she descended the stairs like she was fleeing a burning building. *Surely that can't be another chapter already? Why is he doing this?*

With her feet almost slipping off the final few steps, she moved to the second envelope in as many days. This time she tore it open where she stood and withdrew the pages. CHAPTER TWO.

Her name was in those printed words, again and again, used in spiteful ways. There were scant, distorted details of her own childhood, not-so-subtle hints that her family had broken apart because of her, and the promise of more misery to come. The words suggested that she had messed with the wrong man, a vindictive, vengeful individual who would not take being mocked lightly.

The text described Sam as the model university student, always keen to learn about her chosen subject of Criminology. But there was a warning.

Sam, as the text laid out, was to learn more of the mind of a criminal from her association with this deranged author than she could ever hope to learn from her classes and textbooks.

A bizarre debate raged between Larry and himself over the next few words. Maybe he was attempting to decide on his course of action. Maybe he was thinking through the clicking of the keys of that infernal typewriter. The dilemma? Whether the full extent of Sam's upcoming punishment should be kept a secret or divulged beforehand. True, she could learn to avoid her fate, but how sweet would it be for the killer to capture her, even when she knew what was coming?

When a train is about to crash, How much notice would someone give its passengers? Thirty seconds? Ten? Would they want time to prepare for certain death, or would they rather know nothing of it, not having those seconds to allow themselves to be utterly terrified? Blissful ignorance surely had a place after all, didn't it?

The rambling continued. If a person could know the exact date, time and circumstances of their own death, would they accept it? Would they fight against it? When considering the balance in the universe, would either make the slightest bit of difference?

The pointless debate raged on. Without the need to read on, the pages would have joined the others in the bin for no reason other than sheer boredom. Mistakes were everywhere and they were distracting and confusing. *Larry's first drafts are terrible. This is nothing like the standard I've read in his previous work.*

As the words rolled on, the author seemed to have come to a decision. Sam would indeed meet her end at the hand of the writer, and she would meet that end despite being forewarned.

In a game of literary cat and mouse, her killer would tell her what was going on, as well as exactly what was going to happen. She would know her fate, but like a frog falling into a deep pot of boiling water, she would be unable to change anything that would keep her alive. She could swim to the sides of the pan, but she would have no hope of scaling the hot, high sides. According to the chapter, she was doomed, and she knew it. The question was whether she would accept her fate.

A lump rose in her throat and tears fell on to her cheeks. Her lower lip was trembling.

This wasn't some story written using her name. It was a very real threat directed at her. Referring to it as a threat didn't seem to do it justice. She shook her head, sending tears flying sideways. *This is a promise to make me pay for his own mistakes.*

Instead of casting the chapter aside, she kept hold of it, returning to her bedroom. With the papers shaking in her hands, she retrieved chapter one from the waste bin. She walked back downstairs, not able to feel her feet touching the steps. Not able to feel much of anything at all.

She walked up to her father, reading at his small kitchen table. *I don't think I can handle this alone anymore.*

~ ~ ~ ~ ~

Street after street, row after row of red brick houses in every possible condition whizzed past. Those same houses looked something closer to new once. The wrinkles around one eye were evident from the briefest of glances into the rear-view mirror. Beauty was in the eye of the beholder, but the effects of age were there for all to see. Like those houses, neglect had added to the aging process. You spent fifty years or more building a life for yourself, but it was easy to feel the bricks crumbling away.

Maybe there was some sign above his head that caused people to keep their distance. Samuel Barkes, builder, occasional father, failed husband. Misfortune had never been far away back then. Maybe he had manufactured some of it.

Maybe he had been a magnet to the rest. Poor choices were made, but everyone made poor choices. They didn't all end up with a ruined life.

Destiny differed across the spectrum of the human race. A failed marriage and failures in follow-up relationships cast a long shadow. Loneliness was the recommendation for the man behind the wheel. It had taken no time at all for the first promise of a healthy relationship to shatter an otherwise peaceful life.

Silent Samantha to his left played the part of the dutiful daughter, following her father's wishes in reporting all of this. She was 'Sam' these days. He still called her Samantha. Two people named Sam in the same house was just confusing. The little girl had loved the name Samantha. That little girl was in there, hiding in the sad looks in her eyes.

Names, of course, had meaning. So did labels. She was child number three, but she was also the only one to have survived to adulthood. It was difficult to love a child when all you could see in them was the pain of the past, those who had gone before her.

He tried to blink away tears, keeping his eyes on the road ahead. *Would her older brother and sister still be here if it wasn't for me? Would they have all been a happy family?* He shook his head. What use was there in casting blame? When a lesson had been learned, why poke around back there as if you'd missed something? Yvonne had her reasons. The reality was that they extended beyond the outwardly obvious. Underlying problems had appeared more pronounced in that poisonous predicament.

The car in front was one of those. Offence couldn't be caused to the sensible by any silver-blue saloon on the road, but this car was different. The additional yellow plate on the back contained the number and details of a local taxi company. Talk 4 Taxis, the same company that was written on the side of that car, was the one involved on that fateful day so many years ago. *Of all the vehicles in front, why did it have to be one of those?*

A taxi, along with momentary neglect, had been at the heart of the situation with Lydia Barkes, aged only five. It was a daddy-daughter Saturday morning at the nearby market.

Samuel had turned his back for a moment, distracted by a possible toy for his little girl. She was usually fascinated by those plastic toy horses with their bright coloured bodies and hair. It only took a few seconds for Lydia to run from the market stall across the cobbled stone paving and onto a nearby road.

There was a screech of distant tyres followed by a sickening thud. There were screams and cries from strangers.

Initially puzzled, he looked to Lydia. She wasn't there. Panic gripped him. Where was she? What had she seen? There had been near-misses before, but this felt different.

Panic turned to wailing remorse as the crowd parted. The unmoving feet in those little pink shoes would haunt him forever afterwards. They had only been bought a moment earlier. She had been desperate to wear them immediately. Those feet were spotted in blood and resting at sickening angles on the ground by the dented bonnet of the silver-blue taxi. A mortified driver opened his car door with shaking hands.

The conversations with Yvonne over the next few days did nothing to ease the guilt. A part of each of them had died with that little girl. They each took turns shouldering the blame and projecting it onto others.

I shouldn't have left you two alone, she had said. *You shouldn't have stopped to look at the toys. You should have learned from the last time, or the time before.*

We should have both taught her better about running off at a moment's notice, he had said. *But she kept on doing it, despite what we said or did.*

The hurt and the anger fizzled out. It should have given way to increased affection. Love would have healed the scars, but Samuel's builder shoulders were somehow not strong enough to accept the tears of his distraught wife.

She cried daily for the loss of Lydia. A numbness and a frequent blank stare may have looked different to her. Maybe she had thought he didn't care. Maybe, when losing himself in memory, when regressing into regret, others had mistaken it for apathy.

They pointed fingers. They sobbed in despair. Had Yvonne not been heavily pregnant with their third child she would probably have left him then. For the sake of the unborn child, attempt number three, she stayed.

The good ship relationship was going down. Water was pouring in, and Samuel had not even mustered the energy to bail them out with the bucket in his hand. Their trust in each other, and the simple expressions of love to each other all seemed trite and insignificant. Nothing worked, so he tried nothing.

The terrible memories dispersed as the sign off to the left confirmed that they had arrived at the police station. The concrete construction, the one that had been there for a generation, boasted an imposing but unsympathetic exterior. The general impression was conveyed by building and officers alike, but no one would know whether officers mimicked the stern building or whether the structure was inspired by imposing officers.

The waiting area looked like a cheap airport lounge but had the air of a busy corridor. So many people passed through on their way to somewhere. Since the sixties little would have changed here. There were modern additions to the old structure, keeping it all just about fit for use. Officers were down in number. Everyone knew that. Not a single uniformed officer had been seen, but people in business attire wandered around and the car park was full to bursting.

The padded yet uncomfortable seats, bolted to the hard, tiled floor, had not changed in over twenty years in any obvious way. Maybe they had been trashed and replaced like-for-like, but that seemed unlikely. The furnishings, the colour of the walls, the straight faces of the men and women behind the glass who welcomed each visitor, all overloaded him with memories of their second-born Lydia, but also of Peter, their first child. He let out a sigh. *Why do I keep reliving it? Why do I punish myself?*

A sad smirk wriggled halfway up his right cheek. *I can't believe this is the first time I've spoken to police in almost twenty years.* He tapped a foot on the hard floor. *Maybe this time I can stop things getting any worse.*

For once, the police could help protect his child instead of merely suggesting the neglect or abuse of her absent siblings. He was the father of the victim, doing everything within his power to protect his daughter. This time the police would be on his side. Samantha had realised her mistake. She had learned. She needed protection. His own need to intervene, to do something to show Samantha the dangers, would not be needed anymore.

PC Spencer, an overweight man in his forties with greying stubble and a permanent look of disappointment on his face, took father and daughter down a short corridor to a witness interview room. The room looked out on nothing other than a car park and half a dozen ugly buildings.

Old flimsy-looking blue plastic chairs were scattered around near a wooden desk that had probably been used to take thousands of statements. The brick walls and an ancient cork noticeboard had all been covered in magnolia paint, probably many times. The only things that provided a variation of colour were the window, the white radiator and white box-like trunking halfway up the wall. The dark blue carpet-tiled floor was no doubt stuck on top of a much older tiled surface beneath. The whole room felt functional as opposed to welcoming, but that was no doubt the point.

Samantha launched into her explanation of events. The responding officer seemed less than convinced at the danger. She produced the chapters she had received and they both looked on, wringing their hands in the same way. It was a trait she must have picked up from him, years ago.

Minutes that felt like aeons passed without a word. Occasional heavy, fast-moving footsteps could be heard the other side of the closed door.

"So, Miss Barkes," PC Spencer said, "you tell me you met this man, Mr Llewellyn, on a train. You then spoke with him in his flat and you agreed that he could use your name and image in a story?"

Samantha nodded. "Yes, that's right."

"Isn't that exactly what he's doing?"

Samantha tilted her head to one side. "In a way, yes, but it's not like that now."

"Because you find the story insulting, you'd like him to stop?"

He could not sit idly by and wait for the girl to be dismissed without due consideration. "Officer, we're here because we are genuinely afraid of what this man might do." Gesturing towards the stack of printed pages they had provided he added, "This is not *just* a story. This is a series of threats."

The officer nodded. He picked up the papers and continued to read over them. Maybe his previous review only covered chapter one. As he read on, concern crept into his features.

He replaced the papers and then put his left hand on top of the pile as if he was patting a dog's head. "I will review this thoroughly, but we're most likely looking at a Malicious Communication offence. Without any means of attribution to the person you believe to be responsible, our lines of enquiry and our means of dealing with this are very limited. You've withdrawn your consent for his use of your name, told him to leave you alone, and he's doing *this*."

He lifted his hand and started to stand up. "I'll send you a message shortly with a crime number after I've recorded it on our system. If anything else happens, please give me a call, and if you feel threatened or in danger-"

"I know," Samantha interrupted, "I call 999."

There was a grave nod from the policeman. "It happens. I'll do as much as I can do, but if he tries anything else, we may be able to take further action."

Chapter 13

"Dad?" she shouted as she approached the top of the stairs. "Are you home?"

No answer. Her right eyebrow and the right corner of her mouth lifted together, like a piece of string that connected the two was being tugged by a puppeteer. *I guess I'm facing things alone.*

She took a deep breath as she stepped down, her dark blue jeans hiding the jittering in her legs to some extent. She let go of the handrail and wrapped her arms around her, the overly long sleeves of the grey sweater slapping her sides. She stepped down again.

She paused, as if the next step could cave in. Like every step was a herculean effort, which to her, was true. She stepped down again saying in a mumbling, trembling voice, "One more step and I'll found out…"

A car horn blared from the road outside, causing her to jump. She closed her eyes and shook her head. *This is insane. It's just paper and ink. Why am I being like this?*

Her foot didn't move on the first attempt. She gritted her teeth and put her foot on the fourth step, looking down at the thinning carpet instead of straight ahead.

She took the next two steps at a faster pace, still staring at the floor, before looking farther ahead.

Her expression brightened. Her arms loosened themselves from her side. She could breathe again. She could see the doormat. "No envelope!" she shouted out, elated, ready to throw her arms up in celebration.

She hurried to the halfway point and then stopped dead, clinging to the handrail. It still felt wrong. "No envelope? Why not?"

Her heart rate raised again. The now-familiar pounding within her chest was back. *Am I getting a break for a few days? Is he trying to trick me?*

Fear and worry had raged through every thought and action for the past two days. Could this game of cat and mouse suddenly come to an abrupt end? Who would start like that and give up so quickly? Was this merely the eye of a storm? There was comfort in thinking that the worst had passed, but it was delusional. It had to be. Was something devastating lurking just beyond the horizon?

Balling her hands into fists, she let out some sort of frustrated battle cry. *I'm going to get breakfast, and I'm going to just get on with my day!*

As she stepped down towards the kitchen, there was a cheerful knock at the door. She stopped and turned her head around. Was there a sensible place to hide? *Would someone intent on killing me knock on a door like that?* She raised both eyebrows and sighed. *I don't know what to think anymore.*

She approached the door like a stupid girl in a horror movie. The girl that ignored the screaming viewers, and who reached for a light switch when she should have been a mile away. She opened the door. Maybe it would be a mean guy in a trilby, pointing a Tommy Gun at her. Some mafia moment would really top off the week.

Instead, there was an old guy wearing a dark green baseball cap and overalls to match, wielding nothing more dangerous than a bunch of flowers. *Harmless.* Her shoulders slumped. *Unless that's how they get you.*

An embroidered patch gave the man's name as Donald. He had a genuine smile on his slightly chubby face, wisps of grey hair peeping out from under the cap. He was probably the cheerful grandad that told the same jokes at every party and did a little dance from the fifties. There was a good chance that he had taken years of delight in delivering flowers.

This one was shaping up to be different from those thousands he had done previously. He handed over the bunch of flowers in his hand and said, "Wait there, this is a bigger delivery than that."

He hurried to the van parked by the side of the road, again and again, returning with two bouquets each time. Six trips later, thirteen bunches of flowers had been handed to Sam, standing there with an expression somewhere between feigned delight and indifference.

There were roses, lilies, daisies, peonies, sunflowers, just about every flower Sam had ever seen in a bouquet. Some were pink, some were bright orange, others purple or a pale yellow. The flowers were colourful and beautiful.

She thanked the deliverer on each handover, careful to read the hand-written card on each as she took possession of them.

She read the first card:

> If my head should fall victim to a heavy blow, even so you'll always be on my mind.

She turned her attention to the second one:

> The very thought of you leaves me breathless, as though I were being strangled.

The third one followed a similar theme:

> Though I hide myself away from everyone, I cannot escape my feelings for you.

On and on they went, until number twelve:

> Though my body be chopped into a thousand pieces, my heart will always belong to you.

The thirteenth was different. This one was aimed at her. She was protagonist thirteen. The card read as follows:

> When life no longer seems worth living, I will be there to end your suffering.

That final card seemed to grow and grow until it was the only thing in the world. Behind it, Donald the delivery man stood, seeming to wait for something. Maybe he waited for a delayed emotional reaction from the recipient of so many flowers. Some show of gratitude. He would have no idea that he had become an accessory to harassment. His only thought would be delivering flowers, imagining his part in some overblown romantic gesture.

"Who sent them?" Sam asked, feigning a smile.

The man smiled back and shrugged. "I don't know. They paid in cash at the florist and didn't leave a name."

"So, you don't know who I should thank for all of these beautiful flowers?" She asked, trying to sound pleased. Everything inside screamed of danger. That danger had spread beyond the once harmless man who delivered mean words. The threat was growing, and it was delivering soon-to-be-dead flowers.

Donald shook his head and smiled. "Sorry. I thought you would have some idea. We don't do deliveries like this very often. You must be very special to someone."

He muttered something about needing to move on to the next delivery with a van full of fresh flowers, and then he left her standing there in her doorway, holding that card.

She closed the door and turned her back to it. The

flowers laid on the floor by the sides, expectant of being placed somewhere visible, displaying their beauty for more of the world to see. She turned the thirteenth card over, still in her hand. Nothing on the reverse, so she flipped it over again in her fingers. *When life no longer seems worth living? Not an if, but a when.*

She collected the cards from each bunch of flowers. *End your suffering?*

There had to be a link between these flowers and Larry. It needed to be clear and obvious for the police to take this seriously.

She sighed. *The police. They will think I'm nuts for complaining about a guy that wants to write a story about me and that has sent me flowers!*

She had worked her way backwards from bouquet number thirteen all the way to the first. With every card in her hand, she turned around. A hallway full of flowers in Manchester. They would not be staying. Sam sighed. *I won't be able to prove to the police who sent these.*

~ ~ ~ ~ ~

Receiving such unwanted attention, even of the floral variety, had proven to be less-than-helpful preparation for a day of university classes. Surely the woman on the receiving end of a bouquet would be delighted that someone cared enough for such a gesture. Not that it ever happened to Sam, at least not until now. Why did the first time have to be this guy? Why couldn't a normal person have showed enough interest, so the idea of receiving a delivery of flowers wasn't tainted forever?

All traces of those things had been removed from the house. No good could come from their staying. The police would have to see the photos on the phone. Dwelling on the matter would only grant Larry another small victory.

The clock at the station showed fifteen minutes until the train arrived. Maybe the nerves, the uncertainty spreading to every inward part like an apocalyptic gloom had picked up the pace.

She looked at her phone, the screen off. Two clear options existed: Join the masses in staring at the mobile device or stay vigilant. The latter was the sensible, if nerve-shredding option to take. So many times, people of all kinds put their trust in strangers by congregating in such close proximity to one another, their only common ground was their need to be somewhere. *Is he here somewhere? Is he watching me?*

Victims, by their nature, were not usually proactive. Maybe that as well could be turned on its head. The first task was to scout out the random people nearby. Get a reading on them.

An old man in tweed with a walking stick. He doesn't look like Larry.

A heavily pregnant woman in a bright pink maternity dress.

A man about my age with a full, scruffy beard, dressed in army camouflage.

Five men and four women, all in jeans and jackets. They're all staring at their phones as if their lives depend on them.

Most were too short, too tall, too heavy to be Larry. Some were women. Could they be ruled out? What if Larry was a Sherlock-Holmes-level master of disguise? What if he could be any one of them? What if he paid any one of these people to do something? She closed her eyes and shook her head. *What a ridiculous idea. Why am I looking out for him everywhere?*

The number of potential passengers increased by the second. No one could keep track of them all. The time had come and gone for the train's predicted arrival. Hundreds of people were thronging the platform. Too many would cram onto this one, despite the next train being minutes afterwards and probably being half-empty.

Constant vigilance took a toll. Fifteen minutes of regarding every person with suspicion had the ability to drain mental and physical resources and to bring on a headache.

The train, several minutes late, finally slowed to a stop on the platform with a shriek of its brakes. The lottery, the guessing game of a hundred passengers, predicting where the doors would end up, had started. They shuffled back and forth with an urgency that was probably unnecessary.

Fortune, for once, smiled down and the door ended up right in front. A hiss accompanied its opening and a step forward was met with a shout from somewhere behind.

"Miss!" came the gruff voice of a stranger, raised to be heard over the noise of a platform of people trying to squeeze onto the carriages. "This is for you!"

An old man's arm, short-sleeved, wrinkled and with a couple of liver spots, shot through the crowd of bodies. The trembling hand held an envelope in front of her face. As eyes blurred and refocussed on the close object, the word SAM was there, written on it by hand.

With an open mouth and wide eyes, she snatched the envelope. The hand disappeared back into the crowd. She turned around but the man responsible had vanished into a sea of bobbing heads.

The next few steps were difficult. Impatient passengers practically pushed her aboard. An empty seat manifested itself at about the point the legs were weakening. She dropped into it.

With her bag occupying most of her lap she examined the envelope. No other markings. The gummed strip designed to seal it had been ignored and the flap had been merely tucked inside, possibly to avoid leaving vital DNA evidence behind, possibly because it was written and prepared in a hurry.

She opened the envelope as the train pulled away. A man was walking down from the far end of the packed aisle, attempting to check everyone's ticket. The single sheet of note paper, a heavy stock of paper in a light cream colour to match the envelope, had a single line typed onto it using the higgledy-piggledy lettering of a manual typewriter.

The words were:

I'm not finished yet.

No other words. No context. The carriage was packed with people, but everyone else seemed to have no problem breathing. Why had it become so difficult? *Is he here on this train? Why would someone else hand this to me? Is he watching me from the shadows, waiting for a reaction?*

There was no sign of him. Not anywhere nearby. Not that it was possible to check the faces of everyone. The man's purpose was to disrupt, upset and strike fear into her, not to literally follow every movement. *Why would he follow me?* The note trembled in-hand. *On the other hand, why would he go to this effort, spend this money on flowers and on someone handing me a one-line note?*

Like a voice from some distance planet, someone spoke.

"Excuse me miss? Can I see your ticket please?" the ticket inspector had made his way through the crowd at impressive speed.

Paranoia took a back seat for a moment. She could only take a breath and shake her head. "Sorry. I was miles away." She presented her ticket to the unimpressed man in uniform.

The rest of the journey was short and bumpy. Maybe the ride had been longer, but thoughts of personal safety, the desire to escape, the need to respond must have occupied every spare second.

The best thing at that moment about modern universities was their ability to attract unusual people like moths to a lightbulb. Nervous footsteps, even mindless muttering did not suggest in that arena that a student was best-suited to some rehab facility. No, even the strangest of people were considered eccentric. As such, the walk to the doors of the university could help anyone in the throng of people to feel anonymous, even her.

The impressive mirrored glass frontage to the University building provided many with an opportunity for reflection. What was the reason for their attendance? What life goals would this institution help them to achieve? Staring at your own feet and scurrying to class seemed to be an equally acceptable option, and the one chosen that morning with the scheduled lecture in Psychology, Crime and Criminal Justice about to commence.

A few footsteps into an open study area with vibrant, random shapes in blue, red and yellow, shuffling past a student support desk, tears were on the verge of erupting from within. The colour scheme, encouraged in every educational refit of the modern era for some reason, stopped way short of having a calming effect.

Her lower lip trembled, joining her knees. The only thing that stopped it was constant movement. *So much for life being back to normal.* She unconsciously stopped a tear from her right eye from travelling down her cheek. *I feel like a girl in a goldfish bowl.*

In an environment built upon principles of challenging convention and self-improvement, it must have been possible to think of something other than certain chaos and self-pity. None of the part-time friends had yet appeared. There was no one to console nor encourage.

Then a recognisable face appeared. Britney, the nineteen-year-old gorgeous blonde waif sister of Harry, walked up to her.

Most probably felt they knew her more than she knew them. She was all over the walls on posters for student representation. She couldn't pick any of her five thousand Instagram followers out of a line-up. There were rumours that she was certain to appear in the university's promotional material. She had no-doubt started those rumours herself. They didn't exactly move in the same social circles. In fact, before that moment, Britney had only ever said a snide remark about her weight.

"Sam?" Britney said more as a question than a greeting. She at least remembered her name.

Sam nodded. The fire of suppressed emotion burned in her throat. Speaking was not yet an option. Maybe the body protected itself against a naked flood of emotions unsuited to such a situation.

Britney held out an arm so skinny it looked as if a strong wind could fracture it. Her hand gripped another envelope that she held out. "I'm supposed to give you this."

A second envelope within an hour. Identical to the first. The same name was written in the same hand on the front, but everything blurred. The floor could have been replaced in that moment for that bumpy, inflated, never-still kind common in bouncy castles. Staying upright became an insurmountable task. She leaned against the wall that luck had put behind her. Swallow. Breathe.

She opened her mouth to speak, to ask one of the questions queuing up to escape, but the girl was gone.

The envelope fell from shaking hands. She sank to the floor until she was sitting. She picked it up. With a slight determined nod, she opened it.

The message was much the same as the previous one:

I'm not finished yet.

I decide when I'm done.

~ ~ ~ ~ ~

The lecture might have been useful. It might have been dull. It might have hit that strange middle ground where it could be both, like some others had been. There was no way for a student to know either way when they were sitting on a floor outside.

As fellow students re-emerged, she picked herself up and found a seat on a bright yellow couch. What were the options? Ignore it all and carry on? Hardly likely. Give up and go home? There was no escape there. This was supposed to be the escape. This was the place that evil should not be infiltrating, and yet students could create a breach.

She withdrew her timetable on a tired piece of paper from her bag. Nothing for an hour then a tutorial in her "Psychology, Crime and Criminal Justice" module entitled "Controlling Crime". She sneered at that title, looking at it now. *If only I was in control.*

Sam closed her eyes for a moment and took several deep breaths. *Let's think about this rationally.*

Would he really be likely to hunt me down in lessons? To put himself where he is so obviously out-of-place and where he would risk being identified as my stalker? He would be ejected or reported to the police.

Course leaders had been updated on every part of the situation before today. They were compassionate, understanding and ultimately no help at all. Lecturers were, however, prepared to keep an eye out to spot anything out of the ordinary. *If he's got to use someone else to get a message to me,*

I'm safe here. Maybe I can do something else about getting home.

A hurried text message to her aunt Stacey had prompted a quick reply. Arrangements for her pick-up could hardly have been easier. The air was less oppressive. The crowds were less threatening. The rest of the day had become manageable, navigable. The train and the notes had almost derailed her, but it was time to get life back on track.

~ ~ ~ ~ ~

The passenger seat of a red Vauxhall Corsa had never felt more comfortable. Shutting the door meant shutting out the world, at least for a little while. The remaining four hours of lectures and tutorials had promised to provide some diversion of thought. They had failed to deliver on that promise.

Aunt Stacey, with her ever-changing hairstyles, sarcastic sense of humour and appreciation for loud punk rock music, was becoming more like a big sister the more time was spent in her presence. Her hairstyle of choice at that moment was a blonde bob with a pink streak. It was an interesting contrast with her white blouse and long grey skirt. She had joked that she was the Paul Pogba of recruitment.

Had Stacey and Samuel Barkes both grown up in the same household? Were they genuine siblings, born of the same parents, both products of the same genetics? Their own ideas and outlooks differed wildly. What had happened to polarise their views so much? Why did they never talk? Why did they complain about each other?

"The key, although it's easier for me to say, I'm sure," said Stacey as she drove the rest of the way home, "is to try to live life as normally as possible."

Sam nodded and rolled her eyes. "I know, I know. I can't let him win."

"Exactly!" she replied with far too much enthusiasm as they came to a stop at a red light.

Another check out of the windows and in the mirror confirmed that Larry was nowhere nearby. The constant checks were becoming exhausting. The third different car to be behind them since university suggested that they weren't being followed.

"It's like what they tell you in school," Sam said. "You ignore the bully until they get bored and leave you alone."

Stacey shrugged. "I never quite understood it, but quite often it seems to work. Sometimes, though, people are just wrong in the head and they don't even follow the simple logic of the bully."

Sam shot a curious look at her as she started the car moving again. "So, you're saying he might not leave me alone, but I just need to live with it?"

Stacey shook her head, keeping her eyes on the road. "Far from it. There will come a point where you can do something that will put a stop to this nutcase. When that happens, you need to take that chance."

"Shouldn't I be leaving that to the police?" Sam asked.

Stacey shrugged and smiled. "They'll do what they've got to do. They're more about investigating and putting people away. You still need to keep an eye out for a moment when *you* can help *you*."

Sam screwed up her face and nodded slowly. Her dad's house was coming into view on the left. "Thank you for the lift," she said, unfastening her seatbelt, opening the door and dangling a leg out. "I couldn't have faced the train journey back today."

"I understand," Stacey said, "Your dad and I don't see eye-to-eye often, but I think he would agree with me on this: Don't let him win!"

Sam climbed out and closed the door before waving Stacey off with a thank you, almost shouted through the open passenger window.

The car pulled away and disappeared into the traffic a hundred yards away. Sam continued to stand there until the vehicle was out of sight. Stacey's drive home from there would be short, with barely more than a handful of streets between one home and the other. Proximity, it seemed, had not helped to repair the rift. She alone made any effort to traverse it, to spend time on both sides without prying into their pernicious past.

The relative solace of her own room was calling. Peace was hardly plentiful, but the moments it manifested could be enjoyed for what they were. Books, movies, online activities could all distract from the realities of a difficult life, like they did for so many others.

But there was something different about the house. Not a big thing. A very small thing. She froze like her right foot had been superglued into place. *Not this. Not now.*

There, sticking out of the letterbox, was something small and cream-coloured. Something had only been partially pushed through, so it was still visible. It was another envelope.

Chapter 14

Sam's eyes opened like the rusty windows to a damaged soul.

The ceiling didn't do anything, no matter how it was stared at. Even doing that used more energy than seemed to be available.

Sleep was a reward that had not come easily. There had been a point in the darkness where the tremendous effort expended in reclaiming requisite rest would remain elusive. Not only had recent days been sucked into some vortex of despair, but the nights were trying to hitch a ride in the same direction.

A wandering mind made shapes from the swirls in the Artex ceiling. Hot and blurry tears formed in her eyes. *I wonder how today will go. Do I dare to hope for any improvement?*

Four words drowned out the local sounds of occasional traffic and singing birds with the constant beat of a metronome. In between each beat there was space for a negative thought.

Three controlling notes.

Don't let him win!

The flowers.

Don't let him win!

He's too clever for the police.

Don't let him win!

Maybe I can change things.

Don't let him win!

But things needed to start somewhere. They couldn't start with a head laying on a pillow. This was probably the point that renewed enthusiasm overcame a protagonist, injecting a new life to help them succeed, so why did the idea of getting out of bed sap every newton of strength?

She rolled onto her side and picked up her phone. The bright light of the screen hit the back of her eyes. It was the little things that made it easy to hate being awake. She glanced at the upper right corner of the screen. *Fully charged and ready for the day, unlike me.*

She could follow a normal Tuesday morning routine, but nothing was normal anymore.

In a sort-of light bulb moment, an idea presented itself from the mush that was her morning mind. *Maybe my way out of this is to stay with her. Larry wouldn't know to look for me there.* She smirked. The idea had legs. *Still in Manchester, but far enough away that he might think I've gone somewhere else.*

Some quick-fire messages to lecturers and support staff would give her a week or so to get over things and to get her head straight. A message to Stacey would surely be sufficient to secure a stay.

She swiped away the lock screen and frowned at the device. Twenty five unread messages. Forty two unread emails. *Something's going on here. People hardly ever send me anything.*

Maybe someone had given out a false email address. Maybe, but apparently not. Some messages mentioned the account "flirty_dirty_hore3". Some were directed to Samantha Barkes.

Graphic sexual messages described all manner of activities. Horrific descriptions depicted bondage, strangulation, forced oral sex and violent rape. It was enough to make an average person's stomach turn. *How could anyone send something so disgusting to a fellow human being? Why would anyone want to read this or even think about it?*

The emails painted the same picture. The same account was referenced. Emails were littered with pictures and videos of naked men pleasuring themselves. A violent rape fantasy video was enough to prompt a tortured cry, which was interrupted by her phone ringing. A call from an unrecognised number.

"Hello?"

"Hi. Is this the flirty dirty whore?" asked a man who waited for no reply before continuing. "Do you know what I wanted to do to you when I saw your nasty profile?"

"Who is this?" Sam asked with an air of impatience, sounding like an offended headmistress. "How did you get this number?"

There was a pause. "Err, you put it on your profile."

"What profile?"

"Your profile on Adult Trash Talk. It's kind of a dating website, but most people don't put their number up like that."

Sam objected, "I didn't put my number on anything. Someone else must have done this."

The voice of the man was nervous all-of-a-sudden. "I'm sorry. I had no idea. I thought this was the kind of thing you wanted. Some people are like that."

"Well, I'm not," said Sam. "Could you please make sure you don't contact me again?"

"Oh, of course. I'm so, so sorry to bother you. I hope I didn't offend you."

The line went dead as the brief, but surreal conversation ended. The tone of that man changed in an instant during their brief exchange.

Sam put her phone down and fell onto her back. She felt tears welling up in her eyes and put her hands over her face.

What's Larry been doing to me now?

After a couple of minutes of letting the tears flow, she moved to her laptop. This was the seedy bit of the internet, the sick, depraved stuff people warn about but never discuss. Overnight she had been signed up to most of those services.

Email addresses and mobile phone numbers that had only been given out to close friends and family were on very public profiles. The home phone number had at least been absent. She breathed out a sigh while looking away. *I suppose I should be grateful that my dad won't need to entertain such bizarre calls.*

Site after site seemed to be chocked full of photos of her, taken from Facebook, Instagram and Snapchat alongside photos of faceless overweight women in lingerie and in sexual acts. The average perverted purveyor of such sites would have no reason to doubt that all of it was her. Without realising it, tears were now pouring from her eyes. *How can someone do this to me? What must everyone think of me now?*

The bio on one site was enlightening.

What was she interested in? Men and women, boys and girls.

What was her favourite thing to do? Take a guess.

What types of depraved sexual activity would she consent to? Just about anything, especially if she was paid.

On and on she read. Everywhere a girl could dare to look, warped versions of Samantha Barkes were smiling back from fake profiles. Larry had not stopped at creating the distorted version of Sam for his own fictitious fantasy. Not only had he hoped to publish his sordid revenge tale around the world. He had gone on to create the vilest version of her before presenting that visage to every depraved pleasure-seeker with an Internet connection.

She put her hand to her mouth. A sickening feeling rose

from the pit of her stomach. She squeezed her eyes tight shut and forced her breathing to slow. A bolt to the bathroom seemed to be on the cards. Coolness broke out on her forehead and neck. Her shoulders slumped. The worst was past. She clenched her jaw and balled a fist from her right hand. *This isn't you. This doesn't have to affect you. No one you know and trust would ever see these.*

An exhausting night led into an exhausting morning, gathering evidence, taking screenshots, making notes, saving emails. Whether or not the police would do anything, gathering sufficient evidence would make any investigation easier.

Next it was making call after call, sending emails one after the other, requesting and demanding that false profiles be removed.

There followed one final call, lasting several minutes, to her mobile network provider, sufficient to request a change of phone number.

"Your current number will deactivate by twelve noon today," she was told. "Your new number will be active at some point tomorrow morning. You'll lose all phone abilities and you'll need Wi-Fi to make contact with anyone."

The new number was scribbled down in the nearest study notebook. Hardly anyone would be getting it. Anyone who was not directly related would just have to deal with it. Maybe if things calmed down, if life returned to something like normal, everyone else could be trusted again.

The clock on the wall said it was almost ten. *Time to finally make it out of my bedroom!*

With every necessary message sent, with apologies to university staff and a polite request to her aunt, the day started here. Maybe there was a way to get free of this mess.

~ ~ ~ ~ ~

Rescue seemed like such a dramatic word, especially given the atmosphere at that moment.

Maybe that was Stacey's plan: Preoccupy the second-guessing guest with old girly movies and pizza. Don't let her think at all about the seemingly never-ending harassment, the garbage online, the damage to her reputation, or the fact that she does not feel safe anywhere.

Distraction was a wonderful thing. If only it was a tactile comfort blanket that could be wrapped around the shoulders. If only it brought warmth and security.

Real life would, of course, return, but several days of recuperation and she would be ready. Some time off-grid in her aunt's make-shift rehab-of-sorts would do wonders.

Stacey's lounge décor was as bright as her hair. An almost day-glow orange feature wall seemed at odds with the three others in light brown that either looked on in jealousy or in disdain at their brighter neighbour. The cream leather sofas took on an orange glow when light bathed the room.

As much fun as it had been eating, watching, chatting with Stacey, time had come along like a practical parent to spoil the party.

The clean stairs in the spotless home were furnished with some odd carpet tiles that felt like islands on each step, or like the disappearing liquid-metal steps leading to an alien spaceship in an old movie.

Stacey had termed the night a sleepover, again trying to soften the mood. Even so, there was no sharing a bedroom, spending the night in girly talk about boys and makeup. The spare room had been tidied and prepared.

The single white lacquered metal bed frame had a flowery headboard and it creaked with every major movement. The only other furniture in view was a small pine chest of drawers, sitting in front of a wall papered with depictions of the flowers of summer. She sneered. *Flowers. Why did he have to send flowers?*

The challenge was to think of anything else when the light went out. The flowers needed to be rooted out, replaced with replays of moments from the cheesy romantic comedy still in the DVD player. The goofball guy who turned out to be the love of the girl's life was loved by many. If only life was so simple. With that thought, she drifted off to sleep easier than had been the case for a number of days.

~ ~ ~ ~ ~

Feeling out of sorts was beginning to feel normal. The blaze of sunshine bursting around the edges of the thin curtains shone a new light on the flowered wallpaper. The room wasn't pink, but it was still too feminine. These days, wasn't everyone supposed to be a bit more gender-neutral? Maybe Stacey, like her dad, had no cares for political correctness. She put on a weary smile. *Maybe I've found something they've got in common at last!*

Sitting up and wriggling her toes against the short pile of the cream carpet, she reached across for her phone, charging on top of the drawers.

She yanked out the cable and swiped away the lock screen, ready to turn away. No text messages. No missed calls. Of course there wouldn't be any. The new number didn't go live for a few hours yet.

Not being a heavy social media user, only a few of the thirty-to-fifty friends on each platform would get in touch to ask about the new number. Her eyebrows raised when she looked at the red circle in the corner of her email icon. Ninety eight unread emails.

The majority were sent because messages hadn't been

answered instantly or at all, as if that was something that required some DEFCON level of concern. *I tried leaving social media alone for a day. I wonder if it will ever do me the same courtesy.*

Most of the messages were a variation on the same question. Some new account in her name, was it hers?

That account was not hers. Neither were the others. *Not again!*

She flopped back onto the bed, laying down again. The pillow felt hard, like it didn't like being headbutted and it was trying to fight back.

As she blinked up at the ceiling, those words came back. *Don't let him win!*

It was growing tiresome now. Was a mantra supposed to get old so quickly? Should it not seem original and decisive for at least a few days, until life could be organised around the principle of the thing?

Screenshots of the accounts, each with a different set of random uploaded images, were reviewed, links to accounts were tapped and every single one was reported to its own service. *Will they even do anything about these?*

The finishing of the task should have brought relief. It should have provided a chance to draw a line under everything that had gone before and start the day anew. There was no breathing of new life into the day. In fact, there was next to no breathing at all. The air became thin, like the room had inexplicably moved atop a mountain as she slept.

With great heaves of her shoulders, she tried to force air into her lungs. The mechanics of breathing seemed to be working but it felt as if nothing was happening. The walls of the bedroom started to close in like an industrial trash compactor. The ceiling too. Pyjamas felt like a straitjacket that was wrapped in a Boa constrictor. A distant dizziness took hold.

It's not a big deal, she would have said aloud if she could have talked. *It's just the latest thing, but it's small. I can deal with this.*

So why the paralysis? Why some new level of fear? When would the air return? Had Larry somehow stolen that too? Wasn't stealing another person's identity and their dignity enough?

With every new, small or even insignificant act, he pushed her further towards isolation and fear.

Don't let him win!

Breathe.

Don't let him win!

There it was. The first lungful of breath in what felt like forever. The clothes, the walls all started to retreat.

It took probably a minute, but the dizziness dissipated. The big hurt-your-lungs sort of breaths were all mum had said about calming down, but more was needed. Too bad they had never discussed the feeling any further.

Another message alert pinged, and she picked up the phone.

Harry: There's another account, but it's private…

The link was sent and within a few seconds she had followed the fictional Sam. It was probably unwise, what else could she do?

More screenshots to take. Send them to the police by email.

Breathing remained steady. The heart did not. Palpitations started in earnest, flooding the body with uneasiness. The world was laughing, and Larry was the one pointing a mocking finger.

A new message, but this wasn't from Harry. This was

from that false account. Disappearing images that flashed for a few seconds and then went. They were pictures of blurred nothingness with words typed over the top. She read them, aghast, as they arrived and watched them disappear.

Sorry you had to change your number.

Do you miss me yet?

Time to cry to the police again?

The last one was a clear picture of a sheet of paper with the words CHAPTER 3 at the top. Added over the top of the blurred text underneath were the words, 'coming soon to a letterbox near you!'

"That's it!" she cried. "How do you deal with bullies?"

All-of-a-sudden she was back in her mum's bedroom in that house in Slough. Her mum was eight years younger, but the same stern look was there. The new school seemed untenable. There had to be an alternative. The look was not directed at her. It was travelling through her as if she could cool new tensions with her icy stare.

She had asked that question. Sam had only shrugged.

Reality snapped back into place. The answer was the same then as it should be now. Through gritted teeth she echoed the next words of her mother. "You fight back!"

Over a week of fear, anxiety, nervousness, panic and worry all mixed together like some sort of perfect, toxic internal swirling storm of indignation. When thoroughly mixed, rage resulted. *I will not let him win!*

She gripped her phone so hard she heard it creak under the strain. Invasion to this level was unfair, unwarranted, uninvited. He needed to be put in his place, once and for all. *Time to reply. Time to tell him exactly what I think of his behaviour.*

Chapter 15

He had been looking at his watch, merely to learn the time, but he had kept on looking.

The second hand ticked from one point to the next, something soothing in its constancy, momentarily transfixing in its repetition.

It was not unusual for Larry to find fascination in ordinary objects and mundane moments. Ideas sprung to mind so often on such occasions.

The first message had arrived seventy two seconds ago. The watch provided only the time and date. It was still sufficient company. He focussed on its face. What made the thing tick? A world of literary success had been founded upon that very question when looking into the faces of his future victims. What pushed them? What held them back? What existed in their lives that could, when amplified, explode in their faces and force them out of the world of the living?

The expected small movement occurred inside the timepiece again and again. Out of its face appeared an apparition of an old, white-haired man, thin-rimmed glasses on the bridge of his nose, his gaunt face and hollow eyes towards the tiny cogs, moving a steady hand to make an adjustment. Dressed in a stale shirt and pressed trousers, his was a dying trade. Time had once been essential in the lives of everyone around him. The ability to learn the time at any given moment was once a sign of distinction, of dependability.

He had escaped death in his prime, but he lived on until Father Time, the provider of his working wage, would become his cruel nemesis. His hand would shake to the point of making the repair of a tardy timepiece untenable. His eyes would fail to focus on those keen details.

Customers would favour electronic devices. He would be left penniless and alone in his old shop, pushing the cold barrel of his war-issued pistol into his temple. His trembling hands would be put to use one final time by pulling the trigger. His old watch, as if mourning his loss, stopped ticking.

Another 320 seconds had passed when another message alert arrived.

The old man in the watch repair shop vanished from view. He looked at his phone with a smirk. *Use this,* his agent had said. *I can get hold of you, and you can always get your messages. You'll find it useful.*

The recent messages told a story. He raised an eyebrow. *I shouldn't have objected for so long. This thing is proving very useful.*

The ability to be interrupted at any moment was a writer's nightmare. Having your train of thought crash into a trash heap of social nonsense would not help any serious student of literature. Isolation was the great paradox of the craft. Loneliness was required to write, but interaction and involvement in the world generated fresh ideas and helped a solitary author to stay relevant.

He picked up his notepad and scribbled down something about the old guy with the glasses before the idea went wherever those ideas went when his mind cleared.

As he finished preserving a skeletal outline, his phone alerted him to another message from Sam. This time, he let himself grin. *Tame words. The insults of a sheltered girl.*

Labelling him a sick freak, a psycho and a nutcase could hardly upset a man such as himself. The fourth message showed more promise. She was getting creative. It at least suggested that he perform a graphic act on himself that was physically impossible.

He turned off the screen and caught sight of an ageing reflection. Another old man appeared. This one looked familiar. The same face from every mirror, withered by time. The man was stumbling, exhausted and thirsty through a desert, ideas like the mirage over the next couple of dunes. Refreshing characters and stories used to be everywhere but somehow life was eroding his imagination. The springs and the well of creativity had run dry. He was left to wander in the wilderness, hoping to find something to sustain him for the next few miles of barren wasteland. Soon, there would be nothing left in his post-apocalyptic postulations.

Life had converged around him over the years. It was all increasingly intolerable. Complaints to anyone would be met with derision, and a scoffing finger pointed in the direction of his place in the bestseller list. Others would feign sympathy at the irritation of welcoming substantial royalties into a bank account. Such a hard life, they would say, with a roll of their eyes.

The face reflected back held more mysteries than most. So many that its owner had yet failed to unravel them all. The ability to see what made others tick was powerless on himself, like a superpower, bestowed upon him only for the benefit of others.

There was no satisfying resolution for the riddles posed by that inner rage, nor an acceptable answer to the inquisition into an inclination to inflict misery on others.

More and more minutes passed without further insulting messages. Silence like this was a precursor to despair. Out of that silence, a sinister voice seemed to be emanating from the typewriter with a mocking laugh. *It's time for your next big failure. Goodbye to the great Larry Llewellyn!*

He shook his head and got to his feet. He walked over to the window. The scene had been seen thousands of times, but it was different somehow. Everything framed by the window joined in the chorus with the typewriter. *You can do whatever you like but you'll never be happy here.*

In a voice that didn't exist, the typewriter continued to taunt, to goad its owner into returning. He frowned, bit his teeth together and took a few swift steps to his chair. He hammered at the keys with an increased intensity that made his fingers hurt, as if the little keys and their attached lettered arms could absorb some of the rage that he exuded. Maybe the force was great enough to punch through the paper, leaving indented lettering on the roller behind.

A feeling scratched at his insides, wanting to get out. Even the wordsmith could not put a label on it. The release valve was the jettisoning of each novel, but the pressure kept building. At that moment, no amount of passionate production of the printed word could produce anything other than a sense of mundane euphoria that passed within minutes. He directed an evil stare at the words he had forced onto the page. *This isn't enough anymore.*

Familiarity flowered into contempt. Contempt continued to frustration. Frustration fuelled anger. Anger accelerated unencumbered towards a full-blown attack on someone or something. Attack afforded him the rush. That rush receded to relief, which returned him to boredom and familiarity. Only minutes after each high, he was falling again, faster and harder than before into an abysmal abyss.

Imprisoned in his room to write, held captive by his need to create, it was all too much. He could do it well. There was always another more gifted, more talented, handsomer, more charming or funnier than he. He could write as well as the man he hated, the one who could produce so naturally. His own material surpassed that of the man who had garnered more hatred than was present in even his own self-loathing.

He spun his chair around, looking out of the window, promising false freedom. *Maybe I could do a J.D Salinger and disappear, but for good. I have the money. This could be the perfect opportunity.*

He closed his eyes and tipped his head back, letting

various new ideas rest in his consciousness for a moment, settling, taking root.

With a bit of planning, some intricate details to figure out, the writing career could finish with a flourish. He glanced at the watch again. Time to move on. Something new and exciting could fill that void. Literary murder was not it. Not now.

The phone buzzed again. The screen lit up and banished the ageing reflection. Every effort in upsetting Sam was starting to bear fruit. *I can learn as much from a person's anger as I can from their grief. Possibly more.*

This new side to her, her reactions to problems, her desire to hide from the world, her need to lash out in response, spoke volumes about her character. Time to record it all in the paper-based version of Sam, the character, the protagonist.

There was a way of coming out ahead in these situations. Playing the victim was easy. Creating them and then killing them was more challenging. Screenshot after screenshot was taken. Replies like "Please leave me alone" or "I would like you to stop contacting me or I'll call the police" were crafted to send Sam over the edge.

He let a wicked smile creep across his face. *Why don't YOU call the police? They'll tie themselves in knots while I do what I'm going to do.*

Sam told him exactly what he could do with those pages about her. The task would involve rolling the pages tightly and possibly lubricating them in some way. Even so, it was almost as challenging as her earlier vulgar request. He scrolled through several of her messages.

> You deserve to meet the fate of one of your characters.

> If anyone deserves a horrible death, it's you.

> Thanks for putting me in touch with sex-crazed perverts. I'll send them in your direction so they can teach you a thing or two.

She said *he* was the one that deserved to be investigated by the police, which of course was true.

The responses started getting more vindictive. They were starting to get threatening, as Larry had hoped.

Turning that screw just a little bit more, applying the pressure, and Sam would be done. She would dig herself into a hole. She would thwart her next few attempts to complain about him and his actions.

One quick call to her through the app, then more messages would surely arrive, and then he could make his next move.

With the events he was about to set in motion, Larry would no longer enjoy the perks of the past few years. The wealth, the fame, the satisfaction, these were hollow anyway.

The typewriter sneered again. The golden goose. The yield up to now had been marvellous. Twelve metaphorical golden eggs. Sam's story would be the last. She would be the one who would mark the end of an old life and the start of a new one. Quite fitting.

He held the phone in his hand, reviewing the screen and occasionally peering past at the machine behind.

I'm sick of the golden eggs, however much the world thinks they're worth.

He smirked. *It's time this goose got it in the neck.*

~ ~ ~ ~ ~

There was a rueful shake of the head from Sam. *I can't believe I fell for it.*

I'm the fish, dangling on the end of a hook. I was lured in by some shiny antagonism until I went for it. This wasn't a nibble. This was a full-jaw bite of the bait. All that was needed was to ignore it. The thing to do was to put the phone down, ignore it and leave the man talking to himself, but that hadn't happened.

The building was the same, but the room was different. Large sound-suppressing panels covered three of the walls. A multi-directional microphone was stuck to the wall near a table. A large black box looked like it could have been an early television prototype with its tiny screen and random flashing lights.

A single sheet of paper was sitting on the table, a photocopy of probably twenty previous photocopies. Details of how the defendant could get a copy of the interview if things went as far as court. A free gift to every suspect, but one that was likely left behind and offered to the next one to find themselves in that room.

The man asking the questions was an off-the-street brand of Constable. He had average length hair on the top of his head but near-shaven back and sides. He had sleeve tattoos and a face like a man who had just found out his dog had died. His name was Paulsen. Sam didn't care enough to remember the rest.

The next words had been heard during TV arrests. She was free to leave at any time though. This was voluntary, apparently. She had a right to a solicitor. She let out a small sigh. *How could things be going so wrong, so quickly?*

"We're here today to talk about an allegation of harassment made against you by a Larry Llewellyn," said the officer who looked less friendly than the others. Did he have any idea of her own complaint against Larry?

"Tell me what you know about that."

Silence. It was time to talk. She shrugged. "I can tell you

that I couldn't take any more. He's been harassing me for days. Maybe you've seen the complaint I made against him several days ago? I've been afraid to leave my home since Monday. I've had to stay somewhere else. I've had to change my phone number. All this week!"

The man nodded, looking through several printed sheets of paper, stapled together. "I know the investigation. I had a chance to review it before you arrived."

"So," Sam said with an air of authority, "you know what he's been doing?"

He shrugged. "The last thing I have on here is from last week."

Sam nodded. "Okay, okay. Let me tell you what's happened since. I've been too afraid to even come here. I get nervous whenever I leave the house because I feel like he's watching me. He had thirteen lots of flowers delivered to my house on Monday, the cards were threatening. He set up adult dating profiles in my name and with my number by Tuesday. I had to change my phone number. He also had people hand me typed notes to cause me distress. He created false social media profiles. He's done all of this. Here."

Sam handed over her phone. "Take a look. I've got all the screenshots and photos of everything. You can see what he's been doing."

The officer sighed and leaned back. "You know, we see this sort of thing all the time."

Sam scowled. "What sort of thing?"

"It's like the bad break-up situation. One person bothers another. They retaliate, it goes on. One calls the police. The other one retaliates by doing the same. We end up with two harassment investigations and neither of them will ever go anywhere."

"A break-up?" Sam's voice was raised. She was losing her

cool. "We were never in a relationship of any kind!"

"That first chapter he sent you-"

"Was a lie!"

He held his palms up. "Okay, let's calm down and take this from the beginning. Tell me what has happened, and what led to you responding the way you did."

Sam spun her phone around on the desk and unlocked it. She opened the pictures, swiped up a few days and used them to guide her through her account of Monday through Thursday.

"I sent the messages to him, but when you see what he's sent to me, and what else he's done, how much distress he has caused me, I hope you can see that I sent them from a place of fear and concern for my own wellbeing."

There was silence for a moment. Maybe he wasn't expecting this sort of response. Maybe it was exactly the response he was expecting.

"We will need to borrow your phone for a few hours to do a full examination. Hopefully, you'll have it back by the end of the day."

"What am I supposed to do in the meantime? I feel like I'm at risk without it, no way to call anyone and tell them if I'm in trouble."

He looked Sam in the eyes and said, "It seems most of this week's harassment has involved your phone. Is it possible that you might even get some peace for a couple of hours if you don't have it?"

He had a point. *Damn such a reasonable argument! Keep a stern face. Don't let him know he's right!*

She rolled her eyes, shrugged her shoulders and relented to the quick examination and return of the phone.

~ ~ ~ ~ ~

A police waiting area was probably never likely to be filled with interesting magazines, quiet, calming music playing or even comfortable chairs. Why would they want people to feel comfortable? Some of the people who sat there would be drunks. Some would be criminals. Some would be whinging members of the public. Why would they want to attract any of those with nice chairs? How long would they expect them to last?

The frustrated desk clerk with the narrow face watched like a hawk. Two hours. How can anyone watch someone for two hours?

The sleeve-tattooed officer emerged from the locked door carrying a small evidence bag. Trapped inside was the phone. The cause of and solution to so many of life's problems.

He pulled a sheet of paper from the side of the small bag like he was doing some slight-of-hand and pulled a pen from seemingly nowhere.

I have to sign to take possession of my own possession.

After handing back the page and the pen, PC Paulsen did the usual "Are you okay" kind of questioning and made a swift exit.

She powered the phone back on, letting it connect and catch up. No more messages of any kind. Not even any social media alerts. Nothing more from Larry. *Maybe he knows I've been to the police again. Maybe he's given up.*

Chapter 16

Television adverts for various universities weren't meant as a guilt-trip. In a way, they were, but they were aimed at the under-achievers, not at the undergraduates. There was a need to neglect Criminology classes to consolidate, to protect against an actual criminal. *Even so, I've not been where I should have been, not focussing on what I need to learn.*

Saturday morning, though, was a gift to the absent student. Nowhere to be. No reason to feel bad about staying at home.

This was day seven. Just under a week since Larry had kicked this whole thing into high gear. Even as the wheels had slowed again, there was no way to feel safe here. This is where the first two chapters were delivered. This is where the flowers arrived in a seemingly endless chain, linked together by a smiling old naïve man.

You're welcome to stay with me when I get back, in a week or so, Stacey had said as she dropped her off last night. *You're just better off not being alone right now.*

There was no rational explanation, but layers of cotton and feathers added a feeling of security that bricks and mortar could not provide. The thick double duvet formed part of the soft-touch fortress constructed around the secondary sofa by the window.

Given the heavy criticism some days ago, the change in her father was remarkable. The sorry sight of his almost twenty-year-old daughter in pink pyjamas, cutting a forlorn figure, huddled in a corner of the lounge prompted no negative response. In fact, comfort had already been offered in numerous ways.

The gap in the duvet offered only a view of the TV, some light green-painted woodchip on the wall and a glimpse of neighbouring red brick chimneys surrounded by heavy clouds. Fine droplets of water were scattered over the window like the early beads of perspiration, like even the window was nervous for whatever may come.

"There's another one!" There it was. A few muffled words through a door communicated everything.

Footsteps grew louder on the hardwood floor in the hallway. It was coming, and he was bringing it.

Her heart rate increased. Her palms felt clammy. Beads of sweat formed on her forehead. Her breathing was becoming shallower and erratic. In those few seconds, dizziness threatened to overwhelm, dragging another victim to a dark nothingness. She flung off the duvet, but the sweats were not a result of overheating.

Another identical envelope was in his hand. He approached but he kept a distance. He held it out like some sort of offering. A shake of the head and an uncomfortable diverting of her gaze later, her dad shrugged and started to open it. He glanced at the first page and scowled.

"This is different," he said as he took a couple of steps closer. "The last chapters, they talked about stuff that had happened, didn't they?"

"With a couple of clear exceptions."

Her dad nodded while also swaying his head slightly from side to side. "I know the whole night-of-passion thing didn't happen, but you know what I mean. They're past tense."

Sam nodded, before staring at him, puzzled. "Why do you ask?"

"There's two here," He said with a slight frown. "Chapter three seems to cover the past week. The flowers, the messages, the social media, the phone calls. But chapter four… He's writing about stuff that hasn't happened, but it's like it already has."

Sam's eyes widened. Every previous symptom returned in a second. "What do you mean? What's he saying?"

He tripped over his words for a moment without adding anything particularly articulate.

"What does it say?!"

He stuck out his bottom lip for a moment, shrugged and said, "It's talking about something crashing through a window, but…"

He turned towards the window and took a step closer to it as he stretched out his left arm.

"No! Don't go towards the window!"

He turned to face her as something hit the window hard, making a frighteningly loud but dull thud. He cowered and raised an arm to protect himself. Only part of a second later, another object hit the window and a deafening crash seemed to drown out everything else. As fragments of shattered glass seemed to hang in the air like water droplets in a monsoon, an object collided with her father's arm, sending him to the floor.

"Dad!" She screamed, darting off the sofa towards him.

"I'm okay," he shouted up from the floor, holding an elbow. "Look out of the window! See who it is! Call the police!"

Sam ran to the window, a gaping, menacing hole in the centre of the large pane of glass. Through it the head and shoulders of a figure disappeared down the street in a dark hooded top. That was all she could see over the roofs of the cars parked by the side of the road.

She turned around. Her dad was sitting up, leaning against the sofa at right angles to the one she had been sitting on a moment ago, holding his left elbow with his right hand. There was blood soaking through his shirt. Crimson drops found their way through the cotton, around his fingers and onto the dark blue carpet, looking black and more sinister as they landed and soaked into the pile.

He was still moving both arms without too much discomfort. Coming through the glass window, the item had slowed down. Maybe it had only caused surface damage.

He looked down, dropped his right hand and was about to pick up the offending item. It was the remaining three quarters of a red house brick.

Sam held out her right palm towards her dad. "Stop!"

He paused and looked at her like a three-year-old reaching for a forbidden cookie jar.

"Forensics will need that. Don't touch it!"

She hurried to the sofa she had occupied when the house was safer, only a minute or so earlier, and she picked up her phone.

Seconds later she was talking to someone at the other end of an emergency line. *I think this qualifies. Maybe the police will take me seriously now.*

~ ~ ~ ~ ~

This time, Sam didn't need to pay the police a visit. They came to her.

There were no broken bones, no shattered joints or any other serious consequences to her father's elbow. There were cuts and there would be bruising, but movement was still good, and the pain was minimal. At least in that regard, the attack had not left any lasting damage. Probably as a means of protecting themselves, the officers finished their First-Aid assessment by suggesting that he get it checked out by a medical professional, especially if anything got any worse.

The responding officer was different to the one she had

seen the day previous. This one was a woman by the name of Kim with short blonde hair, a cute round face, wearing a business suit and a big smile. Beside her was a fresh-faced response officer in uniform. He was tall and blond with a wide face and wider shoulders. There was an enduring expression on his defiantly chubby face that reminded her of a puppy, full of an eagerness to do well, masking a sort-of nervous inquisitiveness.

Kim, on the other hand, was cheerful, almost to the point of being jolly, and yet she was compassionate and understanding. The woman acted like she was hosting afternoon tea. She gave the impression that despite Sam's worst fears, that life could go on. Yet, when she considered the man who was making the victim's life a misery, a darkness filled her eyes as she asserted herself. She was keen to point out that the victim was the one in charge. There was always a choice. Not always in the circumstance, but at least in the reaction.

Sam nodded as Kim spoke, reassuring them both. *I can either let this consume me, or I can let it define me and my future reactions.*

Each of them was sitting on the edge of a sofa seat like some creature was lurking, waiting to attack if they let their guard down. The truth was that only a few minutes could be spent sweeping up the glass before officers had arrived. Sam had barely managed to free up enough space for the four of them to sit down, only able to brush the glass to the floor, leaving a glistening coating over almost the entire carpet, like the first frost of winter, but with a crunch when stepped on that was more like autumn leaves.

Sam looked at the window, covered with a large wooden board, thanks to a helpful neighbour. It would keep the weather out until the insurance company could send someone to replace the glass. The weather had improved the moment it had been installed. The ground was drying, and the sun was out, but no one would be able to tell from the evidence available in that room. The light overhead had to be switched on so they could see anything.

"We're recording criminal damage and a further instance of harassment, based on what you've told me." She held out a leaflet that looked like it had come straight from a laser printer. "These are your incident and crime references, which I've just added to our system using my tablet. I wrote them on the back."

Sam stared at the words on the front for a moment, fixating on "Victim of Crime", and then she instinctively turned it over to make sure Kim was telling the truth. Sure enough, three different crime references were listed.

"Which one do I quote when I call you?" She asked.

Kim shrugged. "It won't matter too much, try to use the one that's most relevant to what's happening. It's probably most likely you'll want the harassment one, which is the second one."

"So, what do we do now?" her dad asked.

Kim's smile drained from her face before she said, "We're taking this very seriously. We'll put a marker on your home address. I would advise looking into some private CCTV, so if this person comes back, we can capture evidence instantly and have other lines of enquiry to follow."

Sam asked, "Do we get a police officer guarding the house?"

Kim had a wry smile. "I'm sorry. That might happen on television sometimes, but the reality is that we don't have the resources to be able to do that. If you do what you can to secure your home and protect yourselves, we'll do the investigation."

Sam and her dad nodded, looking at each other.

"One more thing," Kim said, "You say you think you know who's behind this?"

Sam nodded, not saying a word.

"I'm hoping forensics will get something from the object thrown through your window. Possibly a partial print or something. Do you have anything else that he might have touched?"

Sam puzzled for a moment before a light seemed to switch on in her mind. "The book!" She said before racing upstairs, thankful that she had not yet thrown away the pile of books, next to the waste bin in her room.

She returned as quick as her feet would take her, with Larry Llewellyn's newest book, complete with his signature from their fateful shared train journey. She was trying her best to hold the hardback by its edges and corners. "He signed this for me."

"There's one more thing," Sam said, "but it probably won't help at all." She ran to her room again and returned with the thirteen note cards from the flowers she had received. Larry would not have touched them, but it was worth checking, just in case they were missing a clue.

Kim nodded, pleased. "We'll check this book and the brick, and we'll also make sure there are no possible fingerprint matches on the papers you've provided so far. If I need to rule out your own fingerprints, or if we get a match I'll be in touch. We will also start enquiries to see if there's a link between this man and the online accounts, but this could take some time. We're talking weeks. Maybe longer"

"But when you know it's him, you'll go and arrest him?" her dad asked.

Kim raised an eyebrow. "Arresting these days is trickier because of the changes in law regarding police bail, but we would certainly have reasonable suspicion, so we would have to speak to him, possibly search his home address."

"What about restricting his movements? Bail conditions?" Sam asked. "It would be much easier if he was arrested, surely."

Kim nodded. "It depends on the number of enquiries we have left to get through. Arresting isn't like it used to be. It doesn't really stop criminal behaviour much these days. Bail is very restrictive for us now, but in these circumstances, I'll try to convince my Sergeant and the local Inspector that an arrest and bail is best here."

"So, do you think that would make him stop?" her dad asked.

Kim shook her head. "Any pre-charge bail conditions we impose, any harassment notices, promises between us and the suspect, they're just pieces of paper. When someone is determined, they'll continue, regardless of what we say."

Her dad nodded, wincing and then looking down at his injured elbow again. "That's why you suggest we get CCTV fitted. The more times he comes back…"

Kim nodded and interrupted, "The more evidence we have of the offences, and the quicker we can get him charged and prosecuted."

With some vague reassurance, Kim was gone, taking the brick, the cards from the flowers and the book in separate evidence bags. The accompanying uniformed officer followed like a dutiful dog padding after its owner.

Without pausing for a moment, her dad picked up his coat. "I'm going to get a CCTV system I can fit today. Are you coming?

~ ~ ~ ~ ~

Fitting the CCTV system was the easy bit. Understanding

how the thing worked was the next challenge. The one-button connection setup worked without issue. There was some online account with yet another set of log-in details where they could log in, see the camera's feed live, and review recorded footage from any device, anywhere. Walking outside, he appeared on the live feed shown on his tablet and smiled. No one would be able to repeat the incident of earlier without the police getting crystal clear footage. *I wish I'd done this ages ago.*

In addition to the camera, extra locks on every possible window and door provided some peace of mind. It may have been like plastering over a structural problem, but a temporary fix was better than no fix at all. He walked back in through his front door, closing it behind him. He played with a lock on the door for a moment. *I won't feel fully secure until that man is in police custody.*

For a few minutes, another face kept appearing on the screen in his hand. The insurance claim had been dealt with immediately, and within hours a new pane of glass was being fixed into place. After nodding his approval at the glass repair, he signed an invoice. An assessor would be sent the photographs of the damage, and they would visit in the next couple of days. He then waved the repairman on is way, and he looked at the remaining glass fragments requiring further clean-up. The sofas and the carpet were not old, but they were certain to be replaced. Once glass got into that stuff, there was no guarantee it would ever be clear of it again. He sighed. *I wish she had met anyone else on that train.*

He looked out of the freshly glazed window and up at the camera. Evidence was what was lacking. Maybe the thing could capture Larry in the act if he returned. The street outside was still, as if it was now aware it was being watched. Video evidence played a part in many investigations. *If the technology had been employed in a different setting, where would I be now?*

Peter had been a bright, cheerful sort of a boy. He had the kind of face you'd wish your firstborn son had. His chubby cheeks and cute nose hinted at a healthy beginning. But man, that boy could cry. There were times when it felt like it would never stop.

Doctors, nurses, social workers and police had all questioned why the six-month-old boy did not wake up one morning. Yvonne, his young bride, was on his side back then. The fire of young love had not yet died down, let alone been extinguished by the upcoming onslaught of despair.

Investigations yielded no evidence to indicate intentional harm was inflicted on the child, but the memory of his own frustrated shake of that baby the night before had haunted him, at that time and ever since.

He had downplayed the incident in an interview, but the reality was that he had overreacted to the child's non-stop crying. It didn't take a police officer or a medical professional to point out that only harm could have been caused, even if no one could prove it.

The phone started to ring, jolting him back to reality and back to that glass-infected lounge. With tears on his cheeks from his memories and the heavy beating of the heart within his chest, he picked it up.

Kim again.

"I thought you might like to know, there was a partial print on both the brick and the book that matched straight away. We've got grounds to speak to Mr Llewellyn. The trouble is, his registered address on our systems is in the Lake District, so we've asked Cumbria Constabulary to pay him a visit there."

"But my daughter has been to his place in Manchester. She told you where he was. He was obviously just here, in this area. Not over there."

"I know. We already tried that address and we were informed by an older gentleman who maintains the building they started refurbishment a week ago. No one currently lives there. He didn't have any forwarding addresses."

Samuel shook his head. No one would see the silent protest, but it was better than criticising a police officer. *A likely story. He's probably just hiding, leading the police on a wild goose chase.*

"Okay," Samuel said. There was nothing to be gained by verbalising his own cynical thoughts. "Thank you for letting us know."

He put the phone down.

"Samantha," he shouted upstairs, "Kim just said they're sending someone to his address to deal with him."

There was no response for several seconds. He waited longer. Still nothing. He walked upstairs and peered through her bedroom door which was slightly ajar. She was lying on her bed, curled up, sleeping. *The news can wait until she's awake.*

Chapter 17

Excerpt from YOU'RE FIRED! By Larry Llewellyn

It felt like a lifetime ago when Joshua had last donned the thick jacket of his uniform. There was a surge of excitement as his right arm found its way through the cold sleeve and the final part of the uniform rested on his broad shoulders.

The appeals, the fights through walnut-panelled employment courts, the long talks with his union representative in all sorts of stuffy rooms had all been worth it for the feeling of that moment. He was where he belonged: A part of the emergency services. Out there to save lives.

No more questioning his judgement. He had learned from his mistakes and he would now prove it.

As the alarm sounded and a bright red light bounced off the walls, he was determined that every decision would be the right one. Every option would be geared towards saving another's life and protecting his own. He shook his head. *I will not make such poor choices again!*

As he and his colleagues crammed into the large luminous red fire truck and made their way to this Saturday night's incident, the recent words of his wife Aurora, in her soft yet stern way, seemed to drown out the sound of the siren and hit him like a backdraft.

Why fight for this job when there are thousands of other, safer options? Why don't you just do something else?

She would never understand his need to be part of the group. The need to save lives rather than merely to protect his own or his own interests.

I want to know you'll come home safe every night, she had also said.

After a loud, hot and uncomfortable journey, they at last arrived at the scene. The restaurant, large, opulent, busy only moments earlier, looked like a scene from Towering Inferno.

Flames lit up every Victorian sash window frame. The old glass of those windows had shattered, and the fire was keen to increase its footprint beyond the London Stock bricks, pantile roof and stone beams that made up that simmering structure and to announce itself to the whole of London.

He went to work and was soon part of the meagre crew throwing gallons of water per second on the problem.

As the flames started to abate, news broke from the onlookers that there were still three people believed to be inside. At least six others were missing. Joshua, without hesitation, followed Phillip into the building, aware that their chances of success were minimal. They had to look. They had to try when lives were at stake.

Battling through a maze of smoky rooms and walls that were hot to the touch, even through the insulated gloves, Joshua almost tripped over a body. Without pause for thought he picked it up, threw it over his shoulder and headed for the exit.

Phillip was there to relieve him of the

burden, carry the person to safety, and to allow Josh to keep looking. No words were spoken in the exchange. There was just a nod of a head each and an understanding that Josh would want to prove himself.

He continued on, he followed somewhat muted sounds, sounds like someone's scared screaming, difficult to pick out in the furious noise of a thousand untamed flames. He made his way down some uneven stone stairs into a low-ceilinged basement. The sound of complaining grew louder.

Down a narrow corridor, a doorway, barely visible through the smoke and dust, led off to the right. In a flash Josh had hurried through the doorway, pausing so he could attempt to shove the door further open. It wouldn't budge, thanks to a collection of debris the other side.

At the moment he set foot inside, two things happened. Firstly, Josh realised that the faint screams he had heard were in fact the whines of a struggling industrial walk-in freezer with the door open, the large unit complaining at its impossible task of keeping everything frozen with heat flooding in through the open door.

The second thing to happen was the collapse of the floor above, slamming the heavy steel door to the freezer closed and piling so much rubble in front of it that no one would be getting in or out any time soon.

Josh pushed against the door. Nothing. He slammed himself against it. No luck. Not even a dent in the large shining metal surface. Each exertion caused him to have to breathe in the super-cooled air. A temperature gauge on the wall indicated that the air temperature was around -10C.

The fans inside were going crazy, blowing colder and colder air into the unit. The freezer was intent on getting back to its standard -18C and staying there, and there was nothing Joshua could do about it.

His clothing was designed to withstand heat. The outfit was flame retardant. The insulation helped protect him against the cold somewhat, but he was still breathing in that air, freezing his insides gradually with each breath. He shook his head in despair. *Why didn't I bring the breathing apparatus?*

He kept looking around the metal box that threatened to become his coffin. He kept exploring all available options, trying to find a way out. He tried to rip at any panel that might reveal a circuit board or control switches. Nothing like that anywhere. Not a single useful wire, fuse or switch was found behind any vent, seam or panel. Every dial, switch and setting used to control and adjust the walk-in death-trap must have been accessible only from the outside, the other side of the heavily insulated walls.

Josh tipped over a small metal shelving unit and picked it up sideways. He jabbed it into the walls, the harsh vibrations shaking right through his arms. He dented the metal, but nothing would give. He could not puncture the Surface. He could not hope to find a way free on his own.

Exhausted, he threw the shelves further into the unit. The exertion had caused him to take more and more deep breaths of that freezing air which started hurting his throat and chest, causing him to wince.

A minute went by, and then another. His insulated clothing was feeling more and more useless. Despite the thick gloves the tips of his fingers were starting to hurt. Sharp pains started in the tips and were shooting back through his arms. He hated breathing in the air as he watched the temperature gauge confirm each falling degree. He watched it fall from -13C to -14C, and on and on it went. Thick frost was starting to form on every surface, including the outer layer of his coat.

He listened for any sounds. Surely a colleague would try to save him. Would they really leave him there to die? Would he be the first fireman ever to freeze to death in a burning building? Would he pay the ultimate price for failing to judge the situation properly?

There were no sounds. No one was calling his name. No one would be fighting against obstacles to drag him to safety. He could not even hear the sound of the fire raging through the rest of the structure.

The falling floor had no doubt put a stop to anyone else entering the building. It would be deemed unsafe.

His colleagues had only just welcomed him back. They would now believe he had already been killed by the internal collapse.

No person in any line of work would be forced to enter. They would believe that their chances of finding any further survivors had fallen much lower. He would be found amongst the rubble after the fire was out.

So many conversations about risk versus reward. Despite ongoing objections to the cold-hearted view, the line had to be drawn somewhere. He had put himself on the other side of that line.

As the pleas from his wife came back to haunt him, Joshua smiled. *I bet she never thought I would go out of this world like this!*

He had no idea how many minutes he had been stuck in that freezer. He was amazed that the huge appliance had found the energy to keep going in such a situation.

He, however, was rapidly running out of energy reserves. The shivering had generated enough heat to stave off the worst effects of the cold, but he was exhausted.

He was hungry, all sorts of food surrounding him on heavy duty metal shelving, but what good would it do? His body wouldn't have time to digest anything unless his life was prolonged beyond the next few minutes. In any case, his hands were so cold that he had lost the use of them.

Starting with his little fingers, the feeling had long gone. His whole hands and both feet felt like they weren't even there. Bashing his extremities off surrounding surfaces and each other did nothing to bring back any feeling. Even moving them was a herculean task.

He sunk to the floor in a crouched position. He tried to think of his wife, of their young child, for whom he worked. Even keeping them in his mind was proving difficult.

He tried to think of their home, its layout, the plans they had. With such a fog in his mind he might as well have been attempting calculous.

He gave up thinking. He gave up shivering. There was nothing more to be done. There would be no rescue. His breathing had slowed to the point that his vision was dimming. There was no way out. There was no return. This perilous predicament would be his last.

He looked up at the temperature gauge. -18C had been reached. The noise of the fans ceased. The hum of the cooling elements stopped. Perhaps the electricity supply had finally given up, but it was too late to save Joshua.

He longed for some of the heat the other side of the door to break into the room and save him.

He fought the fire department and won, giving him the opportunity to fight with a freezer and lose. He came roaring back, only to leave once again. This time, with a whimper that was akin to the whine of a hard-working walk-in freezer.

Chapter 18

Nestled in a forest on the side of a small hill just south of Mount Skiddaw, anyone would be forgiven for driving right past the place. Unless someone looked for it, they would see nothing special about the structure nestling in the trees. With trees in full leaf, anyone could bypass the property on the nearest main road without even knowing it was there.

Yet, the front of the property had a slightly raised and perfect, unobstructed view of the River Derwent below, the small town of Keswick in the distance, and the southern end of the large but surprisingly shallow Bassenthwaite Lake, frequented by keen fishermen.

The fence and gate were probably a half-measure short of the kind found on a medium security prison. In an area typical of quaint little cottages let out at extortionate prices to American and Far Eastern tourists, the security measures were excessive.

Not a single house along the A66 looked like this one. It looked new, and it was huge. There were still some pieces of wood and a few broken pieces of red brick against one side of the substantial block paved driveway, but the property otherwise looked neat, new and finished.

The house appeared to have been built entirely from a light brown local-looking stone. Generations of people had used chunks large and small, hewn from the local quarry. Maybe this owner was sympathetic to that.

Home improvement TV shows had pointed to the plight of those trying to build with local materials. Quarries were closed. The costs involved in using the nearest stone were often astronomical. The sad state of local industry was that raw materials could be shipped from Germany or Eastern Europe, often working out quicker and cheaper. As long as it looked like the local stuff, what difference did it make?

There was a smooth gentle-sloping, grey slate roof capping the structure, matching the nearest, but not-so-near houses. The nearest neighbour was in fact almost a mile away.

Despite the intrusion of any remote neighbours being an unlikely event, there was a stone wall to match the house which was topped with a sturdy silver-coloured metal fence, complete with spikes atop each metal pole, around the perimeter. A large, solid, double-width metal gate at the entrance to the property completed its impenetrable look. A fortress in a forest. The place screamed loud and clear *I like where I am and what I am, and you are not welcome!*

A silver panel, about the size of a shoe box, on the wall next to the gate had a camera, a speaker and a large call button. Someone inside controlled entry and didn't like surprise visits.

On this damp Tuesday morning, the Sergeant had already attempted to talk her way past the gates with no success. Two officers back at the station were tasked with seeking court authority to enter the premises and to search it. They returned within an hour with a signed piece of paper.

PC Sizewell was a year into her employment. If someone called her 'young and keen' one more time, she might explode with rage. They all acted like life started when you started at the Force. Some colleagues were probably jealous of her thin and athletic figure. Some of the men, as primitive as the day is long, would look on her frame of five and a half feet with different eyes, allured by the natural red hair that dropped to her shoulders when it wasn't tied back.

Police officers came in all shapes and sizes. She had to remind herself of that anytime she told anyone she was sworn in. Fair enough, she had a figure that suggested she would put up less resistance than a pile of twigs when pushed, but there was an inner core of strength that most had never seen. Every PC did not need to be tall, strong and have perfect eyesight. If that was the case, then with today's entry requirements, the constabulary would be lucky to add three newbies to their ranks every year. She smiled to herself. *I love it when people underestimate me. It gives me the edge.*

Until the locked gate had been encountered, the day had been full of bright, cheerful promise. Any day that started with a first-time contact lens success and a heart-stirring run had turned out to be a good one.

She watched on as her female companion for the day, PS Denton, tried again.

The Sergeant was possibly five years her senior with a wide, stern face, sharp angles to her chin and nose, and eyes that would not have looked out of place on a wild cat. She had very short jet-black hair, a figure borne out of years of exercise, more exercise and some small excesses in some sort of delicate balance. She was spritely and always seemed to bounce on her feet when most would stand still.

The woman was fearless and clever. She had heard stories about her. You had to be brave to even step across the line on to her bad side. She was also the most enthusiastic, and possibly the most manic person PC Sizewell had ever met.

Granted, the signed warrant from the court did not always mean instant and unobstructed access to a property, but it was something official to show. This morning's visit was one of those occasions where it made no difference at all.

"It's faulty," came the voice over the intercom. "I can't open it. I told you that earlier."

"Then we'll have to get someone here to fix it," PS Denton shouted over the rain which had come out of pretty much nowhere to hammer the roof of their car.

With a beep the conversation ended. No amount of discussion through the intercom (that seemed to be working perfectly) would gain them access.

PC Sizewell stared through the trees towards the lake and blew out a laboured breath. *All that initial training, but no one warned me that there would be so much waiting!*

On her radio again, PS Denton called the same officers who had handed over the warrant and disappeared.

"You'll need to go back again," she said. "The stubborn so-and-so is claiming he can't open the gate. We need authority to force entry, and we need a gate technician."

The reply was unintelligible, but somehow Sergeant Denton understood.

"There's a sticker at the bottom of that box and another one on the gate. I'll take a look."

She climbed out of the car and peered at a small rectangle at the base of the control box, and then she walked to the gate and stared at another small white box at the very top.

After hurrying back to the car and slamming the door she got on the radio again.

"Huntsdale Gates, based in Sheffield. You might need to find someone more local or we'll be outside this man's house for the next twelve hours!"

After an hour of watching the rain ease and then become heavier and then stop completely, a black van showed up, followed by a second marked police car. He walked up, plugged a cable into the bottom of the box, stuck the other end into his phone and tapped away. The electronic wizardry foiled the tough security almost immediately and the gates started to open.

"Hallelujah!" said PS Denton with a hint of sarcasm as she started her engine. She wound down her window and shouted her thanks at the technician, already retreating back to his van.

All four officers drove onto the large driveway in their two marked cars. PC Sizewell stepped out of the car and turned around, taking in a lungful of air at the same time as the view. The sun was now beaming down over the lake. The trees in the distance were swaying. A perfect blue sky was being gradually shoved to the right by some small but dark clouds to the left. *I wish every house we visited was as nice.* She raised her eyebrows and let out a long sigh. *I don't think I would ever tire of a view like this.*

She dutifully followed her Sergeant as she approached the solid wooden door that looked as if it had been reclaimed and repurposed from a medieval castle. Unsurprisingly, there was no answer when she knocked, when she pressed the doorbell, or when she pounded her fist on the door.

"Mr Llewellyn!" shouted the Sergeant. "It's the police! Please open the door or we may have no other option but to force our way inside!"

There was a series of clicks, suggesting the release of a lock on the inside of the door. Even so, it must have been close to a minute before the door creaked open at a speed reminiscent of clichéd haunted house movies.

There was no need on this occasion to employ the "big red key". The threat of forcing their way inside was likely an empty one. A judge would need to really believe those threats to kill, and at the moment a broken window and a few typed insulting and threatening words did not seem to be enough. The suspect, however, would not be aware of such limitations to their powers.

Instead of a pale-faced, unimpressed butler with a towel over his arm that seemed to be inevitable, a rather thin, slightly unwell-looking but otherwise handsome man was stood the other side of the doorway. He was close to six feet in height and probably around his mid-forties, but it was difficult to be sure. He was wearing a dark brown towelled dressing gown and slippers that matched. The hair atop his tall-looking head was a mixture of black and grey and he wore a frown and a fake smile that seemed to say *Why are you bothering me?*

"Thank you for fixing my gate. It saves me the repair bill, I suppose." He put on a charming smile. "Now, what is this about?"

"Are you Mr Larry Llewellyn?" Sergeant Denton asked.

He nodded. "I am. Do you mind telling me why you've sent a small army to my house, and why you need to speak to me so desperately?"

"Could we discuss the matter inside?"

He gave a meek nod and turned to walk further into the house, waving his hand in a beckoning gesture. All four officers stepped across the threshold, the last one closing the door behind him.

"Mr Llewellyn, I'm Sergeant Denton. You're suspected of being involved in the harassment of a female in the Manchester area. This has included a number of serious threats." The man looked at her with a mixture of confusion and apathy but remained silent. She continued, "This is PC Hunt and PC Ramsay. They are here to search, while PC Sizewell and I have some questions for you. Do you have any objection?"

Mr Llewellyn didn't seem to know what to say. What could he say? If he refused, he was likely to be arrested and a search carried out anyway whilst he was questioned in less amenable circumstances.

The two other male officers were both tall, well-built and stern with dark hair and stubble on their square jawlines. They looked like something that rolled off a police production line. Without delay they disappeared down the hallway.

Larry looked concerned. "What are they searching for?"

"As I said, we have received a report of harassment by you of a female. Her name is Samantha Barkes. She has received documents containing threats that were typed using a manual typewriter, and criminal damage has been caused to her property."

Larry looked either worried or puzzled. It was difficult to tell. The more they spoke, the more a natural charm seemed to exude from this man. It was as if he was incapable of anything meaner than a clever quip. Sitting there, questioning him like a suspect, felt as foolish as questioning James Bond over terrorism offences.

PS Denton continued, "We will get an account from you with any details you can provide regarding your involvement in any of this, and they'll just make sure there's nothing lying around that obviously points to this crime. Has that put you at ease at all?"

Larry shrugged. "You won't find anything to do with this Samantha person because I don't know who that is."

"Have you ever met anyone by that name?" PC Sizewell asked.

Larry shook his head. "Never."

"Not even on a recent train journey from London to Manchester?" asked PC Sizewell.

He shook his head again before looking at some distant point that wasn't there. "I don't even remember the last time I had to take a train. It's certainly been years."

"Do you use an apartment in Manchester, Mr Llewellyn?" PS Denton asked.

He again shook his head. "This house is the only property I own."

"Have you owned or rented one previously?" She asked.

He thought for a moment. "I owned a small property a

long time ago. I can't remember exactly where."

There was a pause for a minute where nothing could be heard but the distant footprints of two people carefully moving items around, checking and replacing them as they had found them.

"Do you have a typewriter?" PS Denton asked.

Larry nodded without uttering a word.

"Could you show us it please?"

They were shown to a room off to the left-hand side of the lounge that ran for the entire length of the house. A well-used, unmade double bed was opposite the door. There was a window at each end. To the left as they walked in, the window looked out over the lake. The sun was disappearing behind a blanket of clouds still rolling in from the left. To the right was a chest of drawers and a wardrobe next to a smaller window through which nothing but trees could be seen.

Behind the door, which opened to the left, a solid corona pine desk was against a plain wall. On top of the desk was a mechanical typewriter that was likely older than all of the trees outside. A stack of unused white A4 paper gleamed, standing out against the backdrop of darker, dusty surfaces.

PC Sizewell withdrew a photocopy of one of the pages sent to Samantha Barkes. Larry offered to re-type several of the same words for a comparison. His shaking hands did so, and he handed her the resulting page for comparison.

She frowned and shook her head. "They're not the same at all. The typeface, the aligning of the letters, the colour of the ink is wrong." She was no expert, but anyone would have come to the same conclusion. She handed the pages to her colleague.

"This isn't even close to being a match," she said to PS Denton, shaking her head.

PC Sizewell further removed and inspected the used portion of the typewriter ribbon. She held it up to the light, looking for any frequently used words or letters that might show through. It was nearly impossible to make out anything, let alone anything useful.

"Are there any other typewriters, laptops or anything similar in the house, Mr Llewellyn?" PC Sizewell asked.

He shook his head. They started to exit the room for the lounge. With everything indicating that they were dealing with an impersonator, the female officers were ready to leave.

"Ramsay, Hunt, are you nearly done?" shouted Sergeant Denton as she and Larry walked back in the direction of the front door.

PC Sizewell stayed behind for a moment. Under the desk, in the wastepaper bin, there was one piece of crumpled up paper. She bent down and fished it out. She rose to her feet, starting to straighten out the single sheet of A4 paper, pressing it against her leg, smoothing it out with the palm of her hand.

She took a step towards the door as she concentrated on the hand-written words at the top of the page. She reached the door when the shock of the discovery caused her to stop and stare. The title staring back at her had just thrown a huge amount of suspicion on the male in the next room.

How Samantha Barkes Might Die

Several scenarios were scrawled over the page. Some crossed out. Some circled, or with arrows and additions here, there and everywhere. She stared at the sheet, recalling the man's words a moment ago. *You've never met her? Why on earth are you writing about her?*

This needed to be shared with her Sergeant. She walked back into the lounge, trying to smooth out the paper more as she walked. She had opened her mouth to speak, ready to point a finger at the page, and then she noticed it. The reason why PS Denton was standing still in the middle of the room.

There was a weak but unusual smell. Now that she had noticed it, the smell became more obvious, like it was crazy that they hadn't noticed it earlier. It was the kind of offensive smell you might get from a sock that had been worn for several days and then left in a public toilet for a couple of weeks. It was not an overpowering smell, but a scent that drifted in from somewhere. They looked at each other with screwed up faces.

"What's that smell?" asked PC Sizewell.

"I'm not sure," replied PS Denton, turning to face the man for an explanation.

Larry, stood behind them, fidgeting with his fingers and clearing his throat. "I've had issues with damp, but no one seems able to sort it out."

"I've had damp before," said PS Denton, shaking her head and screwing up her face even more, "but it didn't smell like that."

From somewhere down a hallway came the echoed voice of one of the other officers. "Sarge, you're gonna want to see this!"

PS Denton looked at PC Sizewell. Her facial features were soft, but her eyes were stern. "Keep an eye on Mr Llewellyn. I'm going to check."

Larry Llewellyn did not seem like a man capable of catching the officer by surprise.

Words from her early training came to mind. *Always keep your guard up. Always stay vigilant. Be ready for anything.*

There would never be recognition nor awards given for

guarding a defenceless old man in these circumstances, but there would be criticism and questions to answer for anyone who failed at such a task. She stood there with arms crossed but not folded, one foot in front of the other, knees slightly bent, still holding the paper but ready to react in an instant if the guy tried anything.

Various sounds travelled down the hallway from apparent confusion to possible concern. Voices grew louder and then became intentionally muffled. After a minute or so, all three returned looking like they were recovering from a visit to the most terrifying of haunted houses.

PS Denton took the lead. She stood before Larry Llewellyn and said, "Mr Llewellyn, I'm arresting you on suspicion of murder."

She took in a quick, sharp breath and fought the temptation to let her shock show on her face. *What's in that room?*

The usual monologue was spoken as fast as possible whilst the suspect was still able to hear every word. "You do not have to say anything, but it may harm your defence if you do not mention when questioned, something which you later rely on in court. Anything you say may be given in evidence."

Asked if he understood the caution, Larry gave a defeated nod, looking at his feet. He looked half relieved and half as if his life had just been ruined. It was an expression they had seen many times.

~ ~ ~ ~ ~

Even after watching that screen in spells for the past four hours, the news was still enough to cause him to stare, open-mouthed at some of the facts coming to light. Of course, these were 'news' facts, not facts as the rest of the world knew them.

His daughter had been spending her day in a state of blissful ignorance, but it was perhaps time to shatter that mood.

He smiled and shook his head, hearing the loud, thumping music, and feeling the heavy beats in vibrations through the living room floor. *Perhaps not so blissful.*

For more than a day, she had shut herself away, studying (as far as he knew), with only her books and her loud music for company, emerging only to grab a quick meal, a snack or a drink. Maybe her sudden regression to being an introverted teenager was her way of coping, her room recreated in her mind as her safe place. She needed one. He looked at the new window, walked towards it and peered out. The newly installed camera stared out into the street. *I think I need a place to feel safe too!*

The news was repetitive, and little else was breaking. He turned off the TV. His shoulders slumped as he turned towards the door. *It's time to further damage this guy's reputation in her eyes, I guess. No sense in putting it off any longer!*

He started to ascend the stairs, his feet pressing down on each one as little as possible, but no amount of creaking could be heard over that music. He hurried his pace and was about to put a hand on her bedroom door, about to knock, when the music died. For a moment there was nothing but complete silence.

Then there was muffled talking. She had received a phone call. The actual words in the stream of her voice travelled through the door but were softened until they were indiscernible. He backed away. He was basically spying on the girl. Even a pace from the door, very clear, very loud words travelled straight through it.

"Arrested? I thought…"

"So…"

"And…"

She was trying to say something to the other person on the call, without much success.

"So, what *can* you tell me?"

He got closer to the door. He almost pressed an ear against it, able to hear a little clearer.

"Is this even about the harassment anymore? What about the notes? The chapters? The flowers?"

Silence.

"You're telling me he's been arrested, it's for something else, but you won't say what?"

More silence.

"I'll do that. Thank you."

The call ended. The call must have been the police, providing an update of sorts, but apparently not one that was very comprehensive. *If I was the police and I couldn't tell her, I'd direct her to a television to watch the news.*

He heard footsteps. That was exactly what was happening, and she was about to find him stood right outside her room.

He hurried away and managed to get to the bottom of the stairs before the bedroom door opened.

"What's going on?" Samantha asked in a loud voice. "What's on the news, and why aren't they telling me anything?"

Samuel turned the television back on and raised the volume. It was showing the same twenty-four-hour news channel he had been watching earlier.

There was an aerial shot of a large house in the Lake

District with a large white tent outside and a seeming army of people, dressed in white, walking in and out and all over the place. Large white text overlaid a red and blue banner at the base of the screen, which read:

AUTHOR ARRESTED ON SUSPICION OF MULTIPLE MURDERS

A news reporter talked over the footage of the property.

"Several bodies have so far been discovered in and around the home. Tests are ongoing by forensics teams to determine the causes of each death."

Samantha stood, watching on, unable or unwilling to talk, no doubt struggling with the enormity of what was happening.

The news anchor continued, "The property and its grounds, where the bodies have been discovered by the police today, is that of bestselling horror writer Larry Llewellyn."

A stock photograph of the man filled the screen. Samantha took a step back from the TV. It was him. The one she had met on the train. The one who was writing about her. The one who had been haunting her in one way or another ever since.

A female voice was heard saying, "We have unconfirmed reports from other news outlets, some of which may be wild speculation, that the bodies discovered so far may reflect those in the works of Llewellyn."

Samuel shook his head. *Unconfirmed reports. A fancy way of saying a whole load guesswork.*

The camera angles changed, showing close-ups of paper-suited people, police vehicles blocking the entrance and wider shots of the house, the gardens and the lake in the background.

The views returned to the news studio where an older

male was sitting at a table with each of Larry's novels in hardback in front of him.

Samantha put her hands over her mouth, and she stepped backwards at a near-glacial pace until the backs of her legs met the sofa. She lowered herself down at the speed of a forklift truck placing a fragile load on a hard floor.

Tears started to form in the girl's eyes. Her lower lip was trembling. Her hands were shaking.

Clearing his throat, Samuel said, "I guess you led them to catch him in time."

Samantha shot her father in look of horror. She looked as if she was physically unable to speak.

"It's a massive shock," he continued, "but this is very good news."

She looked at him with a straight face, again not uttering a syllable.

"He can't come after you anymore, can he? There's no way they're letting that man out of prison."

His daughter looked torn. She was relieved that this evil man had been stopped from ruining and taking any more lives, but she would also be devastated once again that her hero was not the person she had imagined. That any person could be so evil.

On the TV an older man with a scruffy white beard was lifting, holding and moving the books around on the table. "If this man has killed the same number of victims as he has written into these very stories, he would be considered to be the fourth worst serial killer in UK history."

A league table of mass-murderers appeared with Larry Llewellyn's name towards the top of the list. He was ahead of Jack the Ripper; he was some distance ahead of Ian Brady and Myra Hindley.

Samuel totted up the numbers of deaths spread across these people. How could they be so crass as to present them all like this, like some grand prize awaited the winner?

He turned to look at his daughter again. With wide eyes she urgently pressed both hands to her mouth and stood up. She ran out of the room, leaving the door swinging in her wake.

She returned a couple of minutes later, looking pale, dazed, unsure of what to do with herself.

Samuel did the only thing that seemed to come naturally, if awkwardly at first. His little girl had been upset, just like she had been way back in those days that she was actually little. He stood in front of her and embraced her.

She almost pulled away before resting into him and starting to sob into his shoulder. He squeezed a little harder. She didn't seem to want to move. He would be right there for as long as he was needed. *It's nice to feel needed again. I've not felt like this for a long, long time.*

~ ~ ~ ~ ~

Having her usual four rest days cut in half, PC Sizewell had enough ammunition in her complaint arsenal. It did not need to be restocked.

What was the point in being called back to work early, just to stand out in the rain? If the call had come so she could help with searching, then that would be fair enough, but this?

Maybe the exclusive club, the one that had the exciting jobs, had entry requirements. Maybe newbie PCs were not allowed. They had to 'pay their dues' first. The assigned task of the day for her, the outcast, was "reassuring the public". It was a fancy way of saying that the newest, least qualified and lowest paid officer had become a security guard, keeping the nosey neighbours at bay, as well as the hounds of the local press.

The few who remained out there were dedicated, no doubt about that. The activity of peering into such a scene with morbid curiosity typically had a limited lifespan. The crowd had thinned, boredom or real life dragging some away. The changeable weather had not encouraged onlookers, many of whom would have to get their gossip from the TV news.

The unspoken opinion of colleagues was ringing in her ears. An officer within their two-year probation should be content with any involvement in such a major crime scene. Some would kill to be where she was (someone had already done a lot of that). Even the Chief Constable was sniffing around, wanting a piece of the action.

That moment, discovering that piece of paper, was a lifetime ago. The page had been bagged and filed away. CPS weren't interested in the harassment and criminal damage charges. They would be thrown into the pot to be taken into consideration if the guy started to co-operate.

The big discovery, the one she had not made, started with the blood on the floor, which led to the body in the freezer. CPS went after the big fish, not small potatoes.

The two intervening days had been filled with searching, breaking apart, finding bodies and adding further charges to the sole resident. It took a long time to forensically dismantle a house, stone by stone. A team were gearing up to dig through the garden and take up the patio. An unknown Detective Chief Inspector was pointing people here, there and everywhere.

Larry Llewellyn had replied no comment to every question in interview. He had no chance of experiencing freedom before a trial, however many months away that was likely to be. The meek but charming, frail but capable-looking man had been deemed a danger to society. *I've thrown away cottage cheese that had looked more dangerous.*

But the evidence could not be denied nor discounted. Three bodies had been recovered from inside the interior walls. Further body parts in the walls and another body was propped upright in a closet. The colourful language of colleagues, many of whom had been serving for over twenty years, was enough to highlight that this kind of thing didn't happen very often. It definitely didn't happen here.

Major crime in London often didn't make national news. In a quiet area, the slightest hint of serious crime seemed to shout louder, inviting a string of news vans as long as the average commuter train. Their destination was exclusivity. Every attempted question by a reporter yielded the same evasive response: "I'm not in a position to comment. Your question would be better directed to our public relations team."

Still, the questions kept coming.

"Can you confirm that the arrested man is Larry Llewellyn, the famous author?" asked one of the crowd.

"How has he killed his victims?" asked another.

A shrill woman's voice bellowed out, "Are the deaths like those in his books?"

A gruffer male voice asked, "Why has he not been suspected of wrongdoing before? Surely his books were a clue?"

Every word, every attempt to squeeze information from her like juice from an orange, was exhausting. The media witch-hunt was on. Serious crimes brought a hysterical reaction. The public had a right to know. The reporters had a right to be there to get answers. The truth needed to be laid bare, so the public were aware of the local threat to their way of life. Someone somewhere would be sharpening their pitchfork and lighting the torches.

She screwed up a side of her face. *I didn't expect the most challenging part of my probation to be standing in the rain and saying nothing!*

Despite the deluge of questions, there was no new information to give. The bodies had been found in the home belonging to Larry Llewellyn and he had not denied taking those lives in interview. Every reporter knew the same, no more information could be offered that could cause the case to fall apart.

She looked at her watch. Seven hours in and only a few minutes' break for lunch. There were better things to do than standing outside on a day like this, watching people in white suits moving to and fro in the distance.

PS Denton bounced over, full of too much enthusiasm for the weather and the situation. "Time for a shift-change briefing in the main forensics tent. Come on."

The gates opened and she walked through. The officer who stood to take her place was short with neat hair. No clues as to their identity, but there were other things to think about.

Breathing a sigh of relief as the gates closed again, she followed the Sergeant into the tent.

There were far more grim details on offer inside the tent than out. The first few seconds of mere observation could glean more information than the press had acquired over the previous three days. The man in the freezer had actually frozen to death. The man in the closet had been strangled. Another had trauma consistent with dying in a high-speed impact of some kind.

Maybe she was pointing out the obvious when she asked, "Has anyone here read this man's books?"

Looks cast in her direction ranged from disinterest to

some clear indication that she was deranged. Some were not shying away from shaking their heads, and some looked at the floor. Such a point was bound to be irrelevant to the investigation.

There had been no thought before blurting out the loud question. Maybe there should have been. Perhaps some time to read the room should have been allowed. She was the lowest rank within the canvas structure, and she had almost shouted above the voices of every other rank in Cumbria Constabulary.

Whatever the long-term effect would be, she had their attention. Speaking loud enough to drown out the panicked thrash-metal-styled heartbeat in her ears she said, "He's written twelve, and each have featured at least one death."

There were more stares, murmurs and blank looks. Maybe the forensics people, the Sergeants, the Inspectors and everyone else there were so engrossed in police work from one day to the next that they didn't have the time to read for leisure. To be honest, how many who worked in scenes encountering death regularly would choose to read fiction based on that very same thing?

A hush descended again. They were keen to hear the next thought from the newbie with the big ideas. "The causes of death that have been determined so far… they match the deaths in several of these novels. I recognise some details."

The murmurs gave way to an explosion of noise and activity.

"Where can I get his books out here?" asked one.

"Get them up on your phone!" shouted another.

Others were flicking through photographs of the bodies, looking determined and more urgent than they had seemed a moment ago.

She furrowed her brow for a moment before a smirk

wouldn't be denied. *How can so many people be blind to something so obvious?*

Chapter 19

The news bulletins on the subject were getting shorter. Reporters looked less-than-bothered. The story had run constantly for three days. They were getting ready to pull the plug. It seemed a story about a mass-murdering famous author had the same shelf life as a store-bought loaf. Headlines on old deaths could only sell papers, keep viewers and prompt click-throughs for so long.

It was possible that bigger issues existed in the world, but they diverted to stories on minor political issues and a traffic accident. By the end of day one the man had already been arraigned, charged, tried and found guilty in the court of public opinion, long before he would have set foot in Court. There was no need to revisit the gory details, especially when the police were keeping so tight-lipped.

Exclusives on news channels and in online articles showed a death toll of five by the end of the first day. That had risen to seven by the end of yesterday. It would keep rising over the coming days until everyone anticipated that it would stop at twelve.

She let out a sigh of relief. Day by day the tension dissipated. The real Sam, the one that used to exist before three weeks ago, was still in there somewhere. *Thank God I'm no longer going to be the thirteenth name on that list!*

The building trade would survive without Samuel Barkes, but maybe he couldn't survive without the building trade. He was returning to work, and neither Sam nor anyone else would convince him otherwise. Besides, who let a bruised elbow get in the way of anything?

She turned off the TV. The quiet could have been deemed a threat. Days ago, it would have been a precursor to something awful. Now it was just peaceful. The perfect place to do some mental gymnastics, attempt a catch-up on missed lectures and prepare for a return to university the following day.

As she exited the lounge, a smile broke out for what felt like the first time in forever. Did smiles always make cheeks hurt so much? *Maybe I'm ready to return to normal life.*

But there was something there, on the doormat. There shouldn't be. It was not possible. The smile had been robbed from her face by that envelope.

Her heart changed into some cannon ball on a chain, being fired again and again, trying to break through her ribcage. Her legs collapsed under her own weight as she lowered herself into a crouch on the floor.

She came to rest, sitting on that cold, hard floor, next to the doorway to the lounge, with her back against the wall. She wrapped her arms around her own shoulders. Hot tears streamed down her cheeks.

Say something. Let someone know. She looked around. There wasn't anyone else there to tell.

There was a scream trying to escape but only the first half-second survived the trip. Her hands started to shake. Then the shakes became more prominent and spread through her arms and up into her shoulders.

With her forehead resting on her knees, she spoke in a strained voice no one else would hear. "Don't be so stupid, Sam! It's just a letter. Don't be scared of a damned letter!"

After a series of deep breaths, the tremors eased. She crawled across the floor and picked up the envelope like it was a live IED. This might pack a punch, but in a very different way. It was stuffed full of paper and it was heavy, just like the others.

The envelope was different. A full, hand-written address on the outside and a second-class stamp in the corner. There was a smudged postmark. She frowned. *This one wasn't hand-*

delivered like the others. How long ago was it sent?

There was a choice to make, holding that envelope. Open it or ignore it. What good would it do? What alleged secrets could be contained when the guy was already locked up? Could anything useful come from finding out the plans of a man who could no longer bring them to pass?

Even so, this was evidence. Maybe that was the thing to do: Take it to the police station. Let them decide what happens with it.

She went from window to window twice, checking all were locked shut. She went out the front door and gave it a shove after locking. Then there was a twenty minute walk to the police station. It had become second nature to look on every passer-by with wariness. They could be anyone, up to anything.

Is he nearby? Is he watching me?

She shook her head. *Of course he isn't. How could he be watching me? He's remanded until trial. This is just… I don't know what it is.*

Temptations were posed by every bench, every low wall, every spot where someone could pause for a breather or to tie a shoelace. All of it was beckoning, inviting a sit-down, to rest. And why not read something while you're sitting here? It must have been strange to see her walking along, shaking her head in disagreement at every possible seat, like they had somehow offended her.

The easy thing would have been to give in. To tear open that envelope, to contaminate the evidence. Had Larry's plan changed? Did he have something up his sleeve? Or was this the embers of a vengeful fire, still warm with fury, refusing to fully die?

But sitting anywhere, opening and reading, it all missed the point somehow. Knowledge was useful. Was it really power, or was it just a minor advantage? No, what was needed was reassurance.

It would transpire that a police officer would take it off her hands, look at it, and give her a knowing, gentle smile. *This sort of thing happens all of the time,* they would say. *Some left-over part of the threat, but don't worry about it.* Maybe.

The door to the station slid open to welcome her. But even being there made everything worse. So much had already happened in that building in the past month, some good, some bad. This would be one of those good visits. It had to be. What other possible outcome could there be?

She would leave in a few minutes, reassured, ready to head to university, carrying on with the rebuild of a life yet again. The walk had been measured, sensible, an even pace. So why was it so difficult to breathe?

~ ~ ~ ~ ~

Of all the times the Monty Python song, "Always Look on the Bright Side of Life" could have popped into someone's head, this was either the most relevant or the most inappropriate. Sitting there, waiting in the witness interview room in silence was maddening. There was little to do but look at old posters on the notice board and poke the edges of your shoes into the ridges of the carpet tiles.

The words of the second verse faded away. It was funny how that happened so often with songs. But Kim seemed to have chosen that moment to speak.

"So, this arrived today?" It was a curious look. She was hiding her true feelings behind a mask of intrigue.

The greeting had been a warm smile and a hug. That warmth had already vanished away.

This was the room where PC Spencer had dismissed her

as being almost delusional. That first police report was scary, and maybe they dealt with so many people that they had forgotten how it felt to have that brush with the law, even when you've done nothing wrong. That downplaying of initial fears, all of which turned out to be warranted, was a lifetime ago.

Slow progress was being made in a room that smelled like someone with poor personal hygiene had slept there last night. Only the most nose-blind could stay comfortable there.

Such a feeling prompted a glance towards the exit. A large poster on the back of the door threatened to come away. VICTIM'S CODE was in huge letters along the top. There was a picture of a blond-haired officer conversing with an upset middle-aged woman. Words and helpful suggestions occupied the lower third, but the whole thing seemed like a low-budget movie poster. Maybe the phrase COMING SOON TO A THEATRE NEAR YOU had been missed off the bottom. The trailer wrote itself...

A group of strangers all fall victim to the same scam. When the man responsible is found dead, when they all refuse to talk, the police suspect foul play. The only way to find the killer is to intercept the group's secret messages. Only then could they hope to crack the victim's code.

"If this has been posted to you," Kim said, bringing all thoughts back to that letter, "there's likely no point in preserving the envelope. A hundred people might have handled it."

Sam nodded.

Kim shrugged. "In any case, we know who sent it now, don't we?"

Kim picked at the self-sealing flap.

"Does this change anything?" Sam asked.

An unhappy shrug followed. "Not really. Signs would point to him sending this before his arrest. It adds to the evidence of harassment, but-"

"But you won't be charging him with harassment, now that all this other stuff has come out."

Kim looked away, and then looked back, suddenly more cheerful. "The good news is that this should be the last of it."

"*Should* be?"

Kim gave a smile and a nod. "I'm confident it's the last thing you'll receive. But I'll get word to the prison to make sure he can't send anything to you from there."

Sam nodded, looking at the floor. "Thank you."

"Shall we take a look?" Kim asked.

This was all taking too long. *That's why I'm here!*

She started to peel the flap back at the invitation of her incumbent victim, but at a frustrating speed. She started at the left-hand edge. By the time she reached the other end, the first bit had once again folded closed.

Why is she being so careful? Sam squeezed her hands tight together. *I feel like ripping into the thing.*

Kim, the calm, confident and compassionate face of the police, was hesitating. Was she nervous? What hope existed if even the officer in charge was reluctant to see what was next?

It took forever to withdraw every page, to place them in a neat pile on the desk, and to check inside to make sure nothing else was lurking in there.

Kim started to read, holding the stack of papers so they leaned on the edge of the desk, staying close to upright.

Kim's right index finger was in the middle of a line near

the top and quickly made its way down. She was scanning or speed reading. Silence reigned for a few minutes. The tick of the clock on the wall became more prominent. Even the sound of Kim's finger moving across the pages was standing out.

Someone said patience was a virtue. Kim must have been raised in a company of unbelievably virtuous women or something. The pace at which she reviewed each page, and then carefully placed each sheet face down on the desk in a pile was enough to make a less patient person scream. *Why am I so impatient, so quick to anger? What has Larry done to me?*

About halfway through the new chapter, a look of puzzlement crossed Kim's face. "This is strange," she said. She then looked up with wider eyes and asked, "This arrived in the post today? It was sent in the past few days?"

"Yeah but I can't tell when because of that postmark."

Kim nodded and then asked, "You've not had any direct contact with him since you sent him a couple of messages long before his arrest?"

Sam shook her head. "No."

"What was in those messages?"

Sam shrugged. "I'm embarrassed to say they were insulting. Not sensible or worthwhile at all."

Kim continued to stare. "You didn't tell him you were coming back to the police after the incident with your dad's window?"

"Why would I do that?" Sam scowled.

Kim looked down at the paper again. "It's almost like he engineered his own arrest. It's all written here, everything that would happen."

Sam frowned. "What does that mean?"

Kim then lifted her eyes from the pages and looked Sam

in the eyes, looking as serious as she could probably manage. "He knew we were coming."

Chapter 20

The hard and creaking chair at a well-worn desk in the operation room was not PC Sizewell's idea of comfortable working.

As it turned out, a lot of effort was required to review a detailed forensic report and to not look puzzled.

The words were technically English, and a lot of the standard words were there, interspersed with multi-syllabic monstrosities. Graphs seemed to show something, but anyone but an expert would fail to make heads or tails of it, even if their life depended on it.

The crackled voices of colleagues blared out on a series of radios, responding to each call and incident as control room staff directed. It was a challenge to hear a request for assistance from a colleague and to not be able to drop everything and help out. That was her world, not this. She looked back at the report and her shoulders slumped. *I miss things being simple!*

Sergeant Denton had been vocal in her support of the young officer, dragging her away from a world of domestic incidents, thefts and hysterical parents. She scrunched up her face with one more look at that indecipherable report. *I don't know whether to thank her or hate her for keeping me here!*

"Make the most of these experiences," Denton had said no more than an hour ago. "They don't come around too often, and you can learn a great deal from them."

She had nodded, asking what she still had to give.

"Your insights so far have been essential. I think you have more to give." She had been walking off down the corridor when she shouted, "Think of how this will improve your prospects when you're done with Response."

The large room with its polystyrene-tiled ceiling probably looked okay when it was first fitted out. It also wouldn't have smelled like feet. Cables hung down in two positions in the ceiling so computers could be connected where they were needed, providing greater flexibility than the power and network ports in the ugly trunking on the walls. One of the windows was cracked. The carpet looked like someone might have died on it, such were the stains covering it. Scruffy, ancient posters were dotted around the walls where the boring paint was clinging on for dear life.

The personnel with whom she was sharing that space had been huddled around desks and computer screens for almost a week, and all of them had far more experience than she had. She shrugged. *I don't even remember the basics of complex investigations. That initial training seems so long ago. I'm in over my head.*

A tall detective in his forties with short fair hair and a loose interpretation of work–appropriate attire had read the report and had then handed it to her for a second opinion. It was an opinion he probably didn't want, but which he had been ordered to provide.

Several pages in, there was nothing new to offer. But that final glance gave opportunity for something to stand out, like it hadn't been there before.

She returned to the detective who had handed her the papers.

"Sir," she started in a polite tone, "It's probably nothing…"

She was looking down at the right page as she held out the report, pointing at a picture showing bruises on the body. "What does this bit mean?"

He rolled his eyes. "Bruises only show up prior to death. The other marks that look like bruises are due to pooling of blood in certain areas."

"What do these areas mean? Are these bruises that are starting to form before blood flow stopped?"

The man nodded, looking at the pictures again as if he'd missed something last time. Without warning, he snatched the pages from her hand and moved to stand up.

Undeterred, she stood by his side and pointed back at the picture.

"So, these new bruises here," she said pointing to one area then moving to point at another, "and these bruises here, they were all formed just before death? Probably as they were dying?"

The detective initially looked puzzled, and then his eyes widened. It was as if a light had just switched on in his mind.

She stepped away from him a pace and asked, "Does this mean what I think it means?"

The detective nodded and almost ran across the room to fetch a colleague.

She looked down. It felt like even her feet were smirking. *Maybe I can hold my own in this crowd after all.*

Chapter 21

The plain wall facing Larry had changed. This one was rough brick and mortar, covered with enough layers of pale paint to dull any detail that may have once existed. This was not the smooth, plastered wall of his own home, nor his former home in Manchester. This was one of the walls of a public area in the prison.

He tapped his feet off the cold, tiled floor. The same flooring that had been underfoot during the remand hearing. A duty solicitor, despite his suave and charming demeanour, could not convince a judge that Larry was not a danger to the public.

"Mr Llewellyn," the judge had said, "the facts here point to your involvement in these deaths. You have offered no explanation for this, and I have a duty to protect the public from you until such times as a trial can be held."

Everyone knew what was coming next. "I see no alternative but to remand until trial."

There it was. Ten minutes in a court room. Freedom, gone. Probably forever. Ideas and plans postponed indefinitely.

Some Barrister would have a shot at a defence at trial, but everyone already knew the result. He threw his head back and looked up at the rough-textured ceiling. *They have enough evidence to convince any jury that I belong in here.*

What if he requested another interview with the duty solicitor? Tell them everything, no holding back. What then? He shook his head. *Nothing but a desperate attempt. That's what they'll all call it.*

The inevitable guilty verdict, however, would be months away. Months ahead of years spent in isolation. He looked to his right and then to his left. *Not the most ideal of situations, but also far from the worst.*

An author could thrive in isolation. He had it by the bucket-load. The word summed up his entire adult life. Fame, fortune and fans brought a falseness to life. The people from each story became real. Those fictitious fellows could keep a guy level, sane enough. They would be even more crucial now. Wellbeing was in the balance. The only freedom was to keep on writing.

Getting a typewriter had been easier than expected. An old electronic BROTHER in a sort of yellow-white and light blue plastic had been gathering dust in a box in the library. The dust and dirt on the thing had been thick. Guards had looked on, possibly puzzled, maybe amused by the sight of such persistence in cleaning the redundant machine. Plastic surfaces were cleaned, the letter wheel was removed and cleaned until it looked new. The new ribbon had been put in, from the fifty or so located in the next box.

One sheet of paper had been provided. Not enough to tell a story, but enough to test every key and most of the functions of the contraption. Every key and every option selected worked without issue. The thing looked pathetic, nothing like the heavy-duty device from his home, but it would do the trick.

The only thing missing had been paper. The offices had loads of it, but they weren't giving it out like candy. Heavy hints had been dropped about the need to sort through old records. Volunteering brought more work, but a prize of enough paper, whenever required.

It had been a slog to work up to that point, but days after arrival, the work could commence. After a deep breath Larry typed CHAPTER SIX and pressed Enter, causing the characters to print at high speed at the top of the page. *Let's see what Sam will do next.*

Chapter 22

Excerpt from IN POOR TASTE by Larry Llewellyn

Tommy's breeze block walls and painted concrete floor bore the hallmarks of his successful year.

He smirked as he thought of old friends and their scoffs.

You're going to be an artist? Didn't know you wanted to die penniless!

What did they know? They could leer from their lucrative positions in investment banking, but they might never truly smile like he had learned to do.

The double garage, now full to bursting point with bespoke works, was a thing of beauty.

It won't make me rich, but I could die a happy man if life carries on like this.

No more monotony. No office politics, the cut-throat tactics, the money that could scarcely be spent because of endless hours at the office.

The nine feet tall bronze sculpture was minutes from completion. He took in the sight of the sharp angles, the briefcase with jagged pages spilling out. The shoeless feet.

He bore a calm look of resignation as he looked upon the pained face of the large man and the hands around the throat. He had found his escape from it all.

He stepped back from it and sighed. *It's*

been fun, my Tortured Man, but it's nearly time for you to go.

There would be no further reminders of his previous life.

The whole thing gleamed in the sunlight streaming through small windows in the top of his garage doors. Months of work, and one more coat of lacquer stood between him and his biggest ever payday.

He let his eyes pan across the works scattered around the space, and at the newspaper clippings stuck to the walls as he moved at a glacial pace around the perimeter.

TOMMY LORENZO UNVEILS SHOCKING ARTWORK read one headline. A charity seeking to raise awareness of child neglect somehow resulted in a sculpture showing a baby in a waste basket surrounded by beer bottles.

Another headline bore the title CONTROVERSIAL LOCAL ARTIST MAKES WAR STATEMENT. Tommy always smirked at that one. 'Victory' was emblazoned on a banner, erected over the smouldering debris of ruined homes and several mangled bodies. The buyer, who parted with thirty thousand pounds, was as mistaken as the reporter. The sculpture represented success in political battles in which winning or losing was more important that any lives ruined along the way. The irony was that the piece was bought by a politician.

The last piece he finished was awaiting collection. 'Heart in the mouth' was designed for a rich English footballer. It was a white bust of the man's head with a bright red human heart in its mouth, complete with red paint dripping down the chin. It signified the feelings that accompanied his biggest moments, the times where being overcome by nerves could be the difference between success and complete failure.

Whether the wordsmiths described his art as bold, ridiculous, pornographic or insensitive, their words didn't matter. *Maybe Michelangelo's David drew the same reaction? Was the Venus de Milo ridiculed for being rude? Did they baulk at a Botticelli?*

Recent history had proven that every time there was uproar for his unusual work, he could pretty much add another zero to the price.

He stopped dead in his meandering around the cluttered space, looking at the editorial piece in a national newspaper. ARTIST FINDS NEW LIFE AFTER ESCAPING DEATH. ADMITS TO BEING TASTELESS.

He was lucky to be alive. The piece summarised the head injury and his will to survive. It highlighted the everyday problems since. He had lived with Ageusia, knowing no cure existed. The infection that added Anosmia to the mix did not change too much. During recovery he had seen others who had been more sorely afflicted than he.

Returning to his final lacquer and polish, Tommy took a step back, taking in the full scale and impressiveness of the bronze figure. As he did so, he nudged the table on which he had left his drink. Working with metal generated immense heat, so it was essential he kept himself hydrated. He picked up the large cup whilst still gazing on his latest work and drained

its contents. The coldness of the drink
surprised him. It almost felt like it was
stinging as it made its way down his
throat.

Seeing his misshapen figure shining back
at him in the metal, he reflected on the
reaction the statue would likely generate.
*Before, my work was crude, sometimes full-
blown offensive. This time, it's just
impressive.*

The buyer would be thrilled. He might
once again generate media attention. It all
helped provide him a living, albeit having
no one with whom to share it. *Maybe that's
the next challenge.*

After several minutes, the heat or
exhaustion of his day's work was getting
the better of him. He moved to his side and
sat down. He was weak, he was dizzy. His
stomach hurt. He tried to collect his
thoughts, tried to decide what he would do
next, but his mind was foggy.

He tried to stand up and had to stay
seated to prevent himself from hitting the
floor. A sharp pain all-at-once seemed to
fill his insides from his stomach to the
top of his throat. He looked at the table.
His large cup of water was still there. He
looked puzzled. *If that's still there, what
did I drink?*

His eyes widened in horror. *I drank the
lacquer!*

He lunged across the table and tried to
get his cup, knocking it over and onto the
floor. He rolled off the table, following
the cup.

The pain shot through him like a thousand

knives on a mission to decimate his
insides. After writhing around for some
minutes, knocking over piece after piece of
fragile artwork, Tommy Lorenzo came to rest
on his back beside the statue that had
proved to be his final work. His hands were
clasped around his throat and a pained look
was written across his face.

It was as if the end of his own life was
imitating his own art. The Tortured Man
stood tall above him. The real-life
tortured man lay expiring on the floor.

Chapter 23

What a difference seven days had made. Nerves had settled. The Fitbit reported a return to a normal sleep pattern. Life was easier without looking over your shoulder. Life at home was promising a more settled future, enough to justify remaining as a resident for the next two and a half years. It would take more than a week to catch up at University, but lecturers had been sympathetic and helpful.

The shelf that once contained the works of the author-turned-monster laid bare, begging to be filled with wholesome literature which had apparently been lacking. No more messages. No more threats. No calls, no false social media accounts, nothing.

But a break from studies, even for three or four weeks, seemed to be enough to turn the mind to mush. Several hours of learning of Criminal Law could have been squeezed into a third of the time before all of this.

The soft pillow hugged half of her face in the darkness. Tomorrow it would be easier.

In every gap between thoughts, parallels were drawn between theory and real-world experience. Theory was great as a starting point, but an actual obsessed criminal mind could not be correctly captured in a textbook.

Thoughts started to silence themselves. They drifted off into a tired obscurity. But a swift descent to sleep was interrupted. Her mobile phone started vibrating and lighting up the dark room.

She lifted up her head and stared at her phone quizzically. *Who's calling? How is the call coming through?*

Clearly the Do Not Disturb mode on the phone needed some work. Maybe the caller was persistent. Maybe there was urgent news, the kind you never seem to get in the middle of the day.

Mustering the energy, she took the call and held the phone to her ear. "Hello?"

Not a word was spoken by the caller. Maybe a misdial. But then there were the sounds of heavy breathing.

Sam ended the call, shaking her head. As her head hit her pillow again, the same thing happened. Another call. This time she said nothing as she answered.

Still nothing on the other end. Only someone breathing.

Maybe there was another noise in the background. Tuning out that person's breathing might reveal clues. Nothing. No other sound. She gave up and ended the call again.

A few minutes later it happened again. Who was doing this, and what did they want?

"Why are you calling me?"

Still nothing from the caller.

"Where did you get my number?"

No response. Just breathing in, and then out, and then in again, the only discernible sound.

For each call, the phone was showing only PRIVATE NUMBER on the screen. With tired, aching limbs, Sam powered off the phone and let her head fall back onto the pillow.

No more interruptions. It was time for some much-needed rest.

But before sleep could overwhelm her, there was a knock at the door. Sam stumbled over to the window and peered out. There was a car in the road with a local pizza delivery logo stuck to its roof. Someone was at the front door holding a large pizza box. She ambled down the stairs and sighed as she opened the door.

"Your delivery," said the man. He was bespectacled and skinny, wearing a black raincoat that might have been used for school only a few months ago. The large pizza box was balanced on the extended fingers of his left hand. He didn't look like he ate much of the stuff. If he turned sideways on, he might disappear.

Loud, large drops of rain hit the cardboard box, creating a constant noise that threatened to drown out the conversation.

"I didn't order anything." Frustration must have shown on her face as well as in her voice.

The man's shoulders slumped. In a defeated tone he asked, "You didn't order a large four cheese, pan pizza?"

Sam shook her head. "Someone's been fake calling me, doing all these kinds of things to me recently. Sorry, but I think you're the latest person to get caught up in that."

Maybe the best thing to do was to take the pizza anyway, stop this being a damp, wasted trip. But what would she do with it? She didn't ask for it anyway. Maybe by saying no, they would turn their attentions to finding the person responsible.

He turned and walked out into the miserable night, carrying the increasingly soggy pizza box back to the car.

With the door closed and locked in both places, bed and sleep were well overdue.

Sam walked zombie-like back upstairs and flopped onto her bed. *What the hell is going on? Who's targeting me now?*

~ ~ ~ ~ ~

What did it matter if she opened her eyes? What was life to be other than a series of disappointments, punctuated by occasional glimpses of hope and happiness which lasted just long enough for someone to tear them away? One night of prank calls had blasted away a week of good-intentioned moving on.

Sleep deprivation and paranoia was again on the menu since the attempted pizza delivery. A couple of blinks later and it was the sort of morning that beckoned all to get up and to do something with it.

If the morning call could be ignored, another knock at the door could not be.

We've got the camera outside. Where's my phone?

She loaded the Wi-Fi CCTV app. The image was so sharp that she could count the hairs in the old man's eyebrows. The name tag proudly displayed the name DONALD. The logo of the flower delivery company on the van behind was also perfectly clear. *Not again!*

A frustrated groan accompanied the crawl from between the sheets and the putting on of a dressing gown. The old man knocked again. Did they ever leave a 'You weren't home' card or leave a delivery with a neighbour for flowers? Maybe if they came from an online delivery company.

She took a breath and then opened the door. "More flowers for me?"

He looked like he had been trying for hours to solve a Sudoku puzzle, only to give it up as a bad job. "I don't know why, but I've got another delivery for you, similar to the last one."

There was no sense in refusing. The man with the gentle face was only doing his job, like the pizza boy from last night.

Sam nodded and took hold of the flowers. Time to put on a fake smile again. "How lovely!"

"There's more," he said, turning around. "A lot more."

Was it another thirteen bouquets? Taking hold of each, the delivery stopped at seven. Not as many on this occasion. No notes. No threats. Nothing but random bunches of flowers, one for each day lived in temporary quiet and misplaced optimism.

Put on a smile. Let Donald leave happy.

As the van disappeared from view, the flowers were dumped, one bunch at a time in the outside bin. As the final bouquet landed on a bed of others, there were more footsteps growing louder.

Approaching the door was a Royal Mail employee with a Special Delivery.

She signed for the package, addressed to her and in a box big enough to provide a fun hiding place for a small child. There was the obligatory thank you before the house and its approach was once again peaceful.

She leaned against the back of the door as it closed. Her eyes did the same. *I don't know how much more of this I can take.*

But the box was still there. Staring at it for over a minute didn't change that. It might as well have been covered with question marks like the Riddler costume from the Batman comics. What was waiting inside? Who had sent it?

More questions wanted answering, and a box was crying out to be opened.

The tape was easy to breach and to cut with a key. Inside was a series of thick black straps stuck together in some random order. There were some very skimpy black lace items that probably passed for some ultra-revealing lingerie and a delivery note with a personalised message.

The billing and delivery addresses were the same. The note at the bottom said, "I bet you know what to do with lingerie and an over-door sex swing, my flirty, dirty whore."

The box seemed to drift a few paces away. It offered no answers, just more questions. She collapsed to the floor, staring, hyperventilating, crying. The familiar loud, fast heartbeat returned. *Is this him? Who else could it be? How is he doing this? What do I do? No one seems to be able to stop this!*

He had to be doing this. Who else would? But he had been arrested. He was remanded in prison. This stuff couldn't be done from there, could it? Newspapers occasionally complained that prisoners were treated more like hotel guests these days, but not to this extent. Did they have access to the Internet and their credit cards?

But that note... She hurried back to the box and picked up the piece of paper. *Ordered from here. Paid for using this address. How could that be?*

No amount of sitting or standing there, looking at the indecipherable delivery could unscramble this puzzle of the package. Even logic was a let-down. *How can any of this still be happening?*

Chapter 24

There had to be a safe place. Stacey had not answered, so the next best place was university.

Nothing made sense. Not the graphs and tables shown in the lecture, not the comments of classmates, nor the email open on the laptop screen.

Kim, the most human and humane of the police employees encountered, had sent a reply. Claims that a call had been attempted were disputed by the phone in her hand. No missed calls. No voicemails. Plenty of signal. Maybe she tried the wrong number.

Criminology Research Methods could have served up a distraction, but the content of the morning's First lecture was bewildering. Instead, only the email could grab her attention. That wasn't a good thing. Especially when it came to one odd sentence.

> Despite the arrest of Mr Llewellyn, our forensics team has discovered evidence that suggests there may still be a risk to you and to your father.

Eyes grew wide with panic. *What does that mean?*

Maybe Larry was not safely locked up as others had said.

Maybe he was attempting to break free.

Maybe he had some unconscionable lawyer who threatened legal action if he was not at least granted bail. *Or maybe he's working with someone else.* She shook her head. *Too ridiculous a thought to even finish thinking!* She paused and puzzled. *Or is it?*

Whatever had been said or taught in that arena had taken a back seat. What did that man know of serious crime anyway? How much fear had he really lived through? The criminal with the personal vendetta had once again taken centre stage.

Musings in a spirit of melancholy over mounting mayhem were interrupted. A small box appeared in the bottom right of the laptop screen. Another new email. *I think that's the first direct contact from dad in about a day.*

There was no reason to fear that email. Not until it filled the screen.

> Sam,
>
> This has not been sent by your dad, but by your future killer.
>
> See the attached. Did you think the story would end with my arrest? What kind of poor excuse for a novel would that be?
>
> Still so much more to tell. The question is whether life is imitating art, or whether it's the other way around.
>
> You'll need to figure that one out.
>
> Sincerely,
>
> Your own personal Grim Reaper.

The large lecture hall was suddenly the size of a box room. Murmurs turned into the yells of an angry mob. She grabbed her laptop and her bag and bolted from the old lecture theatre.

The same yellow sofa, occupied much earlier in this ordeal, had been empty, like it was waiting to provide minimal comfort at that exact moment.

The laptop was opened again but with trembling hands. What was in the attachment? There was only one way to find out. A double-click and the thing started to open. A second passed, and then another. No change. A small wheel spun where the cursor had been, and it seemed content to just keep on spinning. As they always seemed to do, the file opened at the point that alternative measures were being considered.

The product of a manual typewriter, it was a series of scanned or photographed pages. Sent by email instead of the hand-delivery method previously used, this was the chapter the police had said would never be written.

The first words CHAPTER SIX were enough to lock every muscle and joint. The only things that still worked were the lungs and they were going crazy trying to empty themselves. With no other option, the obvious thing to do was to read on.

The chapter introduced a new character. It was a person Sam knew well. It was her rescuer the last time things had gone wrong. The woman who wasn't answering her phone.

Aunt Stacey had been a loving, happy influence on Sam throughout her life, even when distance made emotional closeness tricky. The random phone calls, the Christmas cards, the birthday presents were the actions that spoke louder than any words between them. There was clear, undeniable, unconditional love from at least one person on that side of the family tree.

Like indigestion, the negativity came back every time it should have gone, leaving a foul taste in the mouth. The horrible words on those digitally reproduced pages hit the eye like a punch to the gut. Eyes, desperate for more punishment, flew across the words describing Stacey's end of terrace red brick home, down to the style of the front door and the colour of the carpet in her lounge.

Paragraphs described garden ornaments that had only been present for a matter of weeks.

The writing described her colourful hair, her sky-blue

eyes, her childlike dimples and her thin figure.

Further descriptions included the red floral dressing gown that she had been wearing on that recent extended sleepover, and the décor throughout the woman's home of the past fifteen years.

He had been there. Then he had written this. This chapter was him showing off, gloating. He was still ruining her life and not even iron bars and high fences could put a stop to it. He would be a thread, woven through the fabric of his victim's life until the whole thing unravelled and burned.

Prison was an obstacle, but the truth was much more obvious. The style of writing exposed the truth. This was not Larry. This was basic, cluttered and clumsy. It was even worse than the others. This was not the work of a best-selling author. None of it had been. It was the effort of someone who fancied themselves as a writer. Larry would no-doubt rewrite from a first draft, but when you used an old typewriter, isn't it all a bit final?

Those imperfect words refused to relent. They would test the limits of the whites of her eyes. The woeful writer described forcing his way into Aunt Stacey's home, knocking her unconscious, tying a rope securely to the top of the stairs, and looping it around the aunt's neck.

Sam's pulse raced as the pages further described the writer waiting until she had regained consciousness, only to be hoisted up and left with panic in her bloodshot eyes, her legs thrashing, her hands clawing helplessly at a nearby wall, and the eventual twitch of the feet of someone who had succumbed to strangulation.

The words then portrayed the killer being calm and composed as he left the house and closed the door. The next chapter in the series would be waiting for the avid reader when she arrived, panic-stricken, at the scene.

With a heart hell-bent on breaking free of her rib cage, she picked up her phone and dialled 999. *Is this real? Is this a joke? What will I find when I go to my aunt's home?*

Chapter 25

The stairs creaked and sagged ever-so-slightly under-foot as he ascended. He could not shift that look of concern from his face. *What if the bannister is not strong enough? What if I didn't wait around long enough to make sure she was dead?*

The manner of execution was simple, clean, but it was fraught with possibilities of failure.

A background in the building trade had provided a good foundation. There was a lot to learn, but he knew enough. Structural integrity had been assessed, but it was not a perfect science. The building work he had undertaken in his own home was a testament to that. Many imperfections had to be discovered and fixed for even the most basic of DIY projects.

No, the rope was wrapped around enough fixed elements that it would have held the body for as long as was necessary. The bannisters in Victorian-Era houses, like the one in which he was standing and the one in her home, they were built to last. They were far too strong for the task for which they had been constructed. Solid and dependable... and very useful for a hanging.

The woman was annoying with her bright hair and loud personality. She was getting in the way. She was becoming a nuisance and she had to go. She was giving Samantha false hope. She was giving her time away from the family home in which she should have been living. She had been written into the story when she had involved herself. All she had to do was keep out of it, like so many previous family situations. No, she had poked her nose in, and her brief cameo had to come to an end.

She would not be missed. There wasn't even polite conversation between her and Samuel. They were related strangers at best. Any mourning would be minimal. In any event, she was out of the picture. Everything had been reset.

He opened the loft hatch and lowered the in-built ladder, pressing down and pushing it into place with a squeak. He picked up the heavy item and held onto the side with his other hand. It had been used extensively over the past few days. There would be no further need for it. The large typewriter would be placed once again where it would gather dust until it was next needed, if ever.

A new love for writing had emerged in recent days. For significant portions of his life, the idea of writing, of storytelling in any of its forms, was appealing, but his focus was elsewhere, and so were his gifts. Being left alone had tuned his mind towards other things. The focus had been on proving something to the world.

Why attempt to tell a story that would be better told by others? *Samantha needs to know what happens when she lets mysterious people into her life.* She had to be afforded that chance to recognise her mistake and to learn from it.

As he put the heavy object in place and climbed down the ladder, he smiled. *I won't need this for the remaining chapters. But before I write, I need to act.*

Closing the loft hatch and descending the stairs, there was one more task to complete. He picked up and moved the bulky silver-effect laptop away from the black Kodak printer, scanner and copier that had been used for business purposes only until just a short while ago.

He walked out to his car, past the deactivated CCTV camera, taking the laptop with him. Placing it carefully on the passenger seat, he returned to the house carrying one last item to confuse the coppers.

He would leave one more thing behind, and then he would take something with him. His best effort was rewarded with the lack of suspicion hanging over him. He had managed to fool everyone. They thought the author had done it. They would find holes in that story. Maybe the prisoner would prove his innocence. It mattered little. He had no intention of giving anything away until Samantha had read, understood and learned from her mistakes. That was his duty. If she failed to do that, then the next few chapters would achieve nothing at all.

Chapter 26

Excerpt from NO WIN, NO FEE by Larry Llewellyn

The frail-looking grey-haired judge took an age to stand up from his chair, obscuring the view of the large royal crest on the panelled wood wall behind him for just a moment. Of course, when the judge stood, so did everyone else. He shuffled along and out of a door a matter of metres away, leaving one of the smaller civil court rooms in the building.

Chris Binns smiled, looking from his light brown hair to his deep blue suit like the guy from the posters. He tapped his crocodile skin-effect brown shoes on the hard floor as he waited for his chance to leave the room and to celebrate. *Another victory.*

His client, looking at that moment every inch of the stressed man with less hair and a bit of a weight problem, was at the end of his ordeal. *How much would be trust me if he knew what I'd done to get us here?*

He looked across at the enemy, the former employer. *So what if this would have been solved months ago if the guy hadn't believed the misquotes and lies? When you drink from a clear stream, do you check whether any animals upstream have already used it as a toilet?*

He looked back at his prematurely balding client and offered a reassuring smile. This would only go one way. It only ever went one way.

No settlement offer would be good enough for his client. The reasons for trial seemed pathetic as he recalled them. *It's your chance to be heard. It's your chance to make him pay publicly for what he did and for what he said.*

He had already racked up the hours so he could claim his costs after the inevitable victory. He smiled. *That 'Binns Wins' advertising campaign can't fund itself.*

Starting as a simple silhouette of himself, wearing his suit, arms aloft in front of a mock ambulance, advertisement after advertisement tugged at the annoyances of so many, bringing a mixed bag of clientele.

The judge announced the result and set an amount of compensation that inspired a gasp or two from those watching on. It was done.

He shook hands with the sweaty claimant and wished him well. There was no need for further pleasantries as he hurried from the building. He wouldn't be paid for politeness now.

He watched his maroon Mercedes four wheel drive beast of a car unlock as he approached, courtesy of keyless entry. He hung his suit jacket inside the rear driver-side door and took his seat, letting his shoulders drop in a state of semi-relaxation, leaning his head back before taking several deep breaths. He stayed like that for longer than he had planned.

He lifted his head, opened his eyes and looked around at the signs, at the windscreen. It wasn't legal to park down that side road, but it was free. He smiled at the same time as furrowing his brow.

Still no ticket. Do they ever check this road?

Chris pressed the start button and the almost three litre engine roared into life. He revved the engine a couple of times, letting the sound bounce of the nearby walls with a menacing echo. He grinned again. *I would like to thank all of my recent clients for this reward.* He started to pull away. *I could not have this car without you.*

Driving at a speed too dangerous for the streets, Chris sighed as he came to a stop at a red light. *I'd forgotten about drinks with the defending solicitor.*

A tradition honoured, and yet despised. He couldn't be the only one who thought so.

Some would socialise regardless of the outcome in court. Chris was different. He put on a face, laughed at their jokes, told a few of his own, but he resented all of them for their mocking his flying solo in personal injury.

There were money making offerings, but this line of work fit him like an expensive suit. Why change?

He patted his trouser pocket that held his wallet, knowing what was inside to the penny. *I need cash for those damn drinks.*

He drove on until he found a cash machine, stuck to the outside of a post office on the left-hand side of a narrow road heading out of town. He almost missed it, courtesy of the fairly abrupt bend in the road.

Knowing no other cars were nearby, he bounced the big tyres of the car onto the curb and stopped just next to the bollards, designed to dissuade the average motorist from using it as a temporary stopping place. *No harm will be done. I'm only here for a few seconds.*

He made his way around the front of his car and stood by the cash machine. He inserted his card and tapped his fingers on the moulded plastic as he watched his platinum card disappear into the slot at a snail's pace. The upkeep of this particular automated telling machine did not seem to be the best.

On attempting to enter his PIN, he found that the number pad was overused to the point of the number eight nearly failing entirely. It took a second attempt of hammering the keys to get the PIN recognised. The machine had some kind of loading message on the screen. It stayed there… and continued to stay there. He pressed his fingers into the surrounds of the cash machine and scowled. *Will I ever get my money?*

After probably a minute and a half doing a task that should have taken seconds, Chris clenched his hands into fists and tapped his toes. *Why the hell is this taking so long?*

He looked at his Rolex. Over two minutes into the time-taking transaction, he was ready to give up. Finally, the machine flashed up with a message.

ERROR. YOUR CARD HAS BEEN REJECTED OR THE MONEY REQUESTED IS NOT AVAILABLE.

Chris grunted and thumped the keypad of the machine, catching the knuckle of his little finger on a raised edge. He pressed a button to cancel but his card was not returned. He pressed every button, thumped it again for good measure, and stormed back to his car.

As he took those few steps, he was staring at a small cut on his hand. A small self-inflicted injury. *I wonder if I can make my own case from this,* he thought with a smirk. *They'll certainly pay for withholding my card.*

His mind was so caught up in the most minor of injuries that he paid no attention to the road. He did not hear the sound of the vehicle approaching. Even if he had, he was arrogant enough to feel they would move out of his way.

Chris also failed to notice the blue flashing lights whizzing along the road, reflecting off every glass surface.

As he reached for the door handle and started to open that door, he finally heard it. He looked up and a cars length away, an ambulance was hurtling towards him at great speed.

In that moment he took in every detail. The registration plate of the vehicle. The bright yellow and green squared pattern. The panicked look on the face of the young male paramedic behind the wheel. The screech of the tyres. The smoke flying everywhere. The feel of that moment of high-speed impact.

He heard the crunch of the vehicle against his own car door, knowing that he was between the two. He heard the door snap free of the expensive car and the impact was at such a speed that Chris was actually airborne for several seconds.

As he flew backwards with his arms flying up, extended to the full as he travelled through the air, he could see blood, his blood, splattered all over the front of the ambulance, creating a kind of halo-silhouette effect, outlining his upper body shape.

Too many thoughts crossed his mind in those few seconds.

Why weren't the sirens going?

Could I sue them for this?

What will happen to my car?

So much for being an ambulance chaser!

After what seemed like forever, Chris hit the floor. The impact hurt more than the collision with the speeding vehicle. He felt his head hit the tarmac hard. His back, his elbows, everything seemed to crunch as he landed in a heap of broken body parts. The ground underneath him felt wet. *Has it started raining?*

He then realised the dampness he could feel would be his own body fluids escaping.

Everything burned with pain, even down to the cheeks of his face. He tried moving his arms and legs while still conscious. The signals were not getting through.

After three, possibly four seconds, even keeping his eyes open seemed to hurt more than anything else. His head screamed in pain. Nothing felt normal.

As his eyes closed, he heard someone running up to the scene but stopping some distance away. "Did anyone see what happened?"

He recognised that line. He had used it on numerous occasions on arriving at the scene of an accident.

He didn't need to open his eyes to know who was speaking. The voice was one he knew well. It was that of James Slater, an aging, less successful lawyer whose office was the other side of the street. It was a man he had faced in court more than once, and each time he had come off victorious.

Everything faded away, and Chris Binns was only partly aware of his surroundings. His house, his car, his winning record, they all drifted into obscurity and irrelevance.

As he lay there, his life ebbing away, Chris knew his first big loss was at hand. It would not be a loss of any petty little legal squabble, but the loss of a life wasted in making easy money from those who had already been victims.

The pain he felt was starting to disappear, replaced by a numb feeling. The automatic act of filling his lungs with air did not seem to be working. He felt himself coughing. His breaths were shorter and shorter. Each one more difficult than the last. Unless someone helped him within the next few seconds, he would not be around for much longer.

He wondered whether the paramedics would prioritise him or the on-board patient they were already trying to get to the nearest hospital. The fact that no one had rushed from the vehicle to his aid gave him his answer.

Maybe those ten to thirty seconds were actually only three or four. Maybe the driver of the ambulance was so overcome by shock that he didn't know what to do.

Chris Binns took what he felt would be his final breath. There would be no suing for damages. There would be no chance to even revel in his latest achievement. Not even a chance to massage the ego of the losing counterpart.

On this occasion, the only person who had suffered significant damages was him, and he had no one to sue, no one to blame.

A life spent in finding blame in the actions of others was futile in those final seconds. With broken limbs and shattered digits, he had no one to point the finger at but himself. As he exhaled for the final time, he was doing exactly that.

Chapter 27

Doubt and trepidation were now constant companions, as real as the people around her. The incarcerated man could still infiltrate her life, destroying it at whirlwind speeds. Maybe the police had jumped the gun. Maybe the man wasn't acting alone. She, however, had next to no one left to whom could be turned.

She hung up the phone. No answer again. She had tried calling her dad enough times that the call list showed double figures. The reason for Stacey not returning her call was obvious. It had been from the moment that email had come through, but denial and hope had been powerful tools until she had seen the body. The once energetic, enigmatic woman was lying lifeless in her own hallway after being cut down.

But there would be no more reassuring hugs, no confident words, no sleepovers, nothing. She could no longer post those positive, life-affirming comments and images on social media, she would send no more funny birthday cards. She would not be on the other end of the phone when there was no one else.

Life wasn't supposed to be like this. A renewed relationship with her father should have conquered all, but he had disappeared when he was most needed. Even her mother was failing to answer her phone. Friends were so distant and so wrapped up in their own lives that they could hardly be turned to in such a moment.

It had taken a good while of staring at tarmac and feet before there was any awareness of the woman by her side. A police family liaison officer was there, attempting to offer comfort, but what could she really do?

Grief could do strange things, it would seem. For one, it had provided the ability to stare at the same square metre of road surface for minutes upon minutes without so much as a flicker of movement, staring at nothing and not seeing it.

Memories of the past played like a projection on the tarmac. It was the way Larry had described using his own imagination. Damn him for talking to her about it. Damn him for talking to her at all.

But this moment was about memories, not about him. There had been shopping trips culminating with multi-flavoured Italian ice cream. There had been movie nights where they ogled the male lead. There had been drives to nowhere in particular for no apparent reason, just to talk.

Emotions clattered and crashed around inside, hushed every so often by a new wave of numbness. Grief, despair, anger, frustration and bitterness were swept away for a moment by another feeling. Hopelessness. That was it. The sense you get when every single part of life is outside of your control. When you're at the mercy of a madman and even the police are clueless.

The author was still in prison. They knew that. They had provided assurances a couple of times already. No one had deigned to suggest a reason why all of this was still happening. They probably wanted the facts before they speculated. That was great, but cold, hard facts were not forthcoming. Enquiries hit dead-ends. They might get lucky and find something, they might find out the accomplice, but could they do it before any of the remaining ruins of the girl's life had been further smashed to pieces?

She continued to sit there, hunched over, hugging herself. *If I was him, how would I be doing this? If I wrote this story, what would I do next?*

Larry seemed to know the police were coming. More than that, he seemed to set them up somehow.

He could have pre-written a handful of future chapters. He could have arranged for someone to execute his plans and exact revenge on his behalf. Perhaps it was that Steve with whom he had traded insults. He had the money through his successful writing career to employ someone for such a task. He had the imagination. He probably had the contacts, gained through years of research.

She grimaced and shook her head. *What a crazy theory. I could hypothesise as much as I like. What's the point?*

The events of chapter six had been played out. The latest part of this appalling plan was about to be revealed. Found within arm's reach of the dead aunt, there was a clear plastic wallet. Within the container, several sheets of paper. Through the thin, sheer plastic, and through the outer envelope-sized evidence bag, it was easy to make out the words CHAPTER SEVEN.

"What's going to happen to that?"

The officer carried the evidence bag away from the scene. He shrugged. "I don't know yet."

"Well, can I read it?"

The officer looked at her as if she was some silly schoolgirl. "It's police evidence"

Sam rolled her eyes. "I can tell that by the *evidence bag*."

The officer continued, "It will be added to everything else we seize and be booked into police property."

Sometimes idiots only realised you were serious when you raised your voice a little. "So when can I read it?"

There was a downward look and a shrug. Not even a verbal response.

"That's about *me*. You know that, don't you?"

The officer continued walking away.

Sam stood still but raised her voice to a shout. "This is my life! It's being destroyed! Do you get that?"

No hint of a reaction.

She sat with her shoulders slumping and a lump in her throat. The random bark of a neighbouring dog was enough to make her jump.

There was no merit in even sitting there any longer. They all knew what she knew. The best course of action, decided by the most clouded of minds, was to plead and pester officers about chapter seven. All they needed to do was to book it into evidence quickly and to find a way to provide her a copy. There would be clues. There would be something to do or something to avoid.

Regardless of the speed at which those words were reproduced, she was a mouse in a shoebox. The lid was on. Several air holes had been poked into it. The killer had that box in a tight grip in his hands and he was ready once more to start shaking it, just to see what would happen.

~ ~ ~ ~ ~

There was a limit to how much a person could tolerate being back in the same place, waiting for answers. Sam was past that point. The police station, again. The waiting area, again. Awaiting answers, AGAIN!

What would the latest instalment have in store? What horrors were going to leap from the page and extinguish another part of existence?

The floor was sticky. Shoes, if left in one place for more than a couple of seconds seemed to want to stay there. In such a public place, questions about the condition of the floor would only prompt answers that nobody wanted.

There was no clock on the wall. Not that any attention was given to the time when she entered and sat down. The wait, while not considerable was more than enough to prompt inner comparisons to a sit-in protester.

PC Spencer, the officer who, some days ago, had originally shrugged off the original complaint, who thought the girl and her father might be jumping to conclusions, walked in the door and took a seat by her side, looking more like a boy being told off than an officer of the law.

"This is now a very urgent matter," he said. "We have rushed several items through forensics and analysis."

A look of shame looked like it had been carved into his face, destined to remain long after this was over. He had more to say but he seemed to be resisting, going through some inner struggle of his own.

He looked her in the eyes and asked, "Have you spoken to your father since you left university?"

Sam shook her head. "I tried. No answer."

"If you do, can you please let me know? We obviously need to speak with him."

Sam nodded. But that look didn't shift from his face. What did he want? He was the closest relative of Stacey, they avoided each other, but there was more to this than he was letting on.

She was handed a photocopy of the latest chapter. The officer stayed by her side as she read.

After a handful of minutes, she almost threw it back at the officer. "This doesn't tell me anything. It says, very badly, that my dad goes missing and that I wait around in the police station feeling unsafe."

He nodded. "In light of the latest developments, our suggestion is for you to stay with someone else."

Well that was stating the obvious. Who really needed to be told that? *Ooh! I'm scared! I'll go to the home that's already been targeted because somehow it'll be safe? I don't think so!*

Larry knew about her dad. He knew about her aunt. He

knew about her old schools and the university. But there was still one place that would be a mystery to the horror writer. But he had hunted down the aunt on his own. If he had done that, what else was he capable of finding out? What else did he already know?

Tears of self-pity threatened to block out any attempt at rational thought. *Is there anywhere I can go where he can't reach me?*

Sam picked up her bag and asked, "Would it be possible to get a lift to my dad's house? I can collect my things and then get on a train and stay with someone."

Seemingly over-thinking, the officer finally relented. He disappeared and was next seen around three minutes later outside the main entrance, exiting an unmarked dark blue Ford Focus he had parked in the public car park. It didn't look like a police vehicle, and that was no-doubt the point.

Her legs seemed to refuse to bear her body's weight as she first got to her feet. Her hands seemed to want to do their own thing. Her head was filled with thoughts of what might happen. After an unknown period in which her feet seemed to be glued to the sticky floor, she pushed onwards.

The walk was short. The drive was shorter. There was barely enough time to doubt the decision all over again. Maybe travelling alone was a terrible idea. But maybe it was the best idea. Head in a direction Larry wouldn't expect.

The PC offered little by way of small talk.

"You have somewhere in mind where you can stay?" he asked. If he had tried, he could have guessed. Maybe he needed to know. Maybe it was some attempt to reassure.

Sam nodded, and then realising he was looking ahead at the road said, "Yes. With my mother, down south."

"And you can be contacted on your mobile phone or by email if we need to get hold of you?"

"Yes."

The reply was abrupt, but another rush of emotion was strangling her vocal cords.

A moment later they were outside the house.

PC Spencer's only movement was to kill the engine. "I'll wait here, and I can drop you off at the station when you've got what you need."

He was finally going above and beyond his duty.

She opened the door and turned to face him. "Thank you."

The next steps were becoming clearer as the door swung open. University would wait. Her aunt was dead. Her dad was missing or busy somewhere. Her mum was on her own. She nodded as she crossed the threshold. *That's where I'm going. I can at least try to protect my mum from being dragged into all of this.*

"Dad?" There would be no answer, but it was worth a try. "Are you home?"

A brief pause and nothing. It was like he had just disappeared. It wasn't uncommon during a busy task at work, but this was pushing the limits. This had been hours. Had he, for some reason, taken himself off-grid?

She hurried upstairs, threw some clothes and a couple of books into a travel bag. She picked up hair straighteners, a hair dryer and various bottles including her usual hair serum, shampoo, conditioner and the typical toiletries for a stay away.

Having one last check around her room, she stopped, her shoulders slumped, and she rolled her eyes. "Where did I leave my phone charger?"

It wasn't in any of the sockets in the bedroom. It wasn't in the hallway. But a few days ago, she had been huddled up on the sofa. Was it there? It was easy to forget where those sorts of things ended up, despite their being used every day, when the mundane was never foremost in the memory.

Slinging the holdall over her shoulder, she hurried down the stairs, chucking her bagged belongings on the floor in the hallway, close to the front door. She then breezed through the white gloss wooden panelled living room door.

She stopped dead before stepping backwards out of the room, shaking and screaming.

Blood. So much blood.

Chapter 28

"You honestly believe that?!" DCI Mercia asked of Kim, the Police Staff Investigator drafted onto the operation. The faces of everyone around the tables in the large meeting room were now turned towards her.

"I think, if we spend our time looking for a link, we might never find one," Kim responded.

"So, you think those murders that Cumbria are looking into are not linked to the events here?"

DCI Nick Mercia was tall, white like he had never been outside in the sun, and bald. Set into his gaunt facial features were dark brown eyes that almost seemed to burn into the skulls of the opposite party when he gave that disapproving stare.

Kim shrugged. "Those murders are years old. The guy they arrested doesn't even seem physically capable of the harassment, the criminal damage or the murder we are investigating here."

"Are you denying that Samantha has a definite link to Llewellyn?" DCI Mercia asked.

"Some of it just doesn't add up," Kim responded. "Like the DMI results."

They turned to face Maisie, the fresh-faced Digital Media Investigator in the corner of the room. She had a symmetrical face complete with the cheekbones of a model, but the expression of a scared rabbit. Her black hair reached to her waist, which seemed unnaturally high. She either had incredibly long legs or her smartish trousers were deceiving.

On her first operation, Maisie looked like a kid standing next to a broken vase, ready to point the finger of blame at a younger sibling. Kim stared at the young woman for a moment. *I wonder if I ever looked as shell-shocked as that.*

"The IP address relating to the emailed chapter resolved to Sam's home address," Maisie said, her voice wavering for those first few words. "As did a number of the false social media accounts."

Before anyone could question what she had meant, she threw herself into a monologue, divulging everything in only a few seconds.

She continued, "The adult dating profiles were also created from the same IP address. The recent Amazon delivery was ordered from her father's account. We also found an order for a Royal P, and old typewriter, billed to that address. I would not be surprised to learn that the print style matches all the chapters and notes received so far."

The murmurs in the meeting room were growing louder. Theories were being prematurely promoted.

After the DCI quietened the room again, he addressed his staff. "Those of you who have a suspect other than Samuel Barkes, you might want to review your evidence. He has gone from person of interest to our main suspect. Find him."

There were again mumblings from people surrounding the table.

The Detective Chief Inspector spoke again. "But there is one more thing we need to discuss in this briefing. Let's move on to the preliminary results from residual DNA that our colleagues in Cumbria have sent on, relating to the bodies recovered. You'll agree that they make for interesting reading. We're not out of the woods yet, even if we find Mr Barkes."

Chapter 29

A search of his cell was far from surprising. He was treated like the criminal that all and sundry believed him to be. They had the power. They could do what they liked.

When the typewriter was taken away from the recreational area, a guard had given him a cruel smile. That almost drew a reaction. He would have gone for him. He would have threatened to add the guy to the list of bodies in the house. Instead, there was a meek nod and acceptance of everything. Who was he to gain any enjoyment from his time there? It was not deserved.

Those final few typed pages, though, meant something. Why did they need those? Why did they feel the need to wrestle them out of his hands?

"It's my story," he protested, feeling his face getting hot. "What harm can that do while I'm in here?"

Prison staff went about the confiscation without uttering a word to the typically tame inmate, but there would be an explanation. This was about the other guy. *What is he doing out there?*

That man had a plan that involved Larry and his writing. Fools followed a doomed plan. When the world fell apart around them, they would cling to some string of potential events that protruded from their consciousness as if it would all hold the key to putting everything right again.

Since the first sight of the high fences garnished with barbed wire, since the humiliating strip search and the donning of the outfit that labelled criminals and inmates, one thought had been lurking in the back of his mind, gnawing away like a rat on a mission. *Tell the truth!*

He shook his head at the invisible introspective request. *The truth will not set me free.*

But what was real freedom? A physical thing, living without restraint? The past few years could provide proof that such freedom was hard to come by, except perhaps in literary escapism.

The iron bars, the guards, the concrete everything were symbolic of trading one prison for another. Such a change could still have been positive. The food was better than popular culture suggested. The guards were not ogres, either. They would chat, they would check on the welfare of every inmate. It wasn't The Ritz, but in a lot of ways it was a step up from the solitudal life left behind.

Location and conditions had been incidental. The tools of his trade could take him anywhere, anytime, getting away from whatever hell had formed his current circumstances. *True freedom is a state of mind.* Larry could exercise that freedom any time he liked. *But my freedom still seems to require a typewriter or a pen and paper.*

Cut off from the means of mental escape, reality would hit, and it would hit hard. The home that had been paid for by his royalties would have been torn apart in the search for the bodies that they would inevitably find. His bank accounts were no longer his. He had nothing.

The search concluded with a walk to a private meeting room. When you were invited to sit down in prison, you did it. He was one side of a conference-type of table, made up of four individual rectangular tables pushed together. The tables were cheap wood stuck on top of tubular metal. Maybe they had been there for years. Maybe they were picked up from an old school that was throwing them out. They looked like they had suffered the punishment of thirty years of kids eating at them, painting pictures only parents would love, undergoing tests, sticking gum underneath, the works.

The walls were a colour that reminded him of ice cream at the beach as a kid. A large clock with a white face and dark blue numbers was covered with a small cage, bolted to the wall above the solid dark blue door. Maybe, every once in a while, things turned violent in here. Those tubular table legs were fixed in the same way to the medium grey industrial-style floor.

Opposite were three men. Each wore a stern look and a cheap suit. Other than the one on the right having blond hair compared to the dark greying hair of the other two, the three men looked quite similar. Not like brothers but probable cousins. Their backs were straight, and each looked like a smile might shatter their face, so they wouldn't take the risk. Each had a layer of indulgence smeared over strong facial features. These were men of the law, high-ranking, looking for answers.

"Mr Llewellyn," the central figure said. "We have some questions for you."

The usual police caution commonly commenced each interview, but nobody uttered the words he had already heard a handful of times. *Does this give me a way out by way of appeal?*

"We have been studying these first autopsy and DNA results from the bodies recovered at your home. We found out a couple of things that you've not mentioned."

Larry shrugged. "Had I said anything, I doubt anyone would have believed me."

There was a slight outburst, almost a laugh from the man in the middle. They were capable of smiles, but not the warm, friendly kind. "Who would believe the word of a man who makes stuff up for a living, right?"

Larry smiled and nodded once.

"The thing is," the man paused and looked down at the papers in front of him. He picked them up, straightened them, and replaced them where they had been without reading a single word. He then continued, "Your writings aren't based entirely on fiction, are they Mr Llewellyn?"

He shrugged again without a word.

The man to the left spoke for the first time, a slight double chin wobble as he spoke. His voice was a higher pitch, but equally authoritative. "You're already in prison, suspected of murdering many people. We believe we have sufficient to convict you of multiple murders. Talking about it now isn't exactly going to make things any worse."

Larry said nothing.

The man in the middle tried again. "Our preliminary results show that more than one person was involved in some of those deaths. What can you tell us about that?"

They were the kind of bland men that someone could stare at for an age without really seeing them. *Is now the time to tell them everything?*

"To be clear, your DNA was found on the bodies," the man continued, "but so was the DNA of someone else."

The man to the right, with the uneven cheekbones and a nose that was almost straight but not quite, joined the interrogation, being held in a conversational tone. "The people all died in similar ways to the victims in your books. That seems like more than… coincidence, given the circumstances. Wouldn't you agree?"

There was a silence. The tick of the clock on the wall grew louder and louder with each passing second, more prominent in the silence. Pleading, imploring and then insisting with its incessant noise that someone do or say something.

The right-hand man continued, "It is our belief that you witnessed these murders, and that you may have been involved prior to writing about them."

"What we're getting at," the man in the middle said,

butting in, "is that you've not told us much, and what you're *not* saying might well reduce your time in here, or in whichever high security prison you end up, *if* you have to end up in one."

There was another uncomfortable pause.

The middle man spoke again. "You have failed to tell us that there might have been someone else involved. We don't yet know which of the two of you was in charge of all of this. Would you care to enlighten us?"

Tears formed in Larry's eyes. What did it matter that this particular interview didn't seem to follow the rules? What could be gained if his solicitor had been by his side? There was a burning need to give them the truth, the whole truth and nothing but the truth.

He nodded slowly once, twice. "I don't really know how to start talking about it," he said.

The man in the middle picked up his stack of paper and riffled through it. He removed a chunk of pages and slid them across the table. It was pre-printed statement paper. "We thought you might be more comfortable writing it first. Then we could talk about it."

The man withdrew a disposable pen from his jacket pocket, placed it on top of the small stack of paper and slid the bundle the rest of the way along the desk towards Larry. "Would you like to write it down?"

Larry nodded and reached forward, collecting the paper and pen, looking at them as if they were old friends. He started writing.

He began with that fateful moment on the hill. Out for a typical early morning run. The speeding car, making not one but several corrections to head straight towards him. His inability to think fast enough, to get out of the way. The period of indecision that had haunted him ever since.

How different might life have been with a better choice at that moment? He wrote of the moment of impact. The fall down the hillside. That moment where he felt his life was over before he had really started to achieve his potential.

The pen began the fly across the paper at speed, as if everything in his head was pouring out of his mind, through his arm and out of the writing implement in a vice-like grip in his right hand. His right arm felt like a garden hose snaking and flying around with the pressure of the water trying to escape. The force with which he wrote his account, years in the making, drove his hand on and on.

~ ~ ~ ~ ~

Before he opened his eyes, he knew he was broken. In those moments before daylight would flood to the back of the retinas causing his brain to scream, pain had already made its way through his legs, his arms, his chest, just about everywhere.

Was he dying? Something had happened. Some sort of collision. He had been out for a run and then… The rest of the tale was beyond reach.

But if he had been left there to die, if someone had hit him, or if he had hit something else, wouldn't the ground be hard, maybe damp and uncomfortable?

Instead, all he could feel, levels below the intensifying pain, was softness.

He opened his eyelids like he was pushing a piano up a flight of stairs. They dragged open and they stayed there. The light streaming through the window to the right, the desk and the door ahead of him, the foot of the bedframe, it was all his. The cream walls, the brown curtains, unchanged.

The renovated bungalow-turned-maisonette, nestled in a beautiful wooded part of the Lake District looked foreign, despite only leaving that bedroom a matter of hours earlier. Had it been hours? Had it been longer?

Maybe, like the updating of the classic Tudor-style structure, he could be rejuvenated, freed from his current pain on that same plot of land.

The white ceiling was smooth, but the plaster was less than perfect. He counted the tiny pits and the bumps. Anything to avoid facing the reality of what was next. Sometimes it was better not to know. Hadn't that been why the Master Suite on the top floor had remained empty for the past few years?

There was that moment out running, on the hill, and then there was this. Why the disconnect? Had he, like some drunken fool, found his way home with no memory of the journey? That must have been it. If he could muster the energy to sit up...

Every nerve ending screamed at once, almost sending him back to sleep. Even a scream was beyond him, escaping as some sort of tortured whisper. He halted and the pain dissipated.

The bedroom, the sanctuary, the hideaway, was now encapsulating its owner, too injured to do anything but glance around.

How did I get here if I can't move? There was time to ponder that question. It wasn't as if he could do anything else.

Running, an attempt to outrun the pain of his past, had been morning routine for years. Ever since the car crash. But today had been different. A strangely brave young man had reached the junction farther down that road. It wasn't him. It couldn't have been. He always went right, down the hill, taking the long way home, going the extra couple of miles. Never left. Never. Not the short road back. Not along that hillside road with the cliff and the steep drop and the view of the valley. It was too painful.

Yet somehow, he was doing it. He had carried on uphill, running towards his past instead of trying to outrun it. One sweeping bend and he would be at the very point where he had been pulled from the wreckage, where he had seen the stains on the road and the remains of the black Mercedes. The recovery had been long and slow. An insurance pay-out and a decision in the family court later, and he was free at sixteen to occupy the family home alone.

Every hurried step climbed that hill on the run, remembering the past without being paralysed by it. Each time the running shoes thudded into the tarmac confidence grew. He would not be harmed by merely being there.

That would have been true on any previous day. On any of the runs over the past two thousand days, he would have finished the circuit in safety.

On that morning, the one time he had chosen to bite the bullet, to tear off the sticking plaster with reckless abandon, that had been the time that it mattered. And yet, he could not remember why. The tape reel was still spinning but the footage was gone. Whatever had broken his body had done a number on his head too.

Rewinding back to the junction and the decision, maybe hitting play again would show more.

No more questioning left or right. No more a prisoner to his past. A left turn, a jog uphill, around a corner and then blackness. Still nothing.

Some would have said he was lucky to survive on that road the last time. Some would have said he was luckier to get the house without the mortgage and to focus his time in the arts or in literature. Some people were wrong. The pain, the guilt, the anguish could not be bought, recompensed with any amount of money or things.

What would some people say about him now, lying helpless in that bed? Was he still lucky? Maybe he was.

Maybe, for the second time, he had cheated death.

Still there was no answer. The incident, whatever it was, had been enough to break up his memory into a jigsaw and to scatter the pieces on the wind. The fragmented remains provided nothing more than a feeling, a seemingly random thought to be explored. *The answer, whatever it is, is in this room.*

The movement of the neck required to expand his field of view was small, but pain still shot through his neck with every slight movement across the pillow. To the left, the chest of drawers and the wardrobe and nothing else. To the right was nothing but the sofa beneath the window. Dead ahead, the door to the left of the desk was open.

But there was someone standing in that doorway. A dark figure, lurking in the shadows, watching on. The silhouette gave away a great deal before the figure moved into the room and into the light. A man of similar height and build, a head of thick, black hair. The same straight nose. Dark brown eyes stared at him, the kind that bored into you for the truth in interrogations.

Similarities ended with a more rounded jaw, larger ears and uneven cheekbones. Of course, that man was standing there, uninjured. A muscular torso was testing the limits of a black t-shirt. There were differences.

A hundred questions tried to escape Larry's lips at once, but the only audible sound was a gurgle from a dry throat. The other man hurried to fetch a glass of water and to gently tip some into his mouth. The shocking cold temperature of the water was almost enough to numb his throat, but it felt soothing, hydrating, amazing.

Larry tried again. "Who are you?" came the croaking question.

The man stood over him, smiling down like a parent watching over a sick child. "You've had quite an accident." He held the glass of water, backing off. "I was there. I saw your fall and I thought I would come to help you."

"Thank you," Larry tried to say but his voice was still not up to much.

Another attempt to sit up was thwarted by severe pain. He screamed out and collapsed back into the bed.

"I would highly recommend resting for the next few days, possibly weeks," came the voice from somewhere just outside the bedroom door as the man walked away.

Larry shook his head. The pain in his neck and head was manageable. His left arm also seemed to be usable. He could have held and drained that cup in the other man's hands.

"I have things I need to do," Larry said. At least the scream seemed to have cleared his vocal cords sufficiently to talk at a sensible volume.

"Ah, yes!" he heard in a loud voice. "Your writing! I know about that."

Larry stared at the open door, puzzled. "You've been looking through my things?"

The man walked back to the doorway and leaned against the frame. "I didn't need to. I recognised you. You're Larry Llewellyn. Up-and-coming author."

"You've heard of me?"

The man let out a short laugh. "Of course. You're talented. Possibly the best stuff I've read for some time."

"Thank you. But how did you recognise me? My picture hasn't been included in anything I've published. How did you know where I lived?"

"I found a wallet in your pocket when I found you by that tree."

Doubt filled his mind. It couldn't show on his face. *I never take my wallet when I'm running.*

There was something uneasy about this man, about this whole situation. This person, unknown to him, was in his home with complete control over him, a helpless victim of a hit-and-run.

"I'm a writer myself," came a proud comment from the man by the door.

"Would I have read anything you've written?"

The warm expression on the face of the man vanished, replaced by a stern coolness. Anger was bubbling away under there somewhere. Larry had hit a nerve.

"No one has agreed to publish me yet," then his face immediately brightened again. "But they will," he added with an over-the-top cheeriness to his voice.

The man left the room, returning every now and then to check on his patient. A hospital could have provided better, more consistent care. A random stranger could not hope to help in the same way. What could be done about it? He was powerless to change any of it. Maybe the carer had some reason for staying away from such places. But some outlaw, some fugitive would hardly hide away in the home of a stranger and nurse them back to health. The caring criminal? The random do-gooder? What was his angle?

Life was no easier, nor was it any more comfortable in the coming days.

Meal after meal, day after day, the man was there, helping him to eat, to drink, discussing the interests of the injured man. His own personal Good Samaritan was too good to be true. *Who would do this? Who would give up their life to look after me, an obscure author? Why?*

~ ~ ~ ~ ~

As Larry continued writing his lengthy statement, two of

the men had left the room, promising to return, leaving only the man in the centre. Above him was the clock, warning with its loud tick that each second of life had something to offer. Time was a thing to treasure, to protect. He could have been writing for a few minutes. It could have been an hour or more. However long it had been, these three men were growing tired of waiting. Yet, they had asked the question. They had offered. They had no idea of the scale of the task of committing it all to paper. Neither did he until he had started.

In truth, this would probably take many statements over many days, as further detail came to mind. For now, he had written the beginning of his sorry tale. By asking him to write it all down, they had opened a box that could not be closed. A box that promised nothing but the dead cat of some Austrian physicist.

Putting the pen down, he slid the initial twelve pages of his statement over and waited. The man in the cheap suit was sitting, reading, somewhere between surprised and disinterested. He held the pages in his hands and placed them face-down on the table as he reached the end of each sheet. The lips of the man almost seemed to be forming the words as his eyes scanned line by line. As he finished the final page, he collected them all together, stood up and left the room without uttering a word.

After some time with nothing for Larry to do but stare at the clock (reminding himself of the length of a second, a minute, five minutes), the three men entered the room and took their seats.

"Mr Llewellyn," said the man in the middle, "You've put together quite the story here."

"Story?" Larry retorted.

There was a single nod from the man. "If you want us to take you seriously, we need to know what *really* happened.

What was your involvement with those murders?"

"I know I've only written about the first one, but-"

"But it's not a believable account, Mr Llewellyn." He interrupted. "Maybe you do not recollect the details. Maybe you've confused the truth with fiction in your own mind. Maybe you're using artistic license, like you do in your books. I don't know."

The man paused for a moment, allowing the harsh tick of the clock to be heard yet again, louder and louder. He leaned forward, every facet of his face looking clear and serious. There had probably never been a sterner expression in the history of humanity. "What I *do* know is that if this was presented in a court of law, you'd be almost laughed at by the jury. Do you understand?"

Larry said nothing in response. He just nodded, looking at his feet. Defeat, even in honesty. *So much for the truth setting you free!*

The man picked up the paper, added more pages from a folder to the side and then straightened the stack. He replaced the paper on the table before moving his chair back slightly with his legs. "We will leave you for a couple of days to finish your account, or to start it again, whatever suits."

He stood up, which was the cue for the men either side to do the same. He leaned over the table and pointed with gusto at the hand-written statement, then pressing the tip of his index finger into the top sheet like he was trying to hammer through it, he said, "Just know this, no one will believe what you've put in here. Everyone in the country will now believe you played at least some part in these murders. This nonsense is as unbelievable as those popular novels you produced."

The men left the room and Larry was accompanied back to his cell, clutching the bundle of pages to his chest like his latest creation meant more than words on a page. Like he was holding a new-born child.

As he returned to the cell and sat on his bed, he put the first draft of his statement next to him. He glanced over at that first page. *What's the point? Who is going to believe a crazy story like that, however true it might be?*

Chapter 30

The screams, long and loud, seemed to echo forever.

Everything was distant, somehow not really there. PC Spencer was a mirage as he charged through the door. Her useless legs buckled until she was sitting with her back to the wall.

All she could do was point a finger to the door, still ajar, in front of her.

He stepped into the room and a second later he swore. He stood for a second, taking in details he didn't seem to want to take in. He stepped out of the room, closed the door and got on his radio.

"Charlie kilo, delta echo one bravo."

Whatever that meant.

A voice on the radio respond with, "Go ahead."

PC Spencer then said, "We have an incident inside the home address of Samuel and Samantha Barkes. I'm at number 374 Rossendale Road. So far?"

A crackled voice came back and repeated those last words. "So far."

He continued, "Samantha Barkes is here, unharmed but in shock. I need additional officers and forensics here urgently please. They'll need to be prepared to deal with a large amount of blood."

He stood there waiting for a reply. A voice came through on the radio after several long seconds.

"Yes yes. Received. I will request for response and forensics to be despatched to your location."

He then left his radio alone and crouched on the floor in

front of her. "I'm just going to check the property is secure." His tone was low and sympathetic. "I'll only be a minute."

What had happened here? Why was there blood all over the lounge? Why was there no body, no signs of a fight or a struggle? Did this have something to do with Larry, and was this why her father was missing?

Somewhere in there would be answers, but that would mean seeing it all again. Not right now. Maybe not ever. The police could deal with all of that.

Seconds later, the officer returned. Maybe it was longer. It was difficult to tell when so much of you felt numb and negative conclusions had been created by a frantic mind.

Maybe it was the panic, but there were no tears. No apparent sadness at all and her father might have been dead. *What's wrong with me? How can I be so heartless?*

~ ~ ~ ~ ~

How many statements had that been now? How many times sitting with an officer, having them ask obvious questions with more obvious answers? Too many. More than most had probably given in their entire lives.

Some tiny woman, a response officer with blonde and slightly pink hair, the face of a pixie and a voice that sounded like nails on a chalkboard was the other side of the small breakfast table. The thing still wobbled. He needed to be told to get rid of it and get a new set that would sit flat on the floor, just as soon as he turned up again.

Focussing on the chair and the table, both rocking on their diagonal legs, was frustrating. The furniture had been the basis of the breakfast routine for months, but it hadn't been annoying until right then. But thinking about them was better than thinking about anything else.

The young officer re-read the last part as a prompt. What happened next? How many times had she asked that question?

"How do I even find the words for all of this?" she asked.

She looked like she had been modelled on a Barbie doll whose hair had been dyed in some paint-related accident. She shrugged. "Just describe it in your own words as well as you can."

"Okay. I walked into the living room and there was blood everywhere."

"What do you mean by everywhere?"

"It was all over the floor. It was on the sofas and the walls. I didn't get a good look. I was terrified and I left the room."

"How did you know it was blood?"

How did I know? I study criminology! I think I know what blood looks like!

Sam cleared her throat. The age-old system of buying time, thinking about the next words. "I could tell by the colour, by the way it was congealing, and by the smell. I've seen blood before but not like that."

There was a nod as the officer's pen scratched and glided across the page at an almost inhuman speed. "Was there any sign of anyone else? Anyone in the room?"

Sam shook her head. "I did not see anyone in the room."

"Any signs of a struggle? Anything broken or out of place?" the officer asked.

Sam shook her head. "Nothing looked out of place. It looked normal, except for the blood, obviously."

"You've mentioned that Mr Llewellyn is still making

contact with you?"

Sam nodded. "I am still receiving anonymous calls, threats, chapters of this story he's writing about me. I reported them."

"Do you think he's able to do all of this from prison?"

Sam sighed and then stared at her. "What other explanation do you have for all of this?"

The woman looked at the floor as if ashamed. There was quiet for a moment, long enough to hear the forensics team scurrying around in the hallway and that front room.

"I'm told," the officer said, breaking the uncomfortable silence, "that the amount of blood in that front room is not as much as it looks. Probably no more than a pint. It just looks worse because…"

"Because it's been used to redecorate my father's house?" It wasn't really a question. No one of sound mind would try to answer it.

The woman stared at the floor again. She did a great impression of a boisterous puppy that had just heard the words 'bad dog!' for the umpteenth time today.

"What I mean to say is that it might not be as bad as it first looks." The woman said.

Sam nodded. "I know. I'm being stalked, harassed. I'm being threatened. By a mass-murderer, no less. I'm being driven out of my mind with worry, missing so much university that my nine grand fees are a waste, my aunt is dead, my dad's blood is all over the living room and he might well be dead too, but it could be worse. I could have that confirmed."

The tears started as if nothing in the world would turn them off again. Heaving breaths left her body and jagged ones took little air back in. Putting everything down in a statement made it all a bit more real. Maybe it was just the repetition. Maybe it was all starting to sink in.

"I'm the last leaf on the tree and there's a damned force twelve hurricane blowing. Everyone else is gone. I've got this feeling that maybe I should just join them. End it all now."

The officer looked up with a sadness in her eyes that wasn't her own. "Maybe we can help you with that."

Silence for a second gave way to distracting confusion. She looked back at the officer. "You can help me with that?"

She looked around, as if her boss had the answer, but there wasn't anyone else there.

"You can help me with ending it all?"

Her eyes widened when the reality of her stupid phraseology seemed to hit home. "I meant we can help you with how you're feeling. Not with… anything else."

Sam could only nod. There was little use in picking a fight.

Venting aside, there had to be a break from putting these events down on paper. There was benefit in doing it whilst everything was still fresh in her mind, but this was too painful.

She stepped out of the room, aiming for the front door. There was far more air outside. Much easier to breathe freely. She dodged past several white-suit-clad people as she went, and she overheard one of them.

"It's not his blood," he said. "We've compared it to DNA taken from some other items of his. Preliminary results show it's someone else's, not in the family, not on our DNA database, so we don't know who it belongs to. Forensics say it might not even be human."

Belonged, Sam corrected in her mind. *Past tense. It's not like they're going to have someone come up to them and say, 'here's your blood back. Thanks for the loan!'*

She stepped out of the front door and on the third lungful, the words hit home. *It's not my dad's blood? That means he's still alive, wherever he is!*

This could have been cause for celebration amid so much misery. This was something to cling to, the closest thing to genuine hope that had arrived in days. But there was more to the conversation, held out of sight but not out of earshot.

"Hardly surprising, given the rest of the evidence."

"You don't think Mr Barkes is being set up?"

"You look at it. Every piece of evidence we have so far, which isn't much, points back to this address. The withheld calls from this number. The online accounts traced back here. We've even found the right typewriter in the loft today. Maybe he's been trying to protect his daughter in some sick, twisted sort of a way. This doesn't look like it was done by that author. How could he? He's behind bars. The dad's lost it, trying to teach his daughter some kind of lesson and he's gone way too far."

How was it this difficult to breathe where the air was plentiful? She ran back into the house, almost knocking over one of the forensics team. No hope. Not anywhere. This was all bad news. Everything was spiralling downward. *It can't be true. It just can't be. He wouldn't do this.*

Her terror turned to rage against the people in that house. They claimed to be there to protect her, to make sure she and her dad were safe. But no one said anything about their suspicions. *How could they know all of that and not say anything? Surely I have a right to know.*

Sam stormed back to the kitchen. "Is this why they're so quick to check this all out? They wanted to search the home for that typewriter? They wanted to prove that it's all ready for some neat conviction of my psycho dad? Hasn't he been through enough?"

The pinkish-blonde officer wore a shocked look before looking uncomfortable.

"You all think my dad's been stalking me?!"

Still no response.

"This is madness. Utter madness."

"We have to follow the evidence," she said.

Sam shook her head and looked at her feet. "I don't know what to do with this. I don't know how you could all keep this from me!"

There were a few seconds of silence.

Sam then nodded. "All those questions about my dad recently make sense now!"

She picked up the bag that had been sitting by the chair in the kitchen. "The statement is going to have to wait. I don't care what you lot think. You're wrong. You have to be. Larry is setting traps and you're wandering straight into them!"

Without another word, she made for the front door. "I need to get away, straighten out my head. I've got to check that the only person I have left, the only one I know I can trust, is okay."

Chapter 31

It was difficult watching your parents die. People pretended to sympathise, to care, but they had no idea. Unless they had seen someone's eyes close, never to reopen, they could not comprehend the thoughts stuck in a broken child's mind. They would never know what he was going through, however much they claimed that they could.

That grief was a special feeling, unique to those few who had their childhood dragged through hell backwards. What did it matter that he had been the means of his own parents' demise? Would grief have somehow lessened if someone else had been the cause?

Even if he had killed them, Liam was still entitled to miss them when they were gone. Was a young murderer somehow exempt from grief? The mourning was real. So was the lamentation, but his was not the blind sorrow of the oblivious, however much it was needed.

Yes, grief could hang like a noose around the neck of the guilty as well as the innocent. But regret came from timing. Sorrow was for the lives wasted, long before he acted, and an entire syllabus of life lessons unattended and ignored. Clever people could be so stupid.

Yes, his mum and dad had worked hard, too hard. Their business was their first child and their only true love.

They had bought a lavish Victorian-era house in a Cheshire village with big windows, trees and fountains scattered throughout the fair-sized but elaborately styled gardens.

They had purchased an expensive car. The car, a slick black high-powered Mercedes-Benz with pretty much every optional extra, felt like it cost as much as the house. The car even had a name: Trudy. 'She' was regarded in almost the same way as their business. Possibly more so.

As a witness to it all, he was nothing more than an accidental addition, an inconvenient infiltration of their perfect little life. Love was shown, but in measured quantities compared to their stuff. Any toy, any gift requested had been duly obtained. Anything to satisfy wants, as long as those wants did not include physical closeness.

The apathy bred resentment in Liam. Attempts to draw their attention on numerous occasions had failed. Parents were not graded but if they were, the walking, talking report card showed nothing but a big red F. What they were doing was not parental. It never would be.

They had, of course, feigned listening and they had made empty promises of change through the years.

Those years had come and gone. There had been no change. It was not a surprise. There came a point where the needs of the boy bystander boiled over. An inner sense of justice demanded that there be a day of reckoning.

Emotions built and built until there was no choice. Logic suggested it was not the right course of action, but when rage ruled, there was little room for common sense.

Any parent could see the disappointment in their child's eyes when they were seen altering the car and locking them inside. They might have been drunk when he put them inside and started the engine, but deep inside they must have known.

They might have noticed the hose attached to the exhaust, poking in through a rear window, if they had been sober. They might have noticed the suicide note on the dashboard.

With their actions over the previous year, they had made it plain that the car meant more to them than their own child. Liam had his revenge, poisoning them in their most cherished possession.

It was a mercy killing. These people lived mundane, sedated lives. They were barely in the world of the living.

The event, an anti-climax, was responsible for that haunting feeling. They were already drunk and asleep. The carbon monoxide fumes would have caused the same symptoms if they had been awake.

Within a few minutes, neither was struggling. Neither had their eyes open. They had drifted off in a peaceful sleep from which they would never wake.

The couple became obscured as the cloud of gasses grew, pressing against the windows, filling every available space, filling lungs. Eventually he would turn off the engine and let the poison in the air float out through the open garage door. He would place their cold hands on his, as close to an affectionate touch as they had managed in months.

Had he ever truly mourned for the loss of his parents? No. Not once. Could that feeling be disappointment at the manner chosen for their death? A definite yes. It was not dramatic enough. It did not look final. They may have never understood why. It was a missed opportunity in several ways.

Pining had only ever been for the lifestyle provided by pretending parents. Regret only reached as far as a distant memory of the big house, the money, the stuff. It all felt like the perfect older brother, the favourite, the star athlete, the high performer, the creator of sibling rivalry and bitter feuds, but he would have taken it.

The timing had been the problem. Another couple of years and life would have worked out differently, but what was to say those two years would have been worth living?

Foster care was tantamount to living in someone else's hell, but crucial lessons were learned.

For instance, there were two very different ways of

fighting back. You could do the obvious, impulsive stuff. You could punch in the face, shove against a wall, smack over the head with a heavy object, any manner of brash, simple responses. The immediacy of the response meant swift punishment. The other way, the clever way, was to bide your time. Calculate your response. To weigh and to measure your opponent. Let them think they were winning. Then, when they thought you'd forgotten, you would make your move.

You stash something in their possessions and report them. You leave a wet patch on the floor, right where they always run at the top of the stairs. You befriend the bigger kid and fill their heads with lies until they exact your revenge for you, letting you watch. Maybe you do all of the above, just to really let rip. They would know, if they survived it all, that you were not a person to be messed with.

Aunt Vicky had been nothing more than a figurehead when she had eventually shown up. She was put in charge of the estate that Liam was due to inherit around three years later. There were no checks, no questions asked. She turned up and the keys to everything were just handed over.

Survival skills were honed and perfected. He could look after himself and she just needed to be there to sign a few things.

She went to work pretending to look after him. She signed a lot of cheques, and some of the stuff had something to do with him. Vicky spent money renovating the property. She had used power of attorney to buy a car for her own use. She was from the same mould as her sister. Spend, accumulate, alienate.

Vicky was a short but thin woman with short, bleached blonde hair atop a permanent look of disappointment on her gaunt face. Her orange tan was fake and topped up daily. There was a sinister hint to her green eyes and her nose looked flat compared to the rest of her face. She had a loud voice, an obnoxious loud laugh and even louder blouses. It was astounding how some had expensive tastes when they refused to work for themselves.

Vicky had married a rich older man many years previous, but the money paid by the guilty man in divorce had all gone. His parents hadn't spent any time with her as far as he could recall. Strange when they had so much in common.

He had seen precious few relatives. The reason became clear on her arrival. Blood-sucking leeches didn't invite everyone to the party. They would keep as much as they could for themselves.

There was no stopping the woman from extracting personal wealth from the estate she should have fought to preserve. Powerless to prevent her regressing into the financially disastrous gambling addict she had become following her divorce, there was something he could do to get rid of her.

Kill number three came easily. A degree of separation dampened the feeling, but it felt a lot like pulling the trigger, pointing both barrels at her head.

Consigned to a rundown flat after the necessary sale of the family home, life was far from ideal. The wallpaper peeling from every wall and ceiling, the worn out and uneven laminate flooring, the cracked single-pane windows all suggested that whatever Vicky was paying in rent for that place was too much. Add to that the night-time shouting, the slammed doors and the traffic noise from the nearby busy road and life in the place was not worth living.

It had been easier than expected to find the most brutal and unforgiving loan shark in that deprived area. Anyone who called themselves 'Flick Knife' would no doubt have a reputation for being anything but reasonable.

It was almost a simple a task to borrow twenty thousand from his organisation. Everyone else had said not to do it.

Find another way to get the money. Find any other way.

He listened to the very clear threat from this guy's right-hand man in a crowded local pub. He agreed to the terms and took the box stuffed with cash. He agreed to five per cent interest per week, and to repay within four weeks.

He gave his aunt's new address but told her nothing of the transaction. He disappeared to a hotel when repayment was due. Vicky had answered the door, she claimed ignorance and the unforgiving debt collector had not taken kindly to her reaction.

On his return she was bloodied and bruised, stabbed in not-so-vital areas of the body. She quite possibly had broken bones in each arm and leg.

The loan shark knew that a dead person could not pay their debts. He had left her some way short of defaulting.

She would survive the ordeal and she would be given another few days to hand over the money. It was a first and a final warning.

Any number of things were possible with an aunt in such trouble. Nursing her back to health was an option. So was calling an ambulance or the police. So was putting the woman out of her misery.

Instead, the response was a simple one. He collected the small metal box she had used to store her cash, as well as the last of his things. "My inheritance," he had said, pointing at the box and looking at the wide-eyed, open mouthed victim. He made sure to close the insecure door behind him, ignoring the desperate pleas. He then climbed on his mountain bike, the most valuable possession that his aunt Vicky had not sold, and he rode away.

The man with the knife would return. He would not be happy when she again refused to pay him anything. According to his reputation, you didn't get a second chance.

Chapter 32

Anyone on the outside looking in, might have assumed that two hours of undisturbed quiet would have been a blessing in such a chaotic life. Not so for Sam.

The only thing peace and quiet brought with it was the opportunity to think, to dwell on current circumstances, to ponder over past mistakes, to resurrect regrets. She shook her head. *I can't think about anything other than what's happening, even though I can't change a damn thing.*

Samuel Barkes was an over-protective father, but the current hypothesis of the police was absurd. Nobody on the planet with a love for their child would put them through such torment just to teach them a lesson about talking to strangers.

Sam shook her head for seemingly the millionth time. *I don't even know why I'm even entertaining the idea. He's not even any good at lying!*

There had to be an answer somewhere between her own crazy theories and the wild police hypothesis. They said they followed the evidence. Did it really lead there?

There had been a disquieting feeling from the moment Larry's face was plastered all over the TV and online articles, like somehow it was not the end. But the other guy behind this couldn't be their prime suspect.

What did the facts say? Larry was in prison. There was no way of him being behind the recent stuff, but he might have started it all. He might have passed the torch onto some obsessed fan, keen to avenge the arrest of their idol. Maybe it was a lone wolf. But the fingerprint matched. Larry threw the brick through the window. He sent the first couple of chapters. Even the facts didn't help.

There was only one conclusion: Everyone was short on

conclusions. No amount of puzzling over these issues would upright a life that had been turned upside down. No figuring out could fix this. Only action could make amends for choosing the wrong friend.

The train carriage seemed to have a lazy quality. Peak travel time had passed, and few headed in the direction of London from Manchester on a Tuesday evening.

The dispersed passengers were reading, watching videos, listening to music, looking out of a window or otherwise resting their eyes. Still, at least none of them were Larry. She shook her head and looked up to the plastic ceiling. *He couldn't possibly be here. Why am I still looking?*

Maybe a distraction from the thoughts, the worries, the impossibility of it all was somewhere within the phone in her hand. Seven dialled calls to her mum. Seven calls unanswered. *Maybe she's busy. Maybe she's driving or working. But what if something has happened?*

Anyone would fear the worst, given the circumstances. This new reality was forever shifting, so fear made sense. It was no longer some unnecessary emotion that blocked the road to achievement. This instinctive mode, caused by treading a trail of trauma, could be turned on its head. Fear led to self-preservation. That instinct might help preserve others too.

She tapped her fingers on the back of her phone. *One more try.*

She hit the call button and held it to her ear. One ring, and then another, a third, fourth and fifth were not enough for an answer. After six was the sound of her mum's voice but it was from long ago when she recorded that outgoing message. She hung up. There would be no use in leaving a fourth message.

Her mum had been happy living the single life in Berkshire for some years. She had trained in hairdressing, beauty therapy and in sociology since the divorce many years prior. She worked in some kind of social services role that had never sounded interesting. It was possible that the job had once again placed an unreasonable demand on her time.

The drab buildings of Milton Keynes did nothing to inspire imagination as they whizzed by. If only something in the fast-moving landscape had been intriguing.

Well-loved stories and books disappeared into an inner black hole of despair. The only ones not to be sucked in were the tales of the instigator, the once-preferred author-turned-stalker. Why not the tales of Winnie the Pooh? Perhaps the Odd Thomas series or the Lord of the Rings Trilogy could have provided respite, but no. Just Larry's tales about death, as if no other stories ever existed.

Maybe memory would do better with recent university classes and assignments... Nothing. Like everything had been erased.

She looked around the train. She half-smirked and raised an eyebrow. *Maybe I can strike up a conversation with a fellow passenger.*

She pursed her lips, looked down at her lap and raised both eyebrows. *That worked out really well the last time that happened!*

There needed to be something other than fidgeting. Her fingers and thumb seemed to act independently as they pressed to call her mother again. She shrugged and held the phone to her ear.

The phone was ringing once… twice… three times. *Maybe give it another couple of seconds.* This time four rings were all it took for the answering machine to kick in. The message she had heard a moment ago had changed. This was new.

"Hello." The message and voice had changed. Her eyes widened with fear. Her jaw dropped open. It was him. It was the voice of Larry, the man from the train; the one with the flat in Manchester where she had stayed; the one who had befriended her, and then insulted her and then vowed revenge. But how?

Every report on the News and from the police said he was behind bars, but in the past few minutes he was there in a terraced house in Slough.

The message continued, "If this is Sam calling, your mother is not able to get to the phone right now. She is busy with something, as you might have guessed from your many attempts to call."

The heartbeat in her ears threatened to drown out any further words. How could he be there so fast? How could he be anywhere other than prison?

"If you'd like to know what your dear mum has been up to, I would suggest you start by checking your emails."

With shaking hands, Sam ended the call and almost dropped her phone. She managed to place it on her lap. Her head sunk into the palms of her hands. *He got to her before I could. What's going to happen now?*

I need to open that email. No reaction. No movement whatsoever. All her fingers needed to do was to tap an icon. Still nothing. It was as if every muscle in her body was rebelling, afraid of what might be found in there.

Time for deep breaths again. Eyes closed, head tipped back. Air filled her lungs until they seemed to expand to fill her whole upper body.

She opened her eyes but as they fell to her phone screen, terror screamed through every thought.

For the briefest of moments, it would have been easier to open a window and lob the phone from the train rather than open the app. Anything seemed a better option.

This was not the time for this. Fear could be useful. Panic would never be anything other than wasted energy. It was time to rise above these emotions. They had controlled action and inaction for far too long. Time for Sam to decide what was right for Sam. Make a choice. Stick with it.

Her mum needed her. What if Larry had not killed her? What if he had hurt her and left her to be found? What if this was one more step in his game, some attempt to lure her into a trap that she could avoid?

My mum needs me. She reached past her own reluctance. *She needs me, and I need to read this to see how I can help her.*

She opened her email app. Right there, at the top of the list, was an email from some random Outlook account with an attachment. She tapped through until she was reading chapter eight.

The typeface was consistent, and the letters were aligned more neatly than previous chapters. This one had been typed on a computer and printed out.

Childish wording, lazy grammar and poor spelling littered the literature. The problem was not the words but the message they conveyed. She put her right hand over her mouth. *It's a story, but it's not just a story. It's become my life.*

The chapter described the narrow street on which Yvonne, Sam's mother, lived. The grey-brown pebble dashed terraced houses. Some were in excellent condition with perfect gardens. Often their neighbours had old fridges, sofas or mattresses surrounded by overgrown weeds occupying the outside space that may have once resembled a garden.

Yvonne's house was neat. It was clean. Understated, like the home of someone who had worked damn hard for it and who wanted to keep it just right.

The house was just left of the middle of a block of six

terraced houses. A small porch had been added, a dark red pantile roof to match the house and the others around it. On closer inspection that pitch was badly built, sloping to one side but still solid enough to not have any structural issues.

The chain link fence had been replaced by a low, dark brown wooden fence with a creaking gate. The front lawn and cheap paving had been replaced with gravel. The combination of gate and gravel had made the approach slower and more difficult for the attacker.

So, they got there first and waited. She would be home from work soon, if this day was like most others. A tree and a bush to the side of the door provided the perfect shelter from view. Neighbours wouldn't see them. When the light had started fading, the homeowner would miss them as well.

After a long, tense wait beside the front door, the woman walked through her gate, closing it behind her, and approached the house like she didn't have a care in the world. She stood by the front door, the key rattling in the cheap lock.

If she looked sideways now it would force an immediate rethink. But she was focussed on getting into the house, giving the front door a shove with her shoulder at the opportune moment. The resident made a forceful but careful entry as the door flung open. She kept hold of the handle so it didn't keep swinging and hit the wall.

As she stepped clear of the door and was about to close it, the intruder threw himself through the doorway. He managed to cover the mouth of the woman before she could scream. She would have no idea who he was, no clue as to why he was there nor about what he was about to do.

Yvonne's eyes were wide. She was sweating. Who wouldn't be scared with a rag stuffed in their mouth from a complete stranger, come to invade their home?

The chapter described the way the attacker hit the

woman's head off the floor until she stopped struggling. He then stood up, closed and locked the door, and returned to his victim.

He described the thin orange floral blouse she was wearing and the tight black jeans. He described the sound made as the fabric for her shirt was torn apart. He went into detail about every single part of his attack, which culminated in the rape and beating of Sam's mother.

The chapter ended with the attacker leaving the house, just prior to the arrival of the victim's daughter.

A frantic look around the half-empty carriage would do nothing to find useful help. *Dial the emergency number. Get the police there!* But what good was calling someone when she couldn't breathe?

Of course she could breathe. The air was the same as a moment ago. *Panic will not get the better of me. Not today.*

The time shown on the phone was several minutes past her mum's usual arrival home. *What if he's there right now, doing this? What if he's sent me his plan and he's hoping to get out before I get there?*

She dialled 999 from her phone. In spite of the tremors in her hands and slight lack of lung capacity, she sent the police to her mother's house. They understood the urgency and spewed out words of calmness and assurance that were probably not remembered by any caller.

The train was minutes from the station in London, but a connecting train was needed. *Not today.*

She would run out as fast as possible and throw herself into the first taxi she could see.

The train approached the station. It couldn't come to a stop quickly enough. Sam already stood by the door with her bags. She tapped nervously at the straps and handles of her bags.

She bounced her feet on the rumbling train carriage floor. *If I'm lucky, very lucky, they'll catch him at my mum's house, stop him and I can make sure the police know who's behind all of this.*

Chapter 33

Maybe there was a reason for every cell in that prison being painted in a dull dark grey. Perhaps it was a neutralising, placid sort-of a colour. Maybe some meathead thought about attacking his cell mate, caught a glimpse of the wall and thought, Actually, I'll be kind. Then again, maybe not.

A brief examination of those brick walls was enough to discover that layer upon layer of paint had been applied over the years. *How many refreshes will I see during my time in here?*

Most of the others bemoaned their fate, locked away, stripped of their freedom. He was different. Arrest and imprisonment had become strangely liberating. No more was he at the mercy of that man. No more under the control of the carer.

The challenge as he laid on that bed was to make more of the latest, newest opportunity to rebuild his life. The last attempt had not gone so well.

~ ~ ~ ~ ~

The days had been bleeding into each other as he laid in that bed, each day becoming less tolerable than the last. The walls of the familiar room crawled closer to him unnoticed with every passing hour, defying any request of the owner of the combined stone, bricks, beams and mortar to abate.

His muscles and the pain in every joint and bone had eased but nausea was the new enemy. The list of impossible tasks was as long as the first day of recovery. Anything beyond sitting up might as well have been a fairy tale. A dizziness danced around his head. Stringing thoughts and memories together was beyond reach, just like the door in front of him. Logic suggested it was possible. Reality was the devil on the other shoulder, shaking its head.

Maybe that fall had resulted in some low-level brain damage. Maybe that current mind fog would be a factor in every facet of his everyday life moving forward. Even thoughts of family, the monumental loss that drove him to write, was like scaling Everest without an oxygen mask. Tears formed in his eyes. *If this is how my mind will work, what future can I hope to have as a writer?*

Maybe he had been bed-bound for months. It could have been merely weeks. There was no clock on the wall. No calendar anywhere. The other man had maintained a distance between the patient and the outside world. Removing access to newspapers, the radio, the computer and the television could have been wise. No one wanted to check off the days they had wasted in slow recovery. The last thing the world out there had provided was a near-death experience. Perhaps some distance was a good thing.

But the world was not really needed. Not now. Not yet. He had his voluntary carer. The mysterious man who introduced himself as 'another guy called Larry', another writer, had been a ludicrous lifeline.

Few options existed other than to trust 'Larry'. This near stranger became everything. He would be there, day and night. He would provide food and everything else needed to sustain life. At least the food was beyond the level of a local hospital. The man could cook. A simple cumin-spiced omelette provided momentary pleasure amid the pain that would not go away.

The other Larry would sit on the seat beside the bed and employ him in conversation daily about writing technique, building believable, convincing characters, creating dramatic dialogue, and anything else to do with his craft that either of them could dream up to discuss, but conversations were short and hampered.

More than once the brief conversations centred around a fixation on the kind of death featured in his short fiction. Why did he feel the need for it? What effect did it have on him?

Questions from the other Larry became more specific to the point of being alarming.

"Larry, have you ever written about the specifics of death? Described every detail?"

He shrugged. "I don't know every detail. I'm a writer, not a mortician."

"But do you find the life draining from the body fascinating enough to study it in more detail?"

Larry furrowed his brow. "What do you mean?"

The carer sighed. "I don't know." He then wore a smile as he said, "I guess so much of the death described in novels is almost cartoon-like. No one seems to give it the attention a big build-up merits. Do you know what I mean?"

Larry nodded with a half-frown. "I think I understand."

The surnameless Good Samaritan said, "I've seen your notebook with your ideas. The irony with which some of those characters would face their death… It's almost breath-taking."

Raising an eyebrow Larry said, "Thank you."

The man slapped his hands down on his thighs as he started to stand up from his chair. "I have an idea of how we can create beautiful works of fiction together. Your writing prowess and my attention to detail. My need to meet my needs."

He shook his head. "No thank you, I would much rather work alone."

"Ha! Not an option!" said the man, the tone in his voice more aggressive out of nowhere. "I've already started something here, and you're powerless to put a stop to it."

This man was intimidating, leaning over Larry who could still not move enough to care for himself.

"What exactly is going on here?" Larry asked.

There was no verbal response. Just a curious stare from the man who claimed to be called Larry. He looked at him. The hair, the mannerisms. The clothes were his own.

"Is that... my shirt?" Larry asked.

There was a shrug. "I spilled something on mine making your dinner."

"And the trousers? They're mine too, aren't they?"

The man smiled. "Same reason. I'll have them cleaned and returned before you're up and about."

"Your hair. The style has changed. Your cologne is a lot like one of mine."

The carer stared at him with a blank look. "What are you trying to say?"

Larry looked away. "I'm not entirely sure."

The patterns of the man's speech were starting to mirror his. Could it be that this man was imitating him? The change had been so gradual, almost imperceptible. *How could I not notice until now? What's wrong with my mind?*

Pieces of a complete picture flew around him like autumn leaves in the wind. Time to reach out and grab what he could and to see if anything made sense. This man, an author, the same forename, his guardian angel and carer. He happened to know where he lived. He knew more about Larry than most of his friends knew. He was obsessed with every aspect of Larry's life. The picture was becoming clearer in an absurd sort of a way.

"Did you...? Have you been poisoning me?" Larry looked

at him with pitiable eyes as he started to run short of breath again. "Is that why I've not recovered yet?"

He stood up straight and turned his back on Larry, taking a couple of steps towards the window to the left. There was a slow applause as he walked.

"Irony of ironies," he said, stopping and turning to face Larry again. "The author who writes about death, but the great Larry Llewelyn took so long to see his own slow descent to lifelessness."

"So that's it? You've cared for me all this time, and now you're going to kill me?!" He had to choose his moments to breathe and to force out a few more words. His breath was still running short. "What sense does that make?"

Expressionless, the other Larry said, "I have no intention of killing you. I think you can be very useful to me, and I to you."

"What kind of sick, twisted person are you?"

"Said the author who wants to write about death?" He held out his hands like a Wimbledon ball boy with nothing to offer a player. "Come on!"

Larry pointed a finger at the man. Even the exertion from such a simple act would leave him exhausted. "That's different. Mine is an attempt to let out my own grief. To solve a problem in my head from years ago. Yours is just…"

"My what is just what, exactly?"

"You seem psychotic… Like you… just want to destroy and tear down. Who saves someone… and then poisons them?"

"I'm only sedating you," his crazy carer said. "As I said, we can be useful to each other. I have a need to be who I am. I don't expect you to understand (well, I maybe I did), but this can be mutually beneficial."

He started to casually walk around the room, glancing out of the windows as he passed them. "I do what I do, you write what you see, we're both sustained by the income from your writing. Then, we start the cycle again."

There was silence for a moment before Larry said, "Who was driving the car that ran me over?"

More silence, and with it a smirk from the man pacing the room.

"You were there," Larry said. "You must have seen them. Who was driving?"

There was a wider smirk on the crazy carer's face. "I think you know that this didn't all happen by chance."

"You are sick," Larry said, tensing his neck muscles to keep his head up, eyes fixed on the man, the cause and solution to all of his current problems.

"You have… some kind of screw loose that makes you want to kill things, possibly people," Larry continued. "You thought from my writing that I would understand you? That I would sympathise? That we could work together? No one would agree to do anything with you!"

The man nodded without uttering another word. He walked towards the door looking deep in thought, as if the brief conversation had changed his entire outlook on life.

As he reached the door he turned back and said, "You don't see it yet, but you will."

Chapter 34

I have to protect my child!

The words hurt. Still.

Even after all the years that had come and gone. Even after many visits, after a substantial amount of time spent trying to be the best possible dad from a distance, those words when Yvonne walked out of his life, taking Samantha with her, still haunted Samuel.

Yvonne had her reasons for leaving. In her mind and in her heart, she had already gone when she walked out of the door for the final time. They had cooled towards each other, but he had done most of the damage. The aftermath of the loss of each child was enough to put any relationship at risk. She needed a rock, a solid, dependable husband to help her to rebuild her life. He was more like a pebble stuck in her shoe, a thorn in her side. The moping, miserable man who couldn't even bring himself to go to work on a morning.

She cried through her grief. Samuel got angry at stuff. Never at people, just at things, but he could see fear in her eyes when she was in the same room.

However much the sorry tale had commandeered dreams, the end was the same. There was no changing it. Yvonne always walked away with the tearful, traumatised young Samantha by her side. Some might expect that a scene seen over and over again might be easier to bear. The truth was the opposite. Each revisit drew more hurt and bitterness from the endless inner well of negative emotion.

Sometimes he just watched each repeat play out. On occasion he had tried to shout back, "She's my child too!" but he awoke every time, shouting the words to no one, hearing them ring in his own ears.

Maybe everyone could pinpoint a moment in which they

suffered heartbreak. Such moments were the most important. They were a chance to hit the reset button on life.

When two thirds of your reason for living goes, you need a new one. The whole series of dreadful events proved to be a catalyst for transformation, for getting over stupid mistakes and becoming more than the broken shell of a person who had spent hours behind that front door weeping.

The new job had provided the energy and enthusiasm to stop the drinking. Small successes instilled a confidence. The past was the past. There was no sense in being embroiled in blaming himself. Lessons had been learned from errors of judgement. Application of those lessons was sure to breed success.

The one exception had been romantic relationships. Maybe more efforts should have been employed to win back Yvonne. He still loved her more than anyone who might compete for his attention and affection in following years. Despite the personal growth and the lessons learned, there had been a reluctance to live through anything like that again. Instead isolation enveloped him. It was the personal coping mechanism for tragedy. Now the default position in life.

It had been years since that moment had haunted any dreams. In the current circumstances, it was understandable that the disappearing car, seen through tear-filled eyes, should make an appearance. All success since that moment, the business built from scratch, the house owned outright, the stable life of a responsible adult, all meant nothing.

There was nothing but complete darkness. Eyes usually adjusted to darkness after a minute or two, but this had been a lot longer and still nothing. Maybe a hand waved in front of the face could provide a faint silhouette. No such luck. Something scraped against his arm before biting down the more he tried to move. His arm was tied to the chair on which he was sitting.

His legs wouldn't move much, neither would his arms. His chest and his neck seemed to be tied back, preventing him from doing anything more than rotating or nodding his head.

Through a series of calculated movements, the restraints had been figured out. There was flexibility from his ankles to his knees but further up, his legs had no give whatsoever. Attempts to move them side to side did nothing but aggravate whatever was holding his knees and legs in place.

Both arms were fastened to the arms of the chair at the elbow and at the wrist. They felt a little looser, like whatever had been used had slackened somewhat. That offered hope for freedom. *If my right arm can come loose, maybe my right elbow can as well.*

He shook, he wriggled, pulled at the restraint on his right elbow until it burned with soreness. It didn't seem to shift.

One by one he tested the durability of each identified point of restraint. He tried his left wrist until it became sore. He tried his left elbow. The same failure occurred with the right. If a hand could get free, there was a chance of getting out of there. The struggle resulted in tiredness and sore muscles. Wrists, elbows and knees would be raw. It would be a few minutes before energy reserves and determination permitted another attempt.

He pulled his ankles inward and felt sharp pains in his knees and thighs. He was held tightly to the chair by something unrelenting and unforgiving. The wrong pull in the wrong direction and a dislocation or a broken bone or two could result. But if that was the price to pay, it was better than whatever else might happen here. People weren't tied up like this for nice reasons. *Stay there. Don't move until I get you your ice cream! Unlikely!*

Inhaling deeply hurt. Maybe it was the thing across his chest. Maybe he already had a broken rib or two. He tensed his neck muscles and tried to pull his head forward. His windpipe closed off, nausea overcame him, and a hotness rushed to his cheeks and forehead. A dizziness suggested he would pass out unless he stopped.

An attempt at a groan got lost somewhere on its way. His mouth was open, and something was stuffed inside. Movements within his mouth failed to dislodge whatever had been crammed in there. His neck hurt like someone was jabbing him with a knife, and his right wrist and elbow complained as he tried to get his hand to his mouth. It wouldn't reach far enough. It wouldn't even be close.

His mouth couldn't open any wider. It couldn't close either. Alternating between straining muscles to open and close did nothing. His jaw and tongue started to ache as the muscles were forced into unnatural positions, all working together to hold some sort of rolled-up rag in place and to prevent him from making any sounds beyond a pathetic whimper.

The darkness was still as deep as ever. Even with all the struggles whilst awake. There was nothing. No sights or sounds. Nothing but darkness and a chair, and a man tied to it who might be destined to fail yet again.

Panic built inside him quicker than he could build flat-pack furniture. Maybe the truth was something different, something worse that he had not considered. *Do my eyes still work? Have I been blinded?*

Until any glimmer of light hit his retinas and created a reassuring picture for his brain to decode, there was no way to be sure.

Maybe the last few moments in his memory held a clue.

~ ~ ~ ~ ~

Rushing in through the front door, there was enough

time to drop off unneeded tools from the morning's job, to pick up a couple of things for the afternoon and then to head out again.

The utility area behind the kitchen at the back of the house held the most frequently used tools. A quick exchange could even allow for a quick sandwich. Samantha was making some sort of noise in the lounge which could be heard through the closed door. Her university schedule was too random to make any sense, or to know when she was at home.

He paused after passing the door. *If Samantha is home, why would the door be locked?*

Perhaps paranoia had set in. Maybe she expected to be captured or injured in some way, in spite of recent deterrents. If she felt safer, what was the harm?

He walked back to the door. *I'd better let her know I'm here and ask if I should lock the door on the way out.*

He breezed through the door, saying, "No classes this morning?" and found a man that he recognised but that he had never met. He was taller than Samuel with dark hair and a squared jaw covered with thin stubble.

The most peculiar thing about the situation wasn't the stranger standing in the front room. It was the guy's dress sense. He was wearing a white paper forensic suit. A strong coppery scent assaulted his nostrils. Small red dots were all over the suit. He was holding something that looked like a large pickle jar filled with blood, and the splatters over the walls suggested that he was using a small scoop-shaped object in his hand to fling it around the walls.

It could only have taken a second or two to stare around the room in disbelief, but it was too long. He recognised him from somewhere. He looked a bit like the man from TV, that nuisance author with a penchant for perishing people. He had reacted to the interruption.

Samuel turned his attention to the blood distributor but instead had a close-up look at his own brass table lamp as it was swung towards his head. There was no time to duck, no time to wish he had bought lighter, breakable items, before impact.

~ ~ ~ ~ ~

Out like a light. That was the expression. Nothing but darkness left behind. How long had the darkness lasted? How long had he even been conscious? It might have been minutes, possibly hours since the collision with the lamp. Time had become some irrelevant, obscure fleeting thing in this place.

A headache thumped against the inside of his skull which had not been there earlier. Somehow the memory of the impact served up a plate full of trauma and a side of pain.

The pain was hard and sharp, located to the right side of his forehead. The point of impact. Such a blow was unlikely to remove his sight, but what did he really know?

Heart palpitations had been a part of his past, forgotten in the reinventing of Samuel Barkes, but they returned, like an unwelcome friend. *What if I never see anything again?*

The years-old line of questioning from Yvonne came to mind. *Are you blind? Could you not see you were putting her at risk?*

On the day their love had officially flatlined and his wife had called it, she had gone out to spend some time with a friend, get a drink and catch up. He had a list of tasks as long as his arm, including the removal and replacement of their bed.

With a busy day, Samantha at six years of age was happy to stay out of the way, playing in her bedroom. That prevented her from being at risk of being hit in the head by the large parts of the old bed.

With the last of the pieces downstairs, he turned around to see the moment that would ruin his marriage and cause his third child to move far away.

Samantha was falling down from the top. Her head was next to the wall and her feet closest to the banister as she rolled down lengthways, unable to stop. She turned over, again and again, each time the look on her face grew into shock and panic. She could do nothing to steady or stop herself.

Samuel charged up the stairs and caught her halfway. She had already fallen far enough to be covered with bruises and to have an arm that was swollen. It was later discovered to be broken.

That was the final straw. Within a couple of weeks, the girls were gone. Following the divorce and a long-distance move, he had only seen Samantha a couple of times a year at best.

Suicide was a consideration on occasion as a life rebuild fell flat. Dating had been attempted before the first break-up had been fully processed. A brief and doomed relationship with a young bimbo called Mandy lacked substance. She was never going to put up with him beyond about a month anyway. No one would have done.

Life offered much but delivered little. Every time he tried to reach out and grab the happiness he craved, it moved farther away, like he was heading towards the end of a rainbow, a trick of the light that was no closer than the blue of the sky.

But what would Yvonne think of him today? Would she blame him again if Samantha got hurt? Of course she would. Despite doing everything he could, someone would believe he was at fault. All they needed to do was look at his history.

His daughter, right now, could be spending time with university friends. She could be at home, wondering why her father wasn't there. But there was the blood all over the walls. How would she have reacted? Where would she have gone? She was at real risk of significant harm. Hell, that author had even promised that he would kill her.

And what was he doing in the house, redecorating the lounge? Was the idea to make Samuel disappear? Why would he be doing that? They had never met, and he would likely be called nuts by the police for reporting a person as being in his house when he was already in prison.

But was it really him? It couldn't have been. A whack on the head did nothing to improve a memory that had not been brilliant in the first place. Could he have actually been a neighbour? A friend of Sam's?

There were questions to answer, but more importantly, there was a young woman to save from the man. Even now it could be too late. Sitting there, bound and gagged was not an option. Making amends, proving to the world, to Yvonne, that he had changed, started right now. But bigger and more important than anything else was the need to save his only surviving child. It was time to do something.

It would have been helpful to know what that something could be.

Chapter 35

Sitting alone in his cell in the dark, Larry had nothing for company but the statement he had written a matter of days ago. No one believed him. He put on a wry smile no one would see. *If it had happened to anyone else, I wouldn't believe it either.*

He moved his eyes towards the pages. It was too dark to read those words, but there was no need to read them. Indelible memories could retell the story at a moment's notice.

It started with the accident, when he was run over. It continued with his recuperation in a bed far more comfortable than the one on which he was sitting.

From that point on, the actual Larry Llewellyn might as well have been dead. Every day he would sit with fellow prisoners around bespoke steel picnic benches, bolted to the floor. Every bland meal provided a fresh serving of self-loathing, summoning again recollections of being shackled to the subduer's schadenfreude.

~ ~ ~ ~ ~

Following the chilling exchange of words with his protector and prison-guard, conversation had been culled over the preceding couple of days.

There was more to learn about this man. Maybe more secrets to uncover, for someone brave enough to probe. Perhaps crossed words during a discussion on cooperation had caused him to be cagey, unwilling to reveal any more.

Hours in the interim had been spent pondering possible predicaments in which his carer could be combatted. Fantasies ranged from the almost achievable to the absurd.

Two days of applied effort, sitting up, moving as much as possible, had allowed for a self-assessment. Not a chance of getting free in that condition.

But surely anything was possible. If he could find one heavy, blunt object to swing, could he get lucky? If the man was distracted long enough by some other task, could he break free? Every thought had been dismissed before it could sit long enough to germinate into any sort of misplaced, hyperbolic hope.

A new morning often brought a fresh outlook on despair. Not today. Before he could be drugged, he would take positive action. It was time to start succeeding at life again. Success had come at key points in his past. Why not now? He was awake. Time to act before enthusiasm evaporated.

Using his arms, he pushed himself until he was sitting up. Pain was present, nagging away, but at such a level it could be ignored. He lifted the duvet and at a speed that would put a sloth to shame, moved his legs until his feet reached the floor. Discomfort increased, but this was the moment.

This was it. This was when he stood on his own and defied the diagnosis of his unwelcome, guessing guest. He held onto the side of the bed as he pushed his upper body forward, adding more and more weight to lazy legs. He took one step, then another. He was walking for the First time in a long time.

About the time of the seventh step, just clear of the bed, his legs might as well have just vanished, replaced by brittle stilts and a pain of epic proportions. The collapse was sudden but somehow in slow motion. There was nothing nearby to grab onto, hoping it would pass. He could only fall to the floor into the useless bag of bones he had become.

He lay on the floor, forlorn, weeping. Nothing had been gained other than some new bruises and a fresh dose of humiliation. What could the future hope to offer one so pathetic? He was trapped in his own home, unable to do anything to break free.

As tears streamed from his eyes, it mixed with the sweat of his face and the drool of his mouth, all of it soaked the carpet beneath. Not only had his strength deserted him at that moment, but it was entirely possible that it might decide to never return.

Just getting out of bed was enough exertion to make him feel like either throwing up or passing out. His captor held the upper hand. Larry barely had the strength to raise his hand. *Unless I can stop this man poisoning me, I'll never be able to get free.*

The other Larry soon returned. He let out a short pity laugh at the sight that greeted him.

He then walked away, returning with a solid wood dining chair which he placed facing the window. He dragged him, exhausted, to the chair and secured the struggling and whimpering man to it with thick rope.

He longed for the bed he had just departed. Instead, his back garden, a simple rectangle of lawn surrounded by trees stared back through the window. The border fence and trees blocked out the whole rest of the world. The nearest neighbour had no chance of peering in.

No one else could see the A-frame ladder next to the classic-style wooden picnic table with built-in benches, both taking centre stage.

Most alarming was the person lying on top of the picnic table, held in place by a large amount of grey duct tape. The man was probably middle-aged, slightly overweight and he was wearing a dark grey tracksuit.

Eyes widened to the point of being painful. The coolness of the air was apparent only in the wider whites of his eyes. His heart pounded like a caffeine-high monkey was trapped inside his chest with nothing to do but thrash at it. His head felt so light that he needed to look down to be sure it was still attached. Every sight and sound were amplified by adrenaline. The natural drug flooding his system could cause nothing more than a pointless pull at the restraints. *Where did he come from? What is he planning on doing with this man?*

The man who claimed the name of Larry walked outside with his right hand holding the top of something heavy. It was recognisable as a bowling ball. The ball was a light blue shimmering kind of a thing that sparkled when the sun hit it.

"What are you doing?" Larry shouted at the window.

The outdoor Larry turned his head, faced Larry and smiled as he walked.

As he leaned slightly to his right under the weight of the object, he climbed the ladder, using his left hand to grip the aluminium frame.

The ladder had been well used to decorate and repair throughout the home. It bore the spots of paint for every colour in the house, past and present. It creaked with every step, so loudly that the sound was carried through the closed window. The sound returned memories of parents painting the lounge years earlier.

"What are you going to do to that poor man?" he shouted. "What's he done?"

Slowly, the man climbed until he was able to rest the bowling ball on the apex. He stood there, hunched over for a few seconds. He then turned and looked back through the window, no doubt checking that the spectator was paying attention.

"Don't do it!" he shouted at the man atop the ladder, but they were wasted words.

He had to look away. Restraints could only do so much, but he could choose not to watch. Yet, there was a welling feeling, building from some dark part of his soul that he rarely let rise to the surface. Somehow this required a witness. Without one, maybe the scene was destined to be repeated. Maybe retribution would result in some horror greater than this.

Without any warning, or any pause for thought, the man atop the ladder in one movement picked up the bowling ball, extended his arms until it was directly above the other man's head, and let go.

"No!" Larry shouted. Before the word had finished escaping his lips, the deed was done.

The heavy ball dropped with immense speed, despite desperate hope that some miracle would force it to hover in mid-air. Less than a second after release, the object had collided with the man's head with a dull, sickening thud that could be heard over the shout.

The sound of the skull caving in was like someone cracking an egg with a thick shell, or like stepping on the world's largest snail. That and the accompanying chorus of cracking wood, the sight of that head snapping back farther than any human head should go, would all echo through his thoughts and memories for the rest of his life.

The struggles and the muffled screams of that man that had gone mostly unnoticed, had stopped the moment the ball made contact before rolling onto the floor and then across the lawn, leaving a thinning trail of dark blood behind it as it moved. The blunt murder weapon came to rest when it had cleared itself on blades of dew-dampened grass, a metre or so clear of the table.

If there was any doubt that the intended victim had met his end, that was dispelled by the lake of blood forming on the ground beneath, covering every plank of wood, dripping through the gaps. So much blood, turning everything a sinister red, like it was trying to claim as much territory as possible on behalf of its corpse.

The man at the top of the ladder stood there, looking triumphant, like some king whose army had just been victorious in a year-long battle. He stood there, watching from his vantage point, fascinated by the rapid pooling of blood and the caved-in head of his victim.

He continued to stare at the scene of carnage as he descended the ladder. He could barely take his eyes off the dead man as he walked back inside.

"You see what I mean?" he shouted as he closed the door. "I think you could do an incredible job of writing that down, every detail."

The raised-voice monologue continued. "I think you could come up with a perfect, ironic, creative story that could culminate in that kind of a death. What do you think?"

No words. Nothing escaped his mouth at all. Any sound cheapened the life and the death of the stranger, somehow betraying him. Hot tears formed in stinging eyes. Shock did many things. Like the kid who survived those years earlier, he was momentarily mute. Whether by design or as a reaction, silence had served him well back then. He had reverted to type.

Maybe the truth was too horrible to speak. Maybe all of this revealed an internal piece, broken loose in tragedy, which longed for feelings incident with death and destruction. It was easy to hate the man and the manner of murder. Hating himself was easier. Another death for which he could do nothing, but this one brought a loathsome fascination.

It was coming. It was obvious. Why had he not looked away? He could not have hoped to halt events. Despite the predicament, the guilt of another's death would be added to the bubbling mixture of wicked homebrewed negativity swirling within.

~ ~ ~ ~ ~

He could only sneer at the laughable statement. Even to its author it was crazy. He had lived it, but he didn't believe it. It took courage to write down that first murder. It would take more to carry on, even in the face of those wishing to discredit him.

The murders continued after the bowling ball incident. Over time there were no secrets between the two men in that house. The incarcerator became the impersonator. Liam, as he eventually called himself, had changed to become the public-facing Larry Llewellyn. His face had adorned the press publications and had been the one seen in television appearances. Royalties went up and up, and so did the cosmetic surgery bills. Even the few who knew the real Larry might even believe the lie.

But Larry had never had many friends. The people he created had meant more to him than any other living being. Those that were genuine flesh and bones had kept a distance. Maybe they somehow knew what he really was.

The only person who had walked into his life and pretended to befriend him had been this guy. The one who forced him to sit in feeble acceptance in his own home. Nothing to do but to keep writing to escape, wishing life was better. Those early days had given rise to jealousy, knowing that this man was reaping the benefits. Liam had put an abrupt end to that way of thinking.

The poisoning had stopped after the second kill, It was expensive and unnecessary. Instead Liam had moved to a more physical level of intimidation. Severe injuries were inflicted that had cemented a fear of the man. Thoughts of retribution or rebellion were rewarded with actual damage. Any entertained notions of escape enraged him.

The house he once called home had expanded several

times to become a fortress from which he could not escape. Movements were tracked. Maybe people were watching. Breaking free could provide only a momentary thrill. The sequence of events would unravel into capture, torture and sheer misery.

The walls of that building represented his family home, his hospital, his prison and his coffin. There had been no exit route. The scrounging birds that visited the back garden ate better than he did. Enough basic food was provided to sustain life. Treats were infrequent, usually to celebrate the completion of the next manuscript. If complaints reached Liam's ears, then beatings would follow. Liam had become judge, jury and punisher in Larry's four-walled world.

The occasional encounter with stainless steel served up a reflection and a reminder of a man, old before his time. Recent years had not been unkind - they had been brutal. He had become the decaying twin of the man enjoying the spotlight.

Freedom had been gradually granted within his home, without any control over what was inside. There was no phone. No Wi-Fi. No TV. No radio. No link to the outside world of any kind. Even the mundane act of collecting parcels from a delivery driver was forbidden.

Exploration of anything farther afield than the back garden was impossible. The online world may as well have been an unexplored wilderness. Liam undertook any research. The conversation, worn thin through repetition, warned of the danger of Larry's discovery. Their house and their world would be torn from them.

The life of a popular author was hectic. Before any given month had begun, two thirds of it had been filled. Meetings with agents and publishers, media interviews, book readings and signings sucked up so much time it was a wonder that any full-time writer had any time remaining to do more of what had made them famous in the first place. Liam, though, still found the time to keep tabs on his terrible secret. Even with Liam gone for days, Larry could not hope to scale the fence and break free. There would be some other horror lined up on or just outside the boundary in any case.

He had been sprung from his prison when the police forced their way into the grounds and dragged him off to a place no more welcoming.

Writing was the escape in two senses. First, it served as a much-needed mental manoeuvring away from a pathetic existence. Second, it was an escape from the dreadful punishment designed and dished out to the reluctant recluse.

Fiction, whilst a reflection of real life, was simple. Freedom was a fantasy which would never be fulfilled. Hope was clutching at those pages like someone clutching at straws. Liam was still enjoying the life that he had furnished. His future, to be forged in a barren prison cell, was unbecoming of the genuine Larry Llewelyn.

Chapter 36

The taxi door flung open and Sam darted out like a greyhound after a fake rabbit. The hiring of a taxi to make the trip, the journey, even the payment took longer than had been expected.

Two unanswered questions were fellow passengers in that car: *Did the police take me seriously? Will I get there too late?*

As the taxi had entered the street, a police car, the van and incident tape answered both questions. Her heart seemed to drop to the floor.

She walked towards the house and opened the squeaky gate like she had done thousands of times before, like this was all normal. She nearly stepped through before she was challenged by a male officer, probably six and a half feet tall with a shaved head and a face. He stepped sideways, seemingly out of nowhere, to block her path.

"Excuse me ma'am, but this is an active crime scene," he said with no sympathy in his voice.

Sam, out of breath from worry and rushing said, "But… I'm her… I'm her… daughter."

The man's face softened more than had seemed possible. He nodded. "Yes, I recognise you now, from the photos."

"Is she…?"

His eyes widened, and his eyebrows did that puppy-dog thing. "She's in hospital. I'm no doctor but she seemed beaten up and abused but very much alive." The guy had given bad news before. It was in his eyes. He was keen to volunteer something in the affirmative this time.

"This is going to sound weird, but did he leave any paper behind, like a typed chapter of a book?"

The officer looked confused and shook his head.

"Has anyone listened to the outgoing answering machine message?"

His eyes darted to one side. He was clearly trying to figure out what either of these questions had to do with their victim. "We've got forensics on the scene. I'm sure they know what they're doing."

Sam forced a couple of deep breaths, in and out. Her thoughts went somewhere else. Her legs weakened. A second later they started to buckle beneath her, like someone had taken out her knees with a cricket bat. The officer caught her and called for a colleague.

"Get her to the hospital. She needs to see her mother, and she might need to be checked over as well."

There was a nod and she was led to a marked car and placed at almost glacial pace on the rear seat.

Sam closed her eyes and leaned her head back. *At least she's alive. It could have been worse.*

~ ~ ~ ~ ~

Those bright green eyes had not looked on her in close to a month. They had seemed brighter back then, with less sadness lurking in there somewhere. There was worry etched into every feature of the girl's pretty if slightly chubby face. How could someone age five years in around thirty days?

"Are you okay, my girl?" she asked, putting her own health to one side. Her own voice sounding in her own ears like it had gone through some sort of ageing machine.

Sam looked confused. "You're the one in the hospital bed and you're asking *me* if *I'm* okay?"

Yvonne smiled. *There's the girl I raised. Always looking out for others.*

"Mum, I'm sorry. I'm so, so sorry!"

Yvonne shook her head. "You have nothing to be sorry for. Nothing at all." The voice she recognised was returning, sentence by sentence.

"But this happened because-"

"It happened because some nutcase was looking for a power-trip. That doesn't make it your fault."

"But it was Larry!" Sam said in a pleading tone.

"Hush, Sam!" she said in a calm but firm manner. "Even if it's the same crazy man that was after you, how does that make it your fault?"

"If I hadn't talked to him on the train and…"

"Did you tell him where I live? Did you give him instructions to find me and do this to me?"

Sam shook her head with tears in her eyes.

"There you have it then," she said, using the motherly soothing tone that had worked with the girl all the way back to infancy. "You need to stop taking the blame for the mistakes of other people, like when you were six. I keep telling you, but you don't believe me. It was *not* your fault."

There was a tear in Sam's eye as she said, "But I was messing around. I fell. I heard you arguing about me."

Yvonne shook her head. "There's more to this story than you know."

There was silence as Sam awaited an explanation that had been forthcoming for over a decade. The whole story had never made it beyond Yvonne's choked up vocal cords, no matter how many times she had tried.

Yvonne sighed, trying to release almost fifteen years of pressure. "Did you know you should have had an older brother and sister?"

Sam looked confused as she shook her head. A child, even an adult, would struggle with such facts coming to light after so long. She would feel betrayed, even if this secret was kept for the best of reasons. But betrayal knew no bounds. Secretive parents and bewildered offspring could fall victim.

"We didn't speak about them when you were around, but the hurt was there."

Sam, sitting by her mother's bedside, reached out a hand and placed it on her nearest arm. "What happened?"

"Not long after we got married, we had Peter, a beautiful little boy…" There were tears in Yvonne's eyes now. Her voice already struggling to stay constant with a lump in her throat. "The trouble was, he cried a lot. I mean a *lot*."

Sam looked on with wide eyes, as if something terrible was heading towards her and she couldn't get out of the way. Like she was tied to railway lines and a whole steam train of unwanted honesty was hurtling towards her.

"Samuel got frustrated. I heard the annoyance in his voice over the baby monitor. No one ever found out what happened, but Peter was lying there the next morning when I went to check on him, not breathing, grey. He was gone."

Yvonne's final few words were high-pitched and barely audible. She cried for some multiple of minutes. Thankfully, there was a box of tissues within easy reach.

It was so many years ago, but the mere mention yet again brought back buried feelings of heartache, of confusion, of disbelief, of worry and upset.

Several minutes passed. Neither of them said anything. There was a gentle, affectionate squeeze on the arm from Sam.

She cleared her throat, took a sip of water, and continued. "Then there was Lydia. She was five. Close to the age you were when the… incident happened at home. She went out to the shops with your dad. He took his eye off her for a second and…"

Sam watched on in a look that was a shaken cocktail of horror and pity. Those painful memories, so private, had never been shared.

The girl's mind was ticking over. There she was, sitting on her own, glancing to her side, dreaming about life with an older sister, trying to imagine a life in which a happy family of five had stayed together. It could have all happened if somehow her dad had been calmer and more vigilant.

"Lydia was run over and killed by a taxi." Yvonne had nothing else to say. Tears were dripping from her cheeks and her chin. She could feel more follow the paths of the previous ones, her cheek like a car windscreen in a rainstorm. Her throat felt like it had swollen to three times the size and her lungs burned. The body was conspiring against the mind, making sure that any further words were impossible.

Her daughter could have been judgemental. She was within her rights to be upset, to accuse her parents of lying to her, or depriving her of the memories of long-gone siblings. But she had nothing but compassion written all over her face.

They shared a tender moment of grief together, right there in the hospital. They were mourning the loss of Peter and Lydia as if their passing had just occurred. Both were wishing that those intervening years had been more like the postcard, made-for-TV family, as opposed to the grim reality of broken homes and lost young lives.

"So, when I fell down the stairs," Sam started, "you felt you could no longer trust him to keep me safe? That's why there was all the arguing?"

Yvonne nodded, tears falling onto her arms now. She shrugged. "But it was more than that, I guess. Something broke in your father after the second child. He seemed…"

The words to finish that sentence all seemed to disappear at once, leaving nothing but an awkward silence. Her only living daughter was staring back, wide eyed, about to cry tears of her own. She was in no state to help out in finishing that thought.

Yvonne took a couple of deep breaths, let a few seconds pass, and tried again. "He was… distant. It was like someone turned off his ability to love me. When you came along, he seemed to put more effort into showing affection to you, but I didn't see any of it. Between the way he felt about me, and his carelessness that led to you falling downstairs, I couldn't take it anymore. I needed to get away and you needed to be safe."

Sam stood up, leaned over Yvonne and stroked her hair while putting on a smile. It looked like the rueful smile you'd see on the face of someone whose lottery numbers had come up on the week they stopped buying the ticket. "I'm okay, mum. You kept me safe. You raised me well."

"The thing is… I can't keep you safe anymore."

~ ~ ~ ~ ~

There was no logical reason for the message to come through to her instead of a more senior officer, but there wasn't time to dwell on small details.

The most important thing was to pass it on to the Senior Investigating Officer for Operation Conceal, and to the officer handling the GMP investigation that started all of this.

She forwarded the email immediately and then ran to find the SIO. She found the short, overweight red-headed man with a goatee and glasses staring at her as he was talking on the phone. It was Detective Chief Inspector Anderton, and it had clearly been years since he had faced any kind of active duty. He looked like the kind of man who spent most of each day in meetings, whose time was precious, and who did not tolerate interruptions.

She hovered for a moment without a word or so much as a gesture.

DCI Anderton rolled his eyes. "Just a minute," he said to the phone. Looking at her, he said, "What is it?"

The tone included the words *this had better be worth it* without them being uttered.

"Sir, I've forwarded you an email about the Llewellyn investigation. There's been a development in Kent that you need to be aware of."

There was a nod and a wave of a hand. It was a non-verbal acceptance that he would need to check the email, and of her being excused.

She returned to her desk and sighed as she sat down. The email was still showing on her screen. *This could change everything.*

~ ~ ~ ~ ~

The test results arrived too late to send the victim of a violent rape on her way. She had spent the night in the hospital bed. Sam made a bed of-sorts from a couple of nearby chairs.

A mid-morning call from the police was ignored as they were in the process of being discharged. It was probably some victim support person making sure she was okay. Maybe they wanted to arrange to take a full statement.

They would have some DNA for the man from their rape kit tests. A description of the man responsible would help, but surely not as much as the name they had been given several times already.

Searching for Larry in the faces of every bus passenger on that bright Tuesday morning made little sense and a lot of sense at the same time. That had been his voice. He had been there. He had to be somewhere.

Clenched fists had pressed the outlines of her mother's keys into her palms during the short journey. They had faded by the time she had collected the little light blue Toyota and parked it in the hospital pick-up zone.

Her mum was moving freely but with caution. Bruises on her face would die down in a couple of days. In time this would be a horrible memory and nothing more. But the reality was not so black and white. Victims of rape relived their trauma over and over again. They would avoid the locations and circumstances of their attack. They could become terrified by someone with a specific hairstyle or a particular type of car. How would someone deal with being attacked in their own hallway? It wasn't the kind of place you could avoid.

With both women in the car, victims of Larry sitting in solidarity, side-by-side, it was time to take the ten minute drive home.

An uncomfortable silence descended. It was like they had forgotten how to have a conversation, despite more than a decade and a half of practice at it. What could they talk about that would bring anything other than misery?

Yvonne reached over and winced in pain as she turned on the radio. It would have been worth the discomfort to ease the painful absence of undoubtedly unwelcome words. It was tuned in to some station that didn't know songs past the eighties existed.

A Carpenters song came on the radio. Her mother's face broadened with a smile.

"I love this song," she said in a tone far lighter than any used yesterday. She started to sing along.

Why do birds suddenly appear every time you are near?

As she sung those words in a voice that sounded much weaker than usual, something stood out. In fact, it was sticking out – of the glove box. The corners of white sheets of paper were there, like they hadn't been there earlier.

"What's that sticking out of the glove box?"

Her mum should have known. It was her car. She shook her head. "No idea."

She reached down and opened it, pulling out a few sheets of paper stapled together. She looked down with a curious look.

"What is it? Aren't they release papers or something?"

Her mum shook her head. "They didn't give me anything like that."

"What does it say?"

"Chapter eight."

A large, flame red 4x4 travelling at excessive speed showed up in a frantic check of the rear-view mirror.

A verse had come and gone in the song on the radio. No one was singing now.

Just like me, they long to be close to you.

She looked again. The car was getting closer. Too close. Why weren't they slowing down? The quiet and winding residential road was a standard width. Room for a car either side but not wide enough for anyone to easily overtake.

On the day that you were born the angels got together and decided to create a dream come true…

Hushed voices burst into hoarse screams as the car

behind slammed into the rear driver-side corner of their little car.

There was a loud bang and the squeal of metal against metal. There was the sound of the little tyres screeching against the road, trying to stay on, failing to stay straight.

The rear window shattered, and tiny glass fragments flew everywhere.

The screams continued as the back of the car lifted from the ground and everything seemed to tip sideways.

The car was heading for a tall hedge, covering a brick wall. At their angle, with little of the car or its wheels in contact with the ground, nothing could be done to change the trajectory. All they could do was brace for impact.

Going straight through the hedge, the little car punched a hole in the tall garden wall. Bricks, dust and dirt flew in all directions. Bagged white clouds inflated at a speed that hurt faces and arms.

With smoke pouring from the front of the car, windows smashed, the dashboard a broken mess of plastic and airbags and white powder everywhere, the stereo still worked.

Just like me, they long to be close to you.

Her mother's eyes were closed. Blood trickled from a wound on her forehead. It was hard to stay awake when everything was forcing her to sleep. Rest would shut off the pain, at least for a little while. Alertness was not worth it. Utter exhaustion covered the waking world like a thick blanket. It would have taken concrete pillars to prop those eyelids open.

Who knew where they would be when they awoke?

Chapter 37

The scenes could only play on repeat, again and again. Some omniscient being had set it playing and had then lost the remote. Gruesome, horrific acts on strangers were on show on the stage of the mind and an encore always ensued.

The term unpleasant did not do justice when watching and documenting a man freezing to death. The adapted freezer included a Perspex panel on the top. Frost interfered frequently but the view of the expiring man, a sight no normal person would choose to see, was largely unobstructed. The movements of the man slowed and became more laboured. The tortured expression on the middle-aged man's face confirmed that the pain intensified. Then, like a switch had been flipped, he relaxed, giving up. Maybe in those final moments, pain gave way to peace.

Spectating as someone succumbed to poison was equally awful. The convulsions, the manic behaviour, the sheer volume of the screams was unexpected. The deep scratches left in their chair showed how adrenaline was working overtime to try to counteract the poison, but to nil effect. Normal muscles and fingernails could do extraordinary things, leaving lasting damage on items made from strong, durable materials.

All of the shouts from one man, even the screams of an angry mob could do nothing to shield the drugged woman, wandering into the path of a heavy goods vehicle. Watching that instantly lifeless body fly through the air was fascinating. The thud of broken body parts, held together only by a loose bag of muscles and flesh, the roll and tumble along the tarmac, made his chest tighten and his throat burn with bile.

With the sanctity of life reduced to some bit-part in a twisted game, the old guy with the heart condition stood no chance. Withholding medication, shocking him, shouting the vilest insults into the man's face, none of it had worked. A strong mind made up for a weak heart.

In the end, forcing the old man into a hunched over position had put added strain on the heart. That had done the trick. The man's arms had involuntarily raised. He had turned various shades of blue and grey. His face twisted into an unusual expression, as if he was eating the world's most sour sweet. It hadn't lasted long before all movement stopped.

There was no further need to witness another's demise. Not that a thing changed with any personal declarations to that effect. It was not *his* curiosity that culminated in another's being drafted into the ranks of the deceased.

Refusing to sanction the next sanctimonious act achieved something worse than nothing. The next victim would die, whether or not he watched. The act would merely be repeated with others until he relented. Less people died when he pretended to comply.

A new version of him emerged from the ruins of both of their lives. The irreverent reincarnation of Larry needed refining, but differences were slight. No one else had known any better as this man claimed the lucrative identity as his own.

The life-taking, less-than-genuine Larry showed no compunction in eroding the mind of the forgotten man with his addiction. Sadly, there was no such thing as a Murderers Anonymous group meeting, held weekly in Kendall's town hall. No one had written a bespoke twelve-step program. There was no sitting across from some random guy named Gerald or Malcolm or Ian who would, in a room devoid of judgement, proudly state, "I've managed to go almost three months since my last kill!"

That week before each kill was the worst. The mood swings, the angst, the short, curt comments, the random spells of lashing out violently.

And yet, when another soul-splitting act had been performed, the man seemed to liven up. It was as if his lottery numbers had come up, at the same time that a gorgeous, bikini-clad young model had driven up to the house in a supercar and had declared that both the car and her would belong to him.

After a time, the effect of the fix would fade. Fear crept into that house, into that bedroom. Things always had a way of getting worse before they got better.

Still, whoever had been told thus far had passed judgement on the lies as well as the lips from which they fell. DNA for both men would be present on every single body. Forensic evidence was certain to show that one man alone had not been responsible. There was an accomplice. Effort would be expended to identify them. But all they needed to do was to read that statement and to take it seriously.

But the statement, running to more than twenty pages, had been called ridiculous by the police officer who claimed he wanted the truth. Changing it was a sacrifice of personal morals for nothing more than a glimmer of a chance of being believed. Even the defence lawyer had declared that it was fanciful and full of fiction and not likely to persuade a jury.

Before you even consider telling anyone, Liam had said, *don't think that you're going to look innocent. The evidence will point to you as much as it points to me.*

What was the point in any of it? What benefit could be found in even carrying on? There wasn't anything left to save, except maybe some dime-a-dozen writing ability.

Ability required motivation, and that had not arrived in any necessary measure until the sixteenth birthday cards had been taken down. Neither parent, engaged in a prickly political debate, has turned their heads quickly enough. The hillside road had demanded more of their attention than they had been willing to give. So had the cyclist.

The reaction had been a swear word, an overcorrection and a view out of the front windscreen reminiscent of clothes rotating in the glass door of the washing machine.

Seat belts and airbags could only do so much when a car had been flipped more times than a stack of pancakes.

Every gargled sound from those throats could be replayed like some twisted on-demand audio service lodged in the brain. An act as simple as blinking could bring back an unwelcome slideshow of blood, broken bodies and fragments of shattered glass.

A broken leg in other circumstances was a big deal. Not there. Not then. Not when staring at the corpses of the only two people who would care about the broken limbs of their offspring.

The panic still spread when the feel of that broken leg, trapped between immovable items, combined with the smell of leaking petrol and oil and a terrifying smell of smoke.

Maybe that shadow was cast by a nearby tree. It could have been a gust of wind that disturbed the broken glass on the tarmac. Yet, the senses, unreliable in such a moment, had painted a picture in the mind of another person, possibly the cyclist, approaching the gaping hole where the windscreen had been. They had watched man and wife bleed out, smiling as the sounds of near-impossible breathing ceased. Panic had given way to terror, and there was no way, even in a thousand recollections, to be sure of what had really happened.

The coroner must have known best when the whole thing had been ruled an accident. The injuries were consistent with the collision. With a broken leg starting to heal and a broken mind far from okay, the cyclist had been mentioned. The notion of someone acting as this mysterious man drew dismissive shakes of the head and comments to the tune of, "he's just grieving for his parents" and "any child might invent something like this and hide behind it in such circumstances".

Whenever he told the truth, no one believed him. Whenever he lied through his writing, he was applauded. The path of least resistance had begun to guide his footsteps.

A frustrated full account of that "accident" had been written. The writing continued, venturing farther from the realms of reality. Changes committed to paper meant little where reality reigned. What if they had left earlier or later? What if rain had been falling and the cyclist had stayed in? What if the incident had happened a hundred yards farther down the road? What if, what if. None of it brought his parents back.

Over time, a sense of relief was to be found in subjecting fictional characters to the most horrendous of acts. Inflicting misery on the people of his imagination was an invisible comfort blanket. That young man who had watched his parents die and had done nothing to help, he had featured. Innumerable iterations had provided opportunity for the being to be killed with paper and pen.

The cyclist had been thrown from a cliff. He had hit the front of that car and flown off down the hillside. He had been confronted by the survivor, broken leg or not, and punched in the face until there was no face left to be punched.

Written with cathartic consequences in mind, no consideration had been given as to the worth of those words. A late uncle had pointed out its merits and had persuaded him to send it to various magazines.

Popularity and acceptance increased with the size of each cheque. The novella named Youth Justice told of a vigilante youth, breaking stereotypes and defeating local criminals, had proved to be a hit, in spite of the brutality of combative situations.

Yet those stories, all of them, were as much a part of history as the final acts of his parents. Prison was the present. No typewriter, no paper, no pen. Just that statement. Stories could still be composed, but the details would need to be laid out in an organised mind instead.

Whatever the result of the legal system, however unfair, nothing would quell the need to write, to create. They could take away a typewriter. They could deprive of decent accommodation. They could make his life a misery. Bring it on.

It all added fuel to the mental bonfire, a fire that could not be extinguished. The ability to lose one's self in story was an author's last great freedom. No one could take that away.

Chapter 38

The woman had deserved her fate. She had not loaned the money, but she had taken enough that had belonged to others, to him.

A fleeting thought fluttered across his mind on occasion since he had left. No longer was he confronted with the barrage of curiosity that had consumed his thoughts in the aftermath. She was doubtless dead.

The bicycle had helped to clear the mind. Pushing on, pedalling hard, covering great distances, and staying in random guest houses had become a new way of life. The intake of clean air, meeting new people, taking in glorious scenes painted by the brush in mother nature's hand, it all made life worth living. Almost.

It had taken only a few minutes of frantic cycling to reach a weathered sign in amongst a burst of bright flowers.

Thank you for visiting Keswick

"My pleasure," He muttered, out of breath as he forced himself onwards, a grimace on his face as he faced another hill climb.

Maybe the next place would be more interesting. Maybe not.

Freedom was a funny thing. People wanted it. They fought for it, sang about it, devoted lives to it. He had it. Just an open road, no ties, no commitments, but a cartful of constraint. An obligation was attached to the gift. *Don't waste such a precious thing!*

Freedom itself was applying pressure, requiring decisions be made. Choices covering a couple of days were insufficient. Such freedom demanded an action plan. Chance had been afforded to bring about real change to a wandering life. Justification was required, like standing before a memorial to those who had sacrificed for that freedom, laying a wreath that explained how such a gift had been properly used.

The remaining two thirds of the cash in his backpack added to that pressure. *What are you doing with your life? What will you do when the money runs out, when you can't afford to hop from place to place, to buy food and clothes?*

He shook his head. The time wasn't right to answer those questions. Somewhere in his past pastimes he might find something worth pursuing. There could be joy in picking up artist's pencils and paints again, in writing or wood carving, despite the almost forgotten failures. Time on a building site had been successful, but it was harder work than was warranted by the pay provided. There had to be a middle ground, a way to gain recognition and remuneration from sensible effort.

Like the pitiful existence of so many, maybe destiny was calling, just to say that a meaningful job in some faceless organisation awaited. Nothing more. No fantastic future ahead. No extraordinary adventure. Just a bland existence, bobbing around in a sea of fellow mediocre beings. Hardly a future for which it was worth living.

Calves burned as the journey up the secluded but steep hillside road pushed ground level farther and farther away. He veered across the road, sometimes to the left, sometimes to the right. It didn't matter on a road like this on a Sunday afternoon. If a careening car threatened injury, then so be it.

He peered over the edge of the hillside whenever he was close to the roads edge. *When it gets high enough, maybe I'll just ride over the edge and see what happens.*

Every muscle burned, ached, screaming out for him to stop. The air felt different, like something special would happen if the body could be ignored for just a little longer.

Maybe life would find a new direction. Maybe it would end. Both options equally valid as the clouds rolled in overhead, dulling the landscape, any remaining optimism vanishing with the rays of the sun. *Who am I kidding? I'll never achieve anything.*

A sheer rock face appeared to the left and the drop to the right became increasingly steep. The buildings, the trees were all shrinking by the minute. *Not yet. Not high enough to guarantee my death yet.*

He moved back towards the rock face. His legs were giving up. They refused to carry the weight anymore, especially if their only reward was death and atrophy. The rock face was imposing, huge. There was no telling where it ended up there. *If I could get to the top, that might be a good place from which to jump.*

The end was in sight. Finally, direction. He pressed down the pedals with sore feet, like he could not move them fast enough. Those muscles would just have to continue screaming out in pain. They would be doing nothing soon enough. A jump from such a high point in the right direction might even miss the road entirely. If so, he could just keep falling. It would all be over. Discomfort in his muscles, disenchantment with life, disappointment in others would be irrelevant.

He swerved towards the drop to his right one more time and peered over, gritting his teeth. *Not far now.*

The top of the cliff was beckoning. He threw every muscle into the hill climb, eyes fixed on the road. A black Mercedes-Benz rounded the gentle corner. They would see him. Would they have time to react? A terrified middle-aged man was driving with a screaming wife in the passenger seat. Cycling on meant a head-on collision; a body full of tired muscles worked together with the common goal of an eternal rest. There was no application of brakes. The handlebars stayed straight and true.

There was a shriek of tyres, a cloud of smoke. The car swerved out of the way, up on to a bank of earth and smashed into the rock face. The car failed to be a safe mode of transport and it pretended to be a carnival ride for the next few seconds. They would not be queuing to ride it again.

A calm fell over the site, seconds after the beautiful disaster unfolded. Glass, once surrounding the spinning wreckage like a swarm of angry bees, had come to rest on the tarmac. The shimmering black paint had been scraped away, like the flesh from the knees of a child who had taken a tumble on weathered concrete. The air was again still enough to hear the birds in the trees.

The cyclist was unscathed. The only one there who had wanted to die had been spared. The air tasted of rubber, smelled of petrol, but it was filled with euphoria. The man, the magnet to death and destruction, had been able to strike again, and there was that feeling again – the feeling that nothing else had replicated in the preceding months.

That sensation was amplified, almost palpable, on the lazy walk to the car. Sweeping glass fragments aside with his shoes, the ground was clear enough of glass to kneel and peer inside. The husband and wife were hanging on, not quite deceased. The remaining life drained from their eyes. That final moment enhanced the experience. Any future fatalities needed to incorporate those few seconds, such was the power it offered.

A tumultuous few minutes had diverted Liam, a man contemplating, even planning his own demise, onto another path. Seconds after his intended death, he was more alive than ever. All-consuming control combined in a delicious feeling that life was, for the moment, still worth living.

Chapter 39

The place was strange but familiar. Even before Sam opened her eyes, the list of possible locations had been narrowed to one.

The sound of water dripping in a distant corner was unusual. There was a drop followed almost immediately by a smaller drop. There would be a pause and the sequence would begin again. Each time a drop hit the floor the sound echoed around the bare walls. It was like a near-silent, slow heartbeat put through some sort of synthesiser.

The smell of dust and damp in the air suggested the space was not in frequent use, and that it was most likely below ground.

The light hitting her eyelids and then moving on suggested a single, hanging lightbulb in the centre of the low ceiling. It was moving, as if someone had disturbed it within the past few seconds.

It didn't matter that neither foot had ever before been placed here. The location was not confirmed by any sort of physical familiarity. The place had never featured in any movie, magazine or photograph.

This was the room. This was the one in that book. It was real.

Words on a page. That's all it had been when Larry Llewellyn was sitting across the aisle on that train.

The harsh single bulb shone a dazzling light into her eyes as they opened. As her retinas seemed to burn, exact details, as Larry had described them, emerged from the blur. Meat is Murder had come to life and she was in it. *The man is a horrible human being, but he or his accomplice couldn't have described this place any better!*

The light bulb, seeming to dull with every second, was swinging in its basic fitting. It was casting dull light and sharp shadows all over the rough concrete walls and floor. This was the basement in which Andrew had died.

Like Andrew, Samantha Barkes was condemned to death as the latest protagonist. However, unlike the butcher, she had agreed to her fate. She had welcomed it, at least initially.

The story, like a dream, brought delight in the misery of a fictional being. What was the harm in letting go of frustrations and stresses, inflicting misery on another non-existent entity? But life had a strange way of imitating art, especially when both were controlled by the same madman.

Her life seemed to be destined to end in this place. No applause would accompany it. Millions would not mourn her fate. Larry had made sure of it. She had studied to know the mind of a criminal. Now she had let a criminal get inside her head and she would pay for it.

The little girl's parents had drifted apart over incidents her father had seemingly been powerless to prevent. The man's inability to come to terms with it all had led to further punishment. Now, despite Sam's tremendous efforts to take control, she would die with her parents helpless to thwart another death in the family.

It hurt to take a breath. She looked down. A thick rope was pressing into her chest. She could feel another part of the rope digging in under her ribcage. Rope further bound her hands and ankles. She could not move, other than to turn her head and to speak.

What if I start screaming, shouting for help? She shook her head. That would be the worst abduction ever if that worked! *We're probably nowhere near anyone.*

The room was not full of clues, waiting to be uncovered, that could ease an escape. The room was mostly empty, but not quite. Another person, tied to another chair, was away to her right. It was her mother. She had been tied to a similar chair in the same way. The difference was the gag around her mouth. She scowled. *He wants me to be able to speak, to be able to scream, but he doesn't want to hear a sound from her?*

Her poor mother, still asleep, was even more battered and bruised. She was in only slightly better condition than the rotten wooden door behind her. Some old storage cupboard raised above the ground the height of a breeze block. It could have been some mystical gate to an old medieval world with its rusted wrought iron hinges and latch.

The woman had already been through hell more than once. The bruises of the latest injustice were probably still coming to the surface. She would find that her nightmares were far from over when she finally opened her eyes.

"Mum!" The whisper was loud enough to echo off the walls.

No response. No movement. No chance to try again. There was a sound from above and behind. A door, possibly closing and heavy footsteps on the untreated, old wooden stairs to Sam's left. The antagonist was making an entrance in a way that almost shouted, "I'm here!"

Maybe it was an attempt to instil fear in Sam. It wouldn't work. It was difficult to muster a feeling of fear when you were already petrified.

Dressed in dark brown workmen boots, light blue jeans and a red t-shirt, the man from the train, the man who had left the answering machine message, who had raped her mother and who had killed her aunt, the man who had made her life a misery, who had framed and then no-doubt abducted her father, and who had threatened retribution in all the worst ways, descended those stairs.

"You're awake!" he said with a smirk. A month ago, those same words were spoken in a much gentler setting. On that first occasion, a fried breakfast and a luxury taxi had been clues to the measure of the man. They would turn out to be red herrings. The real person, unmasked, with a sinister face and an evil heart, was not the hospitable type.

"I suppose," he continued, "you have some questions for me."

Sam shook her head. "Not really."

He shrugged and walked up the stairs again at a steady pace, closing a heavy door at the top. Again, the only sound was drip-drip, drip-drip. If only the captive's heartrate could seem so at peace with the world.

The sound of the drip seemed to amplify with repetition, like it put more effort in when it knew someone was listening. Before long, it might have drowned out a jet engine starting up. It was maddening.

He returned, carrying something large, plastic and bright blue. Like a man setting up for some non-event meeting, he put the flat object down and pulled parts from the underside. It stood up, proudly announcing itself as a family picnic table from the kind of camping trips she had never known.

The legs were joined in pairs. One side seemed to be more problematic than the other. It still didn't look right, but maybe it was the uneven floor on which it was resting. He pressed down hard on the table and a smirk suggested that he was happy with it.

Without a word, the man ascended the stairs and returned a minute or so later. This time he brought a dark red metal fold-up chair which he placed behind the table, opposite Sam. Like a set-up for the world's weirdest interview.

He disappeared up the stairs again, almost running this time. He returned carrying a copy paper cardboard box which he placed on the edge of the table.

Off he went again. This time the object in his arms was a

familiar one. The old black typewriter, the one from the apartment in Manchester. He hefted it into place in the middle of the table in front of the chair.

He approached the base of the stairs again. How many more times would he do this? Was he bringing a whole house-full of furniture down here, one trip at a time? Would it not have been easier to tie her and her mother up somewhere on the ground floor?

The final time, he brought down another box, the size of the last one. It was the sort people used on TV to pack treasured belongings when moving to a new house or when clearing out a desk on dismissal. This box had no lid. Objects protruded, one of which could have been the handle of a hammer.

He took a seat, he webbed his fingers together, and then he leaned his chin on his fingers. He stared at Sam. "You look upset."

A straight stare was directed back. "Wrong again."

He looked puzzled but said nothing. He just cocked his head to one side a few degrees.

"I'm angry. Furious, in fact."

He nodded. "Good… good!"

He reached forward, opened the paper box and withdrew one sheet of bright white paper. He fed the single page into the barrel of the typewriter and twisted at the side until he was ready to type a first line. He grabbed the corners of the typewriter and shuffled it around before his fingers hovered over the keys.

He looked up. "Furious, you said?"

Sam shook her head and sighed. "I'm not going to do this."

He smiled. "You are already." He held out his arms,

almost fully extended, the palms of his hands facing upwards. "It doesn't look like you have many other options really, does it?"

Sam smirked. "I know you want me to be scared of you, but you're pathetic."

His arms shot back to his sides. He raised his hands to the height of his head before slamming them down onto the table as fists. The table shook, looking like it could topple if that was done a couple more times.

"Pathetic?" he questioned in a loud voice. "You've no idea what I am!"

Sam laughed. "I know what you are. You're a fraud."

He stood up, pushing the chair backwards with the backs of his knees with a force strong enough to send it clattering on the concrete floor. He walked over to Sam and stood in front of her.

"You think I'm a fraud?" he said, sounding intrigued.

Sam shrugged. "You're not the real Larry. He's in prison. He's the real writer, too, isn't he?"

His body stayed still but his head moved backwards, like he had just been the victim of a slap in the face. "*I'm* a writer. I've sold millions of books around the world-"

Sam interrupted him with a laugh. "You say those two things like they're connected. I've got you figured out."

He walked back to the table, picked up the chair and resumed his previous seating position, ready to type some sort of rudimentary dialogue. "What have you figured out exactly, my dear?"

"You made a fortune off the back of the real Larry. You look a bit like him, but you're certainly not him. I can see it now."

"It's my picture in those books-"

"Because you've cheated your way to being famous!"

He was glaring at her, biting down hard. "I've been writing the story about you: The one that's had you so terrified."

Maybe he was flustered. Maybe the anger fed it, but a rush of confidence surged through her, urging her on. *Don't let him win!*

She could wind him up, antagonise him. Maybe she could make him do something stupid, make a mistake that could trip himself up. *If he's going to kill me anyway, it's not like the situation could get any worse.*

"The only thing I was terrified of," Sam said, rolling her eyes, "was having another dreadfully written chapter land on my doorstep!"

He pointed a finger at her. "I know the effect it had. You knew I was watching. I know you were running scared. No one is that good an actor."

Sam shrugged. "Frightening me is the easy part… but writing it in a believable way? That's not you. The grammar… the spelling… any primary school kid could tell you the quality of the writing was horrendous in places."

The flaws in the bold approach started to manifest themselves. A confident victim would need to be humbled. Maybe that's what that other box was for. Upsetting the man had put her here in a round-a-bout sort of a way. Would the same approach do anything to change that? Could the same things lead to a different result?

"You can do whatever you want to me, but you're not Larry. You never will be."

"I *AM* Larry!" he shouted back. "The world knows who I am! *NO ONE* knows who *you* are!"

Sam curled up the right side of her mouth and sighed.

"The people of the world think they know you, but they don't know you at all, do they? That's why you've spent the last few years changing yourself to be more like him. Those bodies in his house. What did you do, and why is that poor man taking the blame?"

There was a short, exasperated laugh. "You've done a good job of putting this together. It's amazing what an average person can do with half a jigsaw puzzle."

"Go on then, fill in the blanks. Get the clichéd monologue out of the way." Sam shook her head slowly while raising an eyebrow. "What's your name? Why was your life so terrible that you had to blah, blah blah?"

Without a word, the man picked a small hammer out of the box, walked over to Sam like he was late for a bus, and threw it down hard until it smashed the little and ring fingers of her left hand.

The scream of pain couldn't be helped. Confidence couldn't hide that.

He crouched in front of her and waited until her tears had subsided enough so she could look him in the eyes. "Are we done with the sarcasm?"

There was silence. The only sound was the drip-dripping of the water. A glance to the right revealed that her mother was awake, trying to struggle against the restraints. Trying to scream. All without success.

Fingers throbbed with pain. Tears again blurred her vision. Blinking had no effect. Nothing could be done to clear it. She could see only rough shapes.

"Liam," he said before a long pause. "My name, before all of this, was Liam."

Broken fingers mattered more for a moment than that conversation.

Another blink cleared enough of her vision to see him again.

"The thing about killing is, it gives you… a rush." Liam's eyes seemed to glaze over as he talked in a romantic tone about taking the lives of others. The tone could cause revulsion in the most patient and understanding of people.

"I found I had a better talent for killing than I had for writing. I guess destiny threw me in the direction of Larry's parents, and eventually Larry as well. I thought about killing him, of course. I was so jealous. But what would that achieve? I had taken lives before that had left me disadvantaged. I wasn't about to do it again."

Liam looked down at his typewriter and started hammering at the keys. He pressed them slower than someone should do when they typed for a living. He also focussed far more on finding each key following the press of the previous one. Had he really used a contraption such as this before?

"We had an arrangement, Larry and I," Liam continued. "It had to come to an end at some point. I could have dumped the bodies in the lake, but this way seemed like a better idea. It was a way of burning all bridges on the way out. To be honest, I've grown tired of all of these games. It's all over now."

Liam continued to give keys a slow, forceful push as he committed some macabre but mediocre memoir to paper. "The harassment, the arrest, your false sense of security and everything that has happened since. My final task before leaving all of this behind is to finish the story I've been building around you."

The pain in those fingers eased. As long as they weren't moving it would probably calm down. Maybe they would yet allow for pin-sharp focus on the horrifying scene being played out. The tears were stopping. The breathing calming down. Talking was again possible, at least for now.

"So, you set him up for everything?... His DNA?... His fingerprints?"

Liam stopped typing, looked at Sam and nodded with a grin.

"What's the plan now? You think you'll just disappear? You think they won't find you?"

Liam slapped his right palm down on the unsteady table. The noise forced a jump and an accelerated heart. The pain in the fingers hadn't been away for long before it returned.

"No, Sam. *YOU* don't get to tell *me* what will happen!"

Liam closed his eyes, took a deep breath, and then continued typing.

"What are you writing about?"

Liam shrugged. "I can't leave the story unfinished, can I? The story about Samantha Barkes, conceited female who wanted to live her own way. But it needs an ending."

He was still tapping away at a snail's pace with a crazed look on his frustrated features.

"And what an ending it is!" he said, pausing and letting his face brighten with a smile before resuming his typing. "I hope I'm happy with it. I have to play both roles, now that my resident writer is out of the picture. I hope I can do them both justice."

He stopped again and leaned back. Another stare in silence.

"Sam was the reason her parents separated. Her accidental nature and the fear of her injury or death drove them apart. I know about the other two. I do my research." He paused and looked at Sam, and then at her mother, and then at the door behind her.

"Now, Sam who had been attempting to save herself from her stalker, will eventually plead for the sweet release of death to save her from torture. Grief over her death reunites the parents who had been torn apart by the past. And Sam finally knows how a killer thinks. She no longer needs her university degree, and then she exits from existence."

Sam didn't respond. There was nothing left to say.

Larry typed another sentence and then stopped, slid his chair back making a horrible scraping sound on the concrete before standing up. He rooted through the box like a kid given the choice of anything from the lost and found. He picked up a set of pliers and walked around the table.

"The trouble with pain," he started, "is that the brain can't let you be in pain permanently. If it had that to deal with all the time, it would give up at some point. It switches nerve endings off and on all the time to protect itself. To feel total pain, you need more and more injuries to be inflicted."

Sam watched on as Liam approached her left hand again.

"Have you ever had a headache, Sam, and then stomped on your foot to see if it would take the pain away? Same basic principle, I suppose."

He opened the pliers and placed her thumb in the jaws. With the hands restrained in that way, there was no way of struggling free. Given time to wriggle, maybe, but no time was provided. Her thumb was stuck there when he squeezed the pliers.

~ ~ ~ ~ ~

Every word was heard through that old, rotting door. Every scream travelled like he was next to her. Liam sounded as if he was the epitome of evil.

The struggle of the past hour or so had not been enough.

No amount of trying to wriggle free had worked. Maybe the ropes were looser. Maybe that was wishful thinking.

Strands of light had chased away the worst of the darkness since the light had been turned on in the next room. The thin ropes were visible and appeared to be as tight as they had felt.

With some ability to move his legs, various attempts had been made to jump or hop towards the door. All of it was too exhausting. Using every ounce of energy had probably moved him a quarter of an inch.

There was movement out there. Someone walking up and down steps, carrying things, heavy things.

Only a matter of minutes ago Sam's voice drowned out the other sounds. His heart had sunk. He had her captive down here. This was no longer just about freeing himself.

The chilling conversation was carried to his ears without obstruction, the psychopath pausing to type something more for his sick little story.

There was anger in his voice. Maybe a chair was thrown. There was a thud and Sam's first scream in pain.

Samuel had clenched his fists. The ropes burned against his wrists, but it didn't matter. He shuffled, he swayed, he jerked himself forwards and backwards, side to side.

Liam went back to the typewriter and carried on hammering at the keys. The noise would mask Samuel's struggles and any noise that might be made in that wrestle for freedom.

With both feet on the floor and his lower legs free, he shuffled both feet as far forward as the pain in his knees would allow. He then strained the muscles in his legs like he was standing up, dragging himself and the chair forward. He repeated this again and again.

He strained and dragged himself forward. Strained and dragged. He used the energy of a jackrabbit and made the progress of a sloth. Even so, he was moving.

Sam was talking again. Liam was answering. As their conversation and the tapping of keys continued, Samuel was edging closer to the door.

With every movement, every exhausting exertion, a mantra accompanied his laboured breathing. *Don't fail Sam like Lydia and Peter! Don't let her die!*

As he neared the door, the conversation grew more heated. There was movement. There was a loud objection from Samantha, and then another scream of pain.

He huffed and puffed for a moment. *Time to put a stop to this!*

He pressed his feet into the floor, tipping it back as far as he dared. He then lifted his feet and let the chair flop forwards until he leaned forward. He slammed his legs into the floor, leaning forward as much as he could.

The extra weight pulled him backwards. The pain in each knee suggested something might be about to break under the strain. Somewhere behind him would be a wall. There was a momentary slump of the shoulders. *This is going to hurt!* He used the backwards momentum of the heavy chair to charge backwards.

He slammed himself into the solid wall behind. The chair cracked and snapped into pieces. Pain shot through his lower back, causing him to wince. The slivers of light showed pieces of wood falling to the ground. *I wonder if my back would look like that in an x-ray later. Assuming I live long enough for medical treatment.*

As the chair fell apart, the rope that bound him loosened to the point that he could almost move freely. Without any further hesitation, and before Liam could inflict any more misery on Samantha, Samuel charged towards the door, leaning in with his left shoulder.

For the second time in a minute, his body had smashed through hard wood. The effects would be long-lasting when the adrenaline wore off.

As the door splintered and its parts flew in almost every direction, the comparatively bright light seemed to almost burn his eyes. The floor was lower. He stumbled and almost lost his footing, feeling something jar in his right knee.

He forced his eyes wide open and launched himself at the shape standing near the table, the target.

The blurry shape ahead of him would be Liam, the tormentor, the liar, the killer. He was facing away from him with a hand reaching for something on the table. He had just turned his head to see the source of the noise when Samuel threw himself into his midriff.

The force sent Liam stumbling forwards until he slammed against the rough concrete wall. The abrupt stop meant Samuel's momentum sent his head into Liam's lower back. The impact caused him to groan in pain.

Samuel stepped back slightly and put his hands around the man's neck. As he pushed his arms inward, he squeezed and forced his knee and shoulder into his back. *No one's going to do this to my daughter.*

Still half tied by the rope, Samuel's movements were restricted. There was a need to put a stop to all of this by any means necessary. Inflicting pain was easy when you hated the guy. Strength and energy waned, however, and soon the strength in his muscles might go completely.

There was no chance to plan ahead, to make sure that the threat posed by Liam had been neutralised. But a next step was needed. He couldn't hold him like this forever. At that moment of indecision an elbow struck the right side of his face.

He staggered backwards, knocking the table, which moved across the floor about a foot, the legs scraping on the rough floor. He put his hand on the table, steadying himself, but the table seemed to offer little by way of suitable support. A full-on lean and it would collapse under him.

Liam turned around and charged at Samuel. Without a thought, Samuel picked up a few sheets of paper from the top of the pile in the box and threw them in Liam's direction. The paper flew and scattered in all directions in the air. It created a temporary cloud, blocking the assailant's view for a moment.

The distraction gave Samuel long enough to duck to the side and to unwind some of the rope from his arms and chest. As the paper fell, he flung his arms at him and wrapped the rope around the man's neck. He was tugging hard at each end of the rope, feeling friction burns on his fingers and in the palms of each hand.

Liam's arms flailed. He tried swinging punches, scratching, pulling, anything, but he seemed to be lacking the strength. He stepped towards Samuel, slackening the rope and he kicked out, catching Samuel behind the right knee, causing his leg to buckle.

Liam threw himself at Samuel this time. Samuel spun around with the force and was knocked hard against the concrete floor, face first. Liam returned the favour of a few seconds ago, trying to choke the life out of Samuel.

The effects of strangulation were felt immediately. After only a few seconds, he had tunnel vision and his face was getting hot. The pressure of the man on his back hurt as much as the hands around his throat.

Ahead of him was a large part of the broken wooden door. Concentrating every bit of his energy reserve into reaching that one piece of wood didn't work. It was agonisingly out of reach, and further attempts would not get any easier.

Try as he might, he would not win this fight on his own.

~ ~ ~ ~ ~

Her father was dying in front of her eyes. With every second, more and more of the inner well of life was drying up. He was only just there, an arm's reach away. She was close enough to see the bloodshot eyes, close enough to hear the throat noises, the gurgles, but still too far away to make a difference.

No amount of screaming, shouting, nor pushing, pulling or tugging at the restraints could do anything to save him. Stamping feet was as impossible as reciting the Greek alphabet backwards when drunk.

It was almost worrying how calm and clear a mind could work when faced with such huge obstacles. Panic had gone on holiday or something. There was time to think, to consider a course of action. Maybe the answer laid outside of the obvious. Maybe the answer was not to struggle with the chair, but to accept it, to embrace it.

She could lift her feet off the floor a little. She leaned forwards as far as she dared, and then backwards. She repeated the motion, forwards and backwards as if trying to move invisible objects out of her way, stretching, straining. Eventually, she was rocking the chair legs.

The rocking of the chair on two legs at a time became more and more pronounced. One more heft forward and she could feel the chair starting to reach its tipping point, she flung everything to the left, spinning it around. Sam and the chair crashed on top of Liam. The high back smashed hard against his lower back, her full body weight making sure it would have an effect.

Liam cried out in pain, and whilst Sam was facing the wrong way, the impact was enough for Liam to loosen his grip on her dad.

Laying there, she was a dead weight, but a good one. If her dad could now breathe for a moment, if he could reach that piece of wood, the balance could once again swing in their favour.

~ ~ ~ ~ ~

The noises immediately behind her were drowned out by the action ahead. The torture of her daughter had her full attention until the moment something burst through that door.

There were wide-eyed looks on the face of her daughter and on the face the man attempting to torture her. Whatever had come charging in, it had been hidden away, able to hear the atrocities committed but unable to do anything.

As the figure flew onto the scene, there was enough about the back of the man's head, the way he ran and his build to identify him. She hadn't seen him in years, but there was no mistaking Samuel Barkes, but the following actions were not consistent with the man she had known. He had never been the kind of man to defy expectation. Maybe that, too, had changed.

Her ex-husband charged past her and every word of criticism, every negative thought directed at the man seemed to fade away as some newer, braver version emerged from that room.

There was once an unuttered wish that he would become a man of substance and principle, that he would be willing to fight to keep and to protect his loved ones. That wish was finally coming true as he threw himself into conflict to save their child.

Being witness to it all, seeing the man she had doubted for decades, might have been marvellous. The transformation could have allowed for a fabulous family reunion, but for one problem.

As the door exploded, chunks of something hit the back of her head. Some bounced off her skull. Some seemed to stick. The force of Samuel's charge knocked her chair, sending her tumbling sideways and backwards.

Instinct forced the tensing of her neck muscles as she braced for impact, but as her back hit the floor, the air seemed to be knocked out of her entire body and her head snapped backwards. The back of her head met solid concrete floor harder than she had hoped. Blinding pain shot through her skull.

A warm wetness seemed to creep around the back of her head. There was a smell of blood and also of a more subtle, sweet odour. The ringing in her ears threatened to drown out every other sound, and her mouth felt as if she'd just licked a sewage pipe. After several seconds, the back of her head felt cold. A few more seconds and it was as if someone were freezing it with liquid nitrogen.

Shivers surged through her entire body. Her fingers and toes went numb.

At the same time, her former wimp of a husband was fighting the monster who had been causing the family such pain.

But Samuel was losing the fight. The object that could turn the tides was an inch from his trembling, desperate fingers.

Sam, clever as always, rocked her chair until she could tip it over, smashing down on the man with the upper hand.

Samuel managed to reach the large piece of wood that had been elusive until that moment.

In one movement, he picked up the wood with his left hand, dropped his right shoulder, pivoted, and swung the wood around in one large arc until it collided with the stranger's face.

The man was no longer on Samuel's back. He rolled off towards the flimsy table. As he did so, Samantha was pushed clear of the action and Samuel followed through with the swinging of his makeshift weapon. It collided with the table leg, causing it to fold inwards. The heavy typewriter on top was no longer supported and the table leaned, teetered and fell towards the man's head. Before he even knew what was happening, the old typewriter, the heavy, cast iron kind, was crashing down on his cranium, crushing it against the concrete.

The copy paper that had remained in the box billowed into the air like a cloud, scattered around the room. It started to float to the ground, one sheet at a time. Some touched pools of blood and instantly turned from white to pink to red. Some attempted to cover some other part of the scene of devastation. It felt like the first snow of winter, covering the dirt and making everything clean and new again.

Blood started to pool around the squashed head like a halo. Her own head quite possibly looked much the same.

Yvonne had finally seen her husband save one of their children, but as an ice cold blast shot through her from her head to every extremity, it would be the last thing she would ever see.

Chapter 40

The decision of the Crown Prosecution Service to continue with their case had been a source of bemusement.

The main culprit had been identified, and he had died in bizarre circumstances. Evidence presented had shown that Liam had done all of this.

Perhaps the lawyers of the CPS had put in so much work that the idea of letting it all go seemed wasteful. From some prosecutor's point of view, there was an accomplice they could go after. All manner of things could be justified with the words "public interest".

True, there was DNA and fingerprints of his all over the bodies, but explanations had been furnished in several lengthy statements. Yes, the man in the dock had been living in the home where the bodies were discovered. Yes, he knew what had been happening. Yes, he had even been involved whilst being falsely imprisoned.

He was standing, once again, in the small glass box in the middle of an ornate wooden panelled court room. In front of him was the bench that had become the temporary home for the prosecuting barrister and his assistant to the right, and his own barrister with their assistant on the left.

As he looked around the room, sat amongst the mixture of old and new wood furnishings and the adaptations made to an aging court, there were quite a number of people. Looking lordly as he deigned to look down on everyone else, the judge in his gown and full white wig looked older than the hills, despite having the wherewithal to use a small tablet computer to competently take notes. The crest, visible in every court room across the country, was the one thing that loomed larger than the stare of the right honourable man beneath it.

Various others moved to and fro, several dressed in a wig and a black gown, seeming to organise and announce everything.

To the right of the judge a grand pulpit-like stand jutted out, looking more suited to a Church of England cathedral. The witness box had been heavily used over the previous few days.

Nearly everything else in that large room was less significant than the twelve people, sitting on two long benches to the far left. Five ordinary men and seven normal women had absorbed the facts and the opinions that had been presented by experts. They had listened to testimony and had taken on board the speeches of each Barrister, each worthy of a stage performance. They had made their decision, and his future hung in the balance, weighed on the scales of justice.

Defence counsel had taken the image crafted by the prosecution of an evil co-conspirator, and they had transformed it. The man, held in his own home by this person against his will, initially injured, and then poisoned and threatened with violence was nothing more than another victim.

X-rays showed badly set broken bones, the result of fighting Liam Kelly while he still had the heart to try. The Defence lamented over Larry's own writing being used to fund the lifestyle of this mysterious and monstrous man, who had targeted the family more than once, as if he had some kind of twisted vendetta or skewed sense of universal justice.

A day and a half of cross-examination followed sincere testimony from the accused. There were nods and sympathetic glances from the jury and even from the judge, but people weren't acquitted on sympathy. They were still people, and people allowed emotion to cloud judgement. Maybe they would look at the cold, stern evidence through the lens of the defendant's soft, gentle demeanour.

Samantha Barkes, once a random reader, was called to the witness box. A story had been started. Two versions had existed. The woman, described as the next victim, looked from the top of her head to her shoes like the Sam imagined and interpreted. Rather than a self-absorbed, conceited creature, a warmth of personality exuded during testimony.

Admiration of the famed Larry Llewellyn and his stories had given way to hounding and humiliation. Threats, attacks on home and family, murder, abduction and mutilation had all been on the menu served up by the real culprit.

Prosecution counsel overlooked aspects of finance. Fraud investigators followed the money, but this money trail was different. Larry's money was not his own. It was all under the control of the man in all of the photographs, the Liam whose only family had died in suspicious circumstances.

As the photographs became newer with each book release, Liam's looks had changed. Cosmetic surgeons and the agent had added to the weight of the defence's case. The changes in appearance could be catalogued. Testimony from the agent confirmed that the man who had attended the London offices was not the one on trial. Maybe the truth had a real shot at making him free, but it was dangerous to even hope for it before the verdict was reached.

Beyond all reasonable doubt, is what the barrister had said. *They need to prove your guilt beyond any doubt at all in the minds of the jury.*

Could anyone who had watched the trial play out really have no cause at all to doubt? True, he was involved, but was he really an accomplice?

The faces of jurors had been a roadmap to their inner thoughts and ideals. Stern, unforgiving looks greeted him on day one. Like they were there as jury in a multiple murder trial and that there must be a pretty good chance he had done it, or they wouldn't have been sitting there. Those faces had hardened further with every day of the prosecution's case being heard.

Yet, as the defence offered a heartfelt and human explanation, the mood in that court room had changed. The barrister was clever. The majority of the jury were women, usually more compassionate than their male counterparts.

Whatever the defence barrister was being paid for the trial, it could be nowhere near enough. This man had taken a case that on the surface had looked impossible to defend. Forcing all present to look beyond the devil in the detail, he had generated a feeling of warmth and sympathy for the defendant. There were times they might have all let out an empathetic 'aww' as some other feature of false imprisonment made it into the public record of the Court. Normal men and women with feelings, with families and with hearts would surely make the right decision.

Three weeks from the jury being sworn in, they were back. They had retired to consider a verdict. Despite debates on television, radio and on social media, they acted as if oblivious to it all. Maybe they weren't. Maybe their mind had been made up before they had first walked through those doors.

But there they were again, filing in, taking their seats. After all of it, the months of build-up, the weeks of the trial, it had all been boiled down to one moment, one bitter pill to swallow. The sombre-looking individuals stared at the floor. Once seated, they were immediately asked to arise for the judge. The futility of court ceremony was laid bare in a way that would have been comical in other circumstances. The clock on the wall showed a deliberation of around five hours. Was that too long for a not guilty verdict? Was it too quick for a guilty one?

Everyone took their seats again, except for one nervous-looking young man in the jury. His next few words would shape the rest of Larry's life. Stuck in the middle of a fog of words that seemed indecipherable, he thought he heard the words 'not guilty'.

He looked across at the defence barrister. He looked over, smiled and winked and mouthed the words, "well done." The judge indicated that Larry Llewellyn was free to leave. He had his life back.

With no home anymore, with nothing but a modest income from historic book royalties, life was to start again from scratch.

All he knew was writing. Could he still do it? Would anyone read or buy it? Had the notoriety of being a defendant in a murder trial been enough to turn a once avid readership sour?

Even so, the idea of having nothing but freedom meant everything. Breathing the same air as everyone else had been a pipedream. Restrictions had been lifted for the first time in his adult life. What to eat, what to wear, what to write, it had all become real, like they were choices that actually mattered. Nevertheless, that promise of freedom, even in embryo, was exciting.

Chapter 41

Sam walked into the almost empty café. The peeling wallpaper, the cracked glass in the front window and the dated interior all spoke volumes of the type of establishment. She paused after a couple of steps, looking for him.

The air wreaked of old cooking oil and stale coffee. Someone with an accent somewhere between Mancunian and Scouse shouted an order to the uninterested-looking cook using colourful language. *Maybe I'm judging, but this can't be the place.*

But he was there, at the back, in the corner. She took a seat opposite.

"This doesn't seem like your kind of place."

He smiled. "Nothing seems like my kind of place anymore. I'm the very definition of a misfit."

Sam raised an eyebrow. "Institutionalised after about five months?"

Larry shook his head. "Hardly. I hated that place. Couldn't wait to get out."

Two basic coffees arrived in ceramic cups with saucers. A chipped plate of average supermarket-quality biscuits was added to the centre of the table with little finesse. From a hospitality point of view, the guy might as well have thrown the biscuits at them and yelled at them to get out.

"There are probably two hundred coffee shops in Manchester. Why choose this one?"

Larry wore a cheeky smile. "No reporters. No one looks twice at this place."

Sam nodded and reached for a biscuit. She moved it towards her mouth and paused. "What couldn't we talk about over the phone?"

She smirked and said in a whisper, "You're not being investigated by the police, are you?"

Larry frowned in the way a friend does when they're pretending to be offended, failing to suppress a lurking smile. He said nothing.

Sam sat up straight and put on a sort of frowning smirk. "Too soon?"

Larry treated the question as rhetorical and reached for something on the floor beside his chair.

He stood up a lever arch file at the edge of the table between the plate of biscuits and the wall.

Sam raised her eyebrows. If she hadn't been wearing such a wide smile her jaw would have dropped much further. "A new one? Already?"

Larry shrugged. "It's been almost three months, and it's not like I can do anything else with my time."

She reached out and hovered her hand above it when it would have been easier to touch it. For some reason she was almost afraid it would disappear if it made contact with human hands.

"Is this… mine?" Sam asked.

Larry nodded. "I'm all modernised. I printed this yesterday from the file on my computer."

Sam stared at it, not moving. Not saying anything.

"Open it," he said.

Sam put the biscuit back on the plate and picked up the file. She pulled it open, tugging the front cover of the binder loose from the protruding rings. She read the first page.

For Sam.

> You went through hell in my name and you deserve better.

Sam shook her head as she closed it again. "I appreciate the gesture, but would you be upset if I said I didn't ever want my name used in fiction ever again, even in an acknowledgement?"

Larry's head tilted to one side before it straightened. "I can understand that. I'll let the agent know to leave you out."

Sam nodded once as she closed the binder again, setting it back on the table. "I appreciate it."

They both reached for and dunked a biscuit in awkward silence.

"You know," Larry started, "Liam might not have met his maker quite so soon if he'd have modernised in like manner."

Sam scowled at him for a moment before her face straightened. Then she smirked. "You think a current laptop would have done less damage?"

Larry raised an eyebrow and nodded.

"Then we have to be very grateful that some people are stuck in their ways," Sam said.

Larry smiled. "They're so afraid of change. They think it will make their life worse. They think it'll be the catalyst that could kill them."

Sam took a sip of her coffee. The harshness of the coffee grounds almost stung her tongue. There wouldn't be another one. The rest would have to sit there, thinking about what it had done. "And those same people fail to see that their own fear of adapting could be the real problem."

"Maybe Charles Darwin had a point a hundred and sixty years ago."

Sam smiled, standing up with the binder in her right hand. "Maybe he did."

Chapter 42

Excerpt from THE PUT DOWN by Larry Llewellyn

James sighed and rolled over in bed, knowing that even at six in the morning, there was no further merit in lying there. Of all of the changes that had occurred in recent weeks since his enforced retirement, his sleep pattern was not one of them.

The reason for his exasperation was not his lack of any much-needed sleep, nor was it the thought of getting up and having to take a handful of pills before his day could begin.

The dog, that feeble creature, was being fed and talked to in his wife's baby voice again before she headed out the door to work. James stared at the ceiling shaking his head. *Three years until Naomi retires. I wonder if the dog will still be here then.*

He let out a short derisory laugh as he pictured Jay-Jay. A golden retriever incapable of retrieving anything. At least not for almost a decade.

The incapacitated canine had been there for so long he had become part of the furniture. How long could he even want to live with such problems? *Why does she insist on having the mutt around?*

James went about the normal routine. He awoke, showered, dressed, had his various heart control, blood pressure and acid reflux tablets and then went to check on Jay-Jay. He looked up to the ceiling and let out a laboured sigh. The dog had eaten half of its breakfast. The half without the crushed pills mixed in. Obviously.

Then he noticed the smell of animal waste, without knowing its point of origin. James let out a growl. This again! *This day is just getting better and better!*

As he doused the area with disinfectant, James wished he was still well enough to work. He felt close to full fitness now, but there was no way back. Not after what he'd been through.

Pragmatic at first about the possibilities, reality had set in. A reality that centred around that dog, past its best, and a new life as its primary carer.

It wasn't as if the dog ever thanked James for his efforts. The licks, the sense of companionship, all affection was reserved for her.

The thought last night and this morning had been *enough of the problems! No more suffering. It's surely more humane.*

One quick trip to the vet would solve several problems. They would save money. James could focus his attention on his new hobbies without the constant need to check on the dog.

His musings on his wife's responses occupied his mind throughout the ill-advised bacon roll for breakfast. She had made her opinion clear during their most recent exchange on the subject.

"But he's hardly got any of his senses left. He's half a dog," he had said.

"Half a dog is still better than no dog at all," Naomi had said in reply.

"He's on as much medication as I am. He's old, he's got too much wrong with him. What does it all say for his quality of life?"

"What about *your* quality of life?"

"What do you mean?" he asked, knowing full well what she meant.

"You've had a heart attack. If it wasn't for doctors, nurses, paramedics and a load of pills every day, where would *you* be?"

He shook his head. "That's not the same thing."

Naomi nodded. "It's *exactly* the same thing. Life is life. What makes yours more important than his?"

"Okay," he said. "When I'm blind, mostly deaf and stupid and I'm falling into the fishpond all the time, you've got my permission to have me put down as well!"

Her reasons kept coming. Jay-Jay was a better companion. He comforted her. He was there for her. He had to stay.

Of all of the hobbies to be taken up by an ex-truck driver with fingers like sausages and a huge bulky frame, most would wonder why James had chosen the latest one.

The freshly dug patch of ground, the seedlings poking up above the soil, all after watching a load of online videos. Maybe he could cross-pollinate and create something truly unique, something to leave behind. A kind of landscaping legacy.

Walking outside, the sky was grey but there was little threat of rain. The temperature was sensible, and it seemed like a nice day to plod around the garden.

He went to his new flower bed to check on the progress of the little buds shooting out from the soil. To his dismay, he could see only bare soil, recently disturbed.

He turned around to see the dog coughing up the immature flowers with mud around his mouth. He clenched his fists. *Is that dog determined to spoil everything I try?*

The dog gave up on the chewed plants and padded off in the direction the pond, no doubt planning on getting a quick drink from the place he should be avoiding. James followed at a quick pace.

He would have called out instructions or commands, but the dog would pretend not to hear. Old dogs, like some old people probably made excuses to justify their behaviour based purely on their age and condition.

James reached the side of the pond as the dog started to lap at the water. He bent down and pulled at the dog's collar.

"Get away!" he said in a loud voice.

Jay-Jay growled and exerted himself to continue.

"No! Bad dog!"

He tugged again, unable to drag the dog away.

He felt himself draw shorter, shallow breaths. He was feeling dizzy. A sharp pain started in both arms and in his chest.

The strength of the once-strong man failed completely, and he fell to the floor beside the pond. He landed on his back, knowing he should be sitting up, but he was unable to move. Except for his arms. His arms seemed to raise themselves as if they had a mind of their own. His fingers tensed and seemed to squash together. The muscles in his body were going crazy as the pain in his chest radiated outwards.

There was no doubt in James's mind that he was having another heart attack. Last time he had just completed a delivery and could get the help he needed quickly. Thankfully there had been an AED and a first aid trained staff member on-site. This time, he was on his own with only an unsympathetic dog for company.

Staring up at the sky, he knew his ticket had been punched. This was his time to leave. No breeding of a new species of flower. No reading of those books he planned to read in retirement. No time to enjoy life without caring for the dog.

He laughed and coughed. The dog. The dog would carry on, no issues at all.

Jay-Jay walked up to James, standing on his arm for a second before backing away. He returned and sniffed at James's face. There was a slight whimper and the dog licked him several times. *NOW I get some affection!*

Everything else vanished away in those painful, dreadful seconds. The dog that he had tried to prevent from falling into the pond once more, the dog that was more broken than healthy, the dog that could not function without significant human assistance, had outlived him.

His eyes closed. There was nothing more

to do but to leave Jay-Jay to wander around the garden, helpless.

As James drifted off, succumbing to the pain, he heard the dog once more lap at the water of the pond by his side. A moment later he heard the splash and felt the cool water hitting his hot face.

The dog had fallen in. Again.

Epilogue

As the train clattered from one set of rails to another, there was a jolt. Not the jolt in the seat from the track shift, but a bump back to reality.

It had been one hell of a year. Even after all this time, there was a luxury in getting lost in one's thoughts. It wasn't too long ago that there was no upside to downtime.

University would wait. She could defer, go back, repeat the first year and then do the rest. There were other dreams to deal with first. There was no point hanging on to them, collecting them like old photographs to one day dust them off when the moment had passed.

Those dreams were being lived, and they had taken her back to London. Admittedly, that meeting was not the stuff of dreams, but it was all part of the bigger picture. With the big thing done, it was time to head home to Manchester.

Her father would be waiting to hear the details of the trip. He listened a lot more these days.

The trip extended to include an open bus tour, a tour of Tower Bridge, a visit to the Houses of Parliament and the Globe Theatre, and some time on the London Eye. There was even a spare seat at the Phantom of the Opera at the West End.

The cities of London and Westminster were not done telling stories. They cried out for more, each street bursting with new ideas. Thrillers centred on the narrow streets were worth exploration. The new notebook was already half-full of new ideas, inspired by every new visage and vista.

Some ideas would be shrugged off. Some would be worth mulling over.

With all the attention fixed on that little book, she almost missed him: The thin man, probably around nineteen with light stubble on his face, thick-rimmed bright blue glasses over his brown eyes and short mouse-brown hair. His appearance, his thin green sweatshirt and black jeans did not draw her attention from across the aisle.

No, there was another reason why this young man grabbed her attention. The book was in his hands. The one that had just been published. The one dedicated to the memory of her mother.

He was halfway through. The boy Peter, his two sisters and their parents had by that point found and explored the large stones near their house: the ones with magical powers. So much adventure still lay in store for him on the remaining pages.

The story was a wish list. It was the kind of family she could have had, minus the magic, if things had turned out differently.

Did it make sense to draw his attention? Would he want to meet the author, take a selfie with her, get an autograph? Maybe ask a few questions?

Would she be able to keep quiet about the ending? Would she blurt out that she had just signed a new book deal to write the next one in the series? She had been published for five minutes. She didn't really have fans yet. Not really.

Sam turned away, smiling. The countryside whizzed by the window.

The train movement, the occasional clack of the wheels on the tracks, all worked together for a grand purpose: Each movement, each rotation, was getting her closer and closer to Manchester, to a dad who had loved her enough to save her life in almost impossible circumstances, despite life-altering injuries sustained along the way.

The smile faded. She rubbed at the fingers and thumb of

her left hand with her right. Medical professionals had declared her digits to have recovered. The damage was now unseen.

Everything that culminated in that incident had started on a train, possibly that same train, from London to Manchester.

One more glance across to the other side of the train.

Maybe she had just caught the man staring at her. He looked away when she moved. She reached for her headphones, put them on and closed her eyes. She shook her head slightly and smirked. *Not today. Who knows what would happen?*

Acknowledgements

Writing a novel of any length is an arduous task. It's an uphill struggle to get from your initial idea to a carefully crafted climax. Breathing life into characters and following them, seeing what they do is the fun part. It's not always what I expect them to do when I start out!

I could not create these novels, and enjoy the ride, without the help and support of several people. These are as follows:

- My wife, Lisa, who seems to love me through everything I do, good or bad, and seems to love everything I write as well (which I'm not sure I agree with, as I'm pretty sure some of it's awful).
- My children, especially the boy who is anxious to be old enough to read my stories, and who comes to me with small story books he produces himself, just as I tried many times when I was his age.
- A mention should also go to my daughter who combines with my son to produce noise sufficient to aid me in developing patience and an ability to concentrate and write in almost any circumstance.
- My parents and in-laws who read and critique my works and help me make them better, making me a better writer along the way.
- Lesley Grainge has provided some of the best feedback I have ever received, which has

helped to improve this book in several ways. Thank you Lesley!

- Tristram Johnson also deserves honourable mention here for reading a book outside of his interests just because I asked.
- Alexander Noot, the next fan of my books (hopefully) who graciously allowed me to use one of his knives in the cover image, despite shrinking it and covering it in blood! He was even prepared to send one to me to use for the photography, such is the level of service you get from this man when you show an interest in his beautiful hand-crafted knives.
- My day-to-day employer that I can't mention by name, who provide me with a job and an income that means I don't have to live in complete poverty whilst living my dream of authoring books.
- Fidus Publishing for believing in me enough to put my material out there for the world to see. I know thus far it's not been seen by millions. The hundreds or thousands so far is enough.

The fact that anyone who isn't related to me can read what I write and enjoy it seems unreal and at the same time validating, so finally, thank you to you, the reader. Without readers, there would be no point in writing anything and I would have to find something else to do with my warped imagination!

About the Author

Will Thurston writes novels, poetry, songs and short stories whenever time permits. He lives and works in a coastal town in England, investigating and dealing with cyber-enabled crime from an office with a sea view, having previously provided Digital Forensic and Expert Witness services to companies and law enforcement in his day-to-day life. His working background has given him experience of law enforcement, legal proceedings, Court cases of all types in the UK, and other disputes that arise within corporate law.

Will lives with his wife and two children and loves the fact that he is supported in his efforts by his family and friends, all of whom are eager to assist in the writing process.

Will's social media details are below. You can also find some of Will's stories on writing sites such as Inkitt and Wattpad.

Twitter: @willbthurston

Instagram: will.b.thurston

Facebook: **www.facebook.com/willbthurston**

Books by Will Thurston

The Replacement Phenomenon

Jake Hingham gets his wish to rewind time to save his brutally murdered little family. When time continues to unwind he seeks to find out why, and to trace the events that led to the death of his wife and two boys.

The Talent Scout

Brian Townley must save his brainchild, the Talent Scout, from falling into the wrong hands. A device that can detect natural abilities in anyone's DNA could be used for good or evil. Will he survive the fight against organised crime to protect his research and his prototype?

The Doll Collector

When PI Dan Castle gets a message that his teenage daughter has been captured, he embarks on a rescue mission in which he hopes to find and bring the Doll Collector to justice. His chase through the disturbing underworld of child abuse could save more lives than one, but can he save his own daughter before it's too late?

Death by Chapters

Sam agrees to be the protagonist in Larry Llewellyn's next gruesome novel. She knows the character will die, but has the man's killing spree merely been confined to the printed page? Horrible truths suggest otherwise, and now she must find a way to stay alive.

Printed in Poland
by Amazon Fulfillment
Poland Sp. z o.o., Wrocław

60789279R00202